LARAPINTA

Annie Seaton

Porter Sisters: 5

Porter Sisters Series

Kakadu Sunset
Daintree
Diamond Sky
Hidden Valley
Larapinta
Kakadu Dawn

Annie Seaton lives near the beach on the mid-north coast of New South Wales. Her career and studies have spanned the education sector for most of her working life, including completing a Masters Degree in Education and working as an academic research librarian, a high-school principal and a university tutor until she took early retirement and fulfilled a lifelong dream of a full-time writing career. Annie has been voted Author of the Year and Best-Established Author in the AusRomToday.com Readers' Choice Awards. In 2016, *Kakadu Sunset* was shortlisted by the judges of the Romance Writers' Association of Australia for the Ruby, in the long book category.

In 2018 *Whitsunday Dawn* was a finalist in the ARRA Awards and also voted Book of the Year in the AUSROM Readers' Choice awards.

Kakadu Sunset, Daintree, Diamond Sky, Whitsunday Dawn and *Undara* were longlisted for the Sisters in Crime Davitt Award.

Each winter, Annie and her husband leave the beach to roam the remote areas of Australia for story ideas and research. She is passionate about preserving the beauty of the Australian landscape, and respecting the traditional ownership of the land. For those readers who cannot experience this journey personally, Annie seeks to portray the natural beauty of the Australian environment—its spiritual locations, stunning landscapes and unique wildlife.

Readers can contact Annie and visit her store through her website, annieseaton.net, or find her on Facebook, Twitter and Instagram.

Also by Annie Seaton

Standalone Books
Whitsunday Dawn
Undara
Osprey Reef
East of Alice
Deadly Secrets
Adventures in Time
Silver Valley Witch
The Emerald Necklace
An Aussie Christmas Duo (two
Christmas novellas)

Porter Sisters Series
Kakadu Sunset
Daintree
Diamond Sky
Hidden Valley
Larapinta
Kakadu Dawn

Pentecost Island Series
Pippa
Eliza
Nell
Tamsin
Evie
Cherry
Odessa
Sienna
Tess
Isla
Also available in three boxed sets
Books 1-3
Books 4-6
Books 7-10

The Augathella Girls Series
Outback Roads
Outback Sky
Outback Escape
Outback Wind
Outback Dawn
Outback Moonlight
Outback Dust
Outback Hope

Pentecost Island Series
Pippa
Eliza
Nell
Tamsin
Evie
Cherry
Odessa
Sienna
Tess
Isla

Richards Brothers
The Trouble with Paradise
Marry in Haste
Outback Sunrise

The House on the Hill series
Beach House
Beach Music
Beach Walk
Beach Dreams

Sunshine Coast Series
Waiting for Ana
The Trouble with Jack|
Healing His Heart

Love Across Time Series
Come Back to Me
Follow Me
Finding Home
The Threads that Bind
Love Across Time 1-4 Boxed Set

Bindarra Creek
Worth the Wait
Full Circle
Secrets of River Cottage
Bindarra Creek Duo
Four Seasons Short and Sweet
Ten Days in Paradise
Follow the Sun

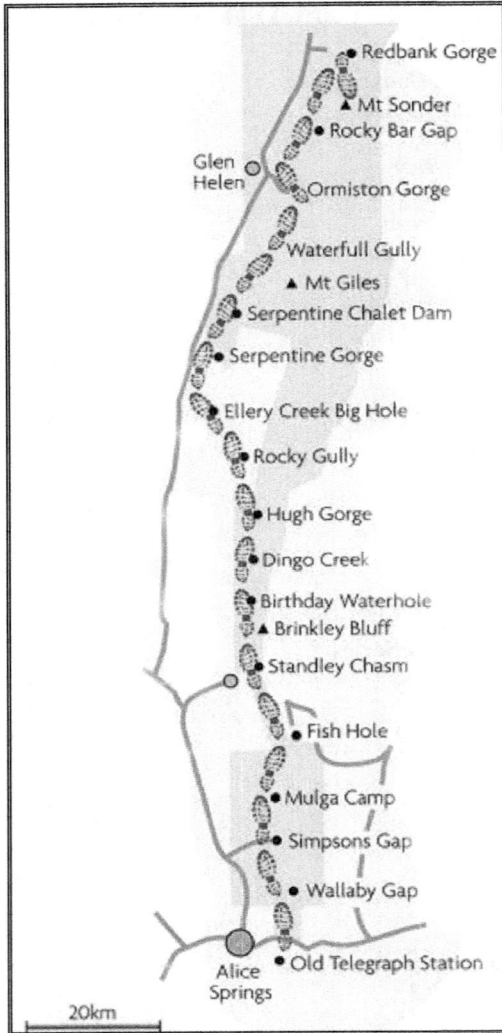

LARAPINTA TRAIL

*As always to Ian, my ever-patient and loving husband.
You are always there for me.*

Brinkley Bluff, McDonnell Range.
At sunrise I ascended the bluff, which is the most difficult hill I
have ever climbed; it took me an hour and a half to reach the
top. It is very high, and is composed principally of igneous
rock, with a little ironstone, much the same as the ranges down
the country.

John McDouall Stuart
Friday, 13th April, 1860

Prologue

Sydney - May

'I think I've found a couple we can trust.' The man turned from the floor to ceiling window of the luxury apartment overlooking Sydney Harbour. Two catamarans were sailing towards the marina and their sails billowed in the already strong wind. The sky was a brilliant blue and there were white caps on the harbour. Tourists were out and about already and even at nine a.m. all the tables at Circular Quay were occupied.

His companion crossed the room and stood beside him. '*Think* isn't good enough, Darley.'

'I'm aware of that. I know how much is at stake. That's why I said "think". When I'm absolutely certain of them, I'll start talking money. They've had a lot of experience around the world, and my contact in Germany gave them a glowing reference. Ten successful jobs and not a finger of suspicion pointed at them, Johann said.'

'And what does Johann get for recommending them?'

'Fifty grand?'

'I'm not made of money.' His voice was cold.

'But you will be if they deliver.'

'Tell me about them.'

'They've been field operatives for Johann's agency for three years. Early thirties. They pose as a wealthy married couple. He reckons they're the best around, and you couldn't do better.'

'He doesn't have my name, I hope?'

'No, you are simply "my employer" in our communications.'

'Good. Make sure it stays that way. I don't trust anyone. Not even you.'

'I am aware of that. I won't let you down. Has she agreed to the trek yet?' Darley ran a hand over his face and looked away.

'No. My patience is wearing thin.'

'She's been looking at the lower and middle end of the market. I've hacked into her email account and also have a tap on her phone. Plus, I have someone following her.'

'Why the hell would she do that? She always goes for the top end of everything.'

Darley shrugged. 'Maybe she likes keeping you guessing. She thinks you're going with her, doesn't she?'

'Yes. It was my suggestion.'

'If she books the lower end one, our operatives can join as backpackers, not connected with each other. If she goes with the expensive "glamping option", they'll go in as the married couple.'

'As long as she doesn't know she's being watched.'

'She doesn't. I can guarantee you of that.'

'Good. She'll go for the glamping option; don't worry about that. Better cover for the couple, if you do end up hiring them.'

'Yes, I agree. The next trek is scheduled for the beginning of June. "Mr and Mrs Smith" are scoping the trail as soon as I advise which trek. What do you think?'

'Jesus! Are they for real? Smith! Who do they think they are? Angelina Jolie and Brad Pitt?'

'They could be. She's a bloody stunner. Looks like a model, not a killer.'

'All right. I'll leave it in your hands, Darley. All I want is an outcome as soon as possible. Before she bleeds me of any more money. I trust you to make the right choice.' The man's smile sent a shiver down Darley's back. 'I am almost tempted to go on the trek myself to make sure the bitch is dead.'

Chapter 1

The McLaren Mango Farm - May

'Ellie, while you're inside, can you grab me one of your hoodies, please? That wind's cool.'

'Have I got one big enough?' Ellie chuckled as she leaned forward and looked out the kitchen window overlooking the veranda. Her sister-in-law, Dee, sat in one of the papasan chairs near the barbeque table looking decidedly uncomfortable.

'Ha ha. Very funny. Wait until you're seven months along,' Dee replied.

Ellie smiled and touched her stomach. 'I've got a few months before I get there. And *I'm* not having twins. Stay there. I'll grab you a pashmina. It'll be more comfortable.'

The family had gathered for an early evening barbeque, and to the family's joy, Ellie and Kane had announced that James was going to have a little brother or sister in November. They hadn't shared their news until she'd safely reached the three-month mark.

Emma came into the kitchen as Ellie turned to go to the bedroom. 'How are you, Els? I was so excited to hear your news.'

'I'm good. I'm over the morning sickness now. Just. I didn't have it with James, and I tell you what, it's enough to make me think twice about another kid after this one.'

'Mum's beside herself out there. I haven't seen her smile so much since Dee and Ryan's wedding.'

'Kane and I told her a couple of weeks ago. But I've been a bit worried about her. She's seemed a bit down the past few weeks.'

'Dad's anniversary?' Emma followed Ellie into the bedroom.

'I don't know.' Ellie opened the bottom drawer of the chest and pulled out a pretty mauve pashmina. 'Could be. But she came good when I told her about the bub.'

'Are you still going to fly?'

Ellie shook her head. 'No. I don't want to risk it. It took me a while to fall pregnant. We've been trying since before Dee and Ryan's wedding.'

Emma looked down but Ellie caught the glint of tears in her eyes.

'Em? You okay?'

'Jeremy and I are thinking about fertility treatment. We've been trying for a baby since your James was born.'

'Oh, Em.' Ellie held her arms open and her big sister stepped in for a hug. 'That sucks.'

'It does.' Emma stepped back and dabbed at her eyes with a tissue she pulled from her pocket. 'You'd think both being doctors we'd know how to fix it, but—' She lifted her slim shoulders in a shrug.

'It'll happen. Maybe when you least expect it.'

'I'm getting on, Ellie. I'll be thirty-three this year.'

'What are you girls doing hiding in here?' Dru, the youngest of the Porter sisters stood in the doorway. 'Is everything okay?' Her high forehead creased in a frown.

'Yeah, we're good.'

Dru shook her head. 'I didn't come down in the last shower. What's going on?'

Ellie glanced at Emma and caught a tiny shake of her head. 'We're just talking about Mum. She'd been a bit low again.'

'Well, I just copped a mouthful from her. I went down to the dam to tell her that the meat's almost cooked, and she was up a mango tree with James.'

'Oh no. I told her last week not to do that. She'll end up falling out and breaking something.' Ellie folded the pashmina neatly into a square. 'What did she say to you?'

'She told me she wasn't ready to go into bloody aged care yet, and she'd bloody well climb trees if she wanted to.'

'What! Mum said bloody?' Emma's eyes were wide. 'I don't think I've ever heard her swear!'

'And in front of James?' Ellie frowned as she led the way back to the kitchen.

'No, she climbed down, and kept her voice quiet enough so he couldn't hear from up the tree,' Dru said.

'Well, I guess that's better than how she was after Dad died, and we couldn't get her out of bed or motivated about anything. Good to see a bit of life in the old girl,' Ellie said.

'For goodness' sake, don't let her hear you call her that. Mum's suddenly got this thing about age. Last time I talked to her, she asked me all sorts of questions. I was worried she was sick and not saying, but she assured me she was fine.' Emma lowered her voice as they reached the kitchen, but it was empty. 'Actually, I've been a bit slack. I haven't called her for a couple of weeks. I've been a bit . . . a bit busy.'

Dru frowned. 'Me either. I've been flat chat at work, and we've been eating out most nights visiting all our favourite restaurants before the tourists hit town. What about you, Ellie?'

A surge of guilt ran through Ellie. 'Me either. We called in to her apartment to tell her our baby news a couple of weeks ago, but that's the last time we talked. Now that James goes to pre-school, she doesn't need to mind him while we both work, and Kane goes into town to pick him up in the afternoons if I'm not home. Do you think she's feeling a bit neglected? Maybe that's what prompted the aged care comment.'

'Maybe. I'll take this out to Dee.' Emma took the pashmina from Ellie. 'And Mum's way too young to be talking about osteoporosis, so don't you dare say anything like that to her.'

'I don't even know what that is, Dr Langford,' Ellie teased.

Emma pulled a face at her. 'Maybe she's been spending time at Dee and Ryan's property. I know she offered to help Dee in the house.'

'Hope so. God, Mum's closer to fifty than sixty, isn't she? I lose track. I don't know where that aged care comment came from,' Ellie said crossing to the oven. 'Dru, can you grab the salads out of the fridge and I'll carry the potato bake out.'

By the time the girls had the salads on the table, and Ryan had helped Dee up from the papasan chair and settled her at the end of the twelve-seater outdoor table, Kane and Connor had filled a tray with cooked steak, sausages and onions.

'That smells great,' Jeremy said as he walked up the stairs to the veranda with Sandra and James beside him.

Soon they were all sitting around the table. The three sisters beside their husbands, Ellie with Kane, Emma with Jeremy, and Dru with Connor. Their half-brother, Ryan was beside his wife, Dee. James, Ellie and Kane's four-year-old son sat beside his nan, Sandra.

'Well, how nice is this?' Sandra said with a wide smile. 'It seems like months since we were all together.'

'I know,' Ellie said as she passed the bowl of green salad to Kane to serve out a portion for James. 'Dru and Emma and I were just talking about that in the kitchen, and how we need to get together more often.'

'That would be nice,' Sandra said. 'Thanks, Ryan, just a small piece of steak. No potatoes for me either.'

'I hope you're not on a diet, Mum,' Emma said.

'No, but I've been going to the gym, and doing lots of walking. Just eating sensibly. At my age, you can't afford to put on weight.'

Jeremy chuckled. 'At your age, Sandra? You're still a spring chicken.'

'Thank you, Jeremy. I'm feeling good. Keeping myself busy.'

Emma and Ellie exchanged a glance.

'How long have you been going to the gym, Mum? Which one do you go to?' Dru asked.

'The one right in the city. I've made some new friends in the classes.'

'That's great,' Ellie said. 'We were worried that we were all too busy, but it sounds like you have been too.'

'I know you all are. I'm proud of how independent I'm getting.'

'And you're looking really well, Sandra,' Dee chipped in. 'I might drive into Darwin and come to the gym with you after this pair are born.' She put her hand on her stomach.

'I hope you don't go too early, Dee. I'll be away for the first two weeks in June. I'd like to be close when the babies arrive, so I can help you out, *if* you need me, although I'm sure Catherine will be up here too.'

'Yes, Mum's coming up about that time, but I won't knock back any offers of help, Sandra. I'd love you to come and stay. There's plenty of room at *Wilderness Station*, and you and Mum get on so well.'

Ellie frowned and put her fork down. 'Away, Mum? First we've heard of that.'

'Exactly, Ellie. I'm your *mum*. I don't have to report in with all my activities, do I?'

Ellie froze and stared at Sandra, holding back the quick retort that came to her lips. She had always been the fiery one of the three sisters, and this wasn't the time or place to cause a fight. 'Of course you don't.' Ellie focused on keeping her voice even as she picked up her fork and paid attention to her meal as she spoke. 'So where are you off to?'

'I'm going for a walk.'

'A walk?' The three girls spoke almost in unison.

'Where to, Sandra?' Kane asked.

'I'm walking the Larapinta Trail.' Sandra sat up straight and her smile was wide. 'The end-to-end walk.'

***

Sandra Porter sat back and looked at her three daughters. The looks on their faces varied from shock on Ellie's to understanding on her sensitive Emma's. Dru, as usual, was an enigma, but she knew her youngest daughter felt a lot more than she ever showed to the world.

Sandra had known the family would be surprised and that wasn't a bad thing. The girls had supported her through the hard times after Peter's death, and it hadn't been until the truth had come out, and her conviction that he had been murdered had been proven true, that Sandra had started on the long, slow road to healing. She knew the girls still worried about her, and had been prepared for this reaction.

Sandra was at a crossroads in her life. Her share portfolio had taken off and she had some serious decisions to make about her investments. Peter's death and the subsequent investigation had left her in a very comfortable position, but she hated spending it on herself. Frank Nichols, her financial adviser in the city, rolled his eyes every time she gave money to the girls.

'You would get much better returns if you follow my investment strategy,' he said every time she had a Zoom meeting with him. 'You need to put some of your money into lithium stocks.'

'The best return is seeing my girls comfortable. I like seeing them spend it.'

It was time to make some changes and make a life for herself, perhaps being the matriarch of the family. She smiled. *Matriarch?* That made her sound ninety.

Ryan caught her smile and he grinned back at her. He was a good man, and she was proud to have him as a stepson, and a member of their family.

Over the past few months, Sandra had accepted that a gap was growing between them, but she knew it was nothing to be worried about. The girls' phone calls were few and far between these days, and she tried not to call them too often. The last thing she wanted was to seem needy. She knew they didn't mean to neglect her, and there was no conflict in the family. In the increasing time she'd spent alone lately, Sandra had spent many nights thinking back to the early years of her marriage to Peter. When the girls were little and they were building up the mango farm, there'd been very little contact with her parents and Peter's family.

That was life. And the family life cycle continued as families grew into their own entities.

Her girls—and Ryan—were creating their own lives, families and careers. When the girls were growing up, they had seen their grandparents in Darwin at Christmas and on family occasions, and that had been about three times a year at best. Each of her sons-in-law had no family—except for Jeremy. His family was in Sydney, but they were estranged. She had been friends with Kane's mother several years ago, but Susan had passed away. Connor had no family either, and Ryan's parents had both passed. Sandra tried to be a mother to the boys as well.

She grinned. Boys? They were all strapping men in their thirties, but each of them cared for her girls, and Ryan, her stepson, loved Dee. She was blessed that they all lived fairly close.

Emma, her eldest, and Jeremy both worked at the main hospital in Darwin. Dru and Connor had their own security business in the city and a beautiful apartment overlooking the park on Darwin Harbour. Ellie and Kane, and her adorable grandson, James, lived on the family farm that Kane had inherited from his mother, Susan. It had gone full circle; when Kane and Ellie had married, the Porter mango farm came back to the family. Ryan and Dee lived a considerable distance away on their cattle station, but still close enough to visit.

Accepting as she was of her girls' personal lives, that didn't stop Sandra worrying about them. Ellie was busy with James and her helicopter flying contract, and now she had a new baby on the way to think about.

Sandra had been worried about Emma lately; she knew she wasn't happy, but like Dru, Emma was a private person and anything that was bothering her, she would keep to herself, but hopefully share with Jeremy.

Dru was just Dru, and the strongest of her girls. Dru had been in her mid-teens when Peter had been murdered, and she'd gone off the rails for a while. Sandra carried guilt over that; Dru had needed her, but Sandra had been so lost in her own grief she had let her youngest daughter roam free.

She glanced over at Dru and Connor and smiled. Dru had married a strong man who loved her very much.

'Mum! Don't just sit there grinning like a Cheshire cat, tell us what this walk is!' Ellie's question opened the dam, and a torrent of questions followed.

'Who are you going with?' Dru asked. 'And what's this "end-to end" mean?'

'That's a long trek, Sandra,' Connor said. He turned to Dru. 'I walked the Larapinta Trail with Greg when we left the Federal Police. It was cathartic. Sandra, it's incredible, but are you sure you're fit enough? It's over two hundred ks, isn't it?'

'Two hundred and twenty-three, and twelve days of trekking. And end-to end means just that. You can do partial treks or you can do the lot. I'm doing the full walk.'

'My God, Mum. You can't walk that far! I couldn't walk that far and you're—' Ellie's eyes were wide and she folded her arms.

'And I'm a lot older that you,' Sandra added sweetly.

Ellie grunted. 'You know what I mean. And don't you have to carry everything? A tent and all your food? I read about that trek in one of the tourist magazines at the airport. I couldn't think of anything worse.'

Sandra ignored Ellie as Connor asked another question. 'Which way are you going? East-west, or west to east?'

'The company I'm about to book with recommend the east to west walk.'

'Phew, you haven't booked it yet. We can talk some sense into you,' Ellie interrupted.

Sandra tried to keep the sharpness from her voice, but failed. 'Ellie McLaren. I am not a geriatric yet. I've still got four years before my sixtieth and I am going to do this walk. And if I want to, I'll climb trees with James too.'

The silence around the table was tense until Emma's soft voice chimed in. 'Ellie, I think it's a great idea. As long as you're with a reputable company, and you're supported, Mum, I think it sounds great.'

'Tell us some more about it, Mum,' Dru said. 'It sounds good. I might even come with you.'

'Oh no you won't. Everyone wants to.' She shook her head. 'Even Frank, my financial adviser in Sydney suggested coming with me. And don't go thinking I'm going to fall in a heap. I've been off any medication for over two years now, and I'm good. Sure, I get sad about your dad, but I've come to terms with it. Where do you think you girls got your strength from?'

'Sorry, Mum. I know I worry too much. So, tell us all about it.'

'I've got two choices. The one like you said, Ellie, where I have to carry a bit of stuff. But not a tent or all my water. There is another one I'd like to do that's a little bit softer.' Sandra glanced at Connor and chuckled. 'More like glamping, but I don't think I can justify the price of that one. I mean I can afford it, it's just a lot of money to pay out for comfort.'

Dru looked across at Ellie, and they both nodded. Ellie nudged Emma and she nodded too.

'That solves a problem for us. You pay for your trip and we'll all pitch in for the upgrade for your birthday.'

'Really? Well, I won't say no, because I know if you're helping me out, you approve of me going.'

'Good, that's settled then,' Ellie said briskly. 'Happy fifty-fifth birthday, Mum.'

'Fifty-sixth,' Sandra said.

Chapter 2

Sydney – Thursday, June 4

Graysen Hughes tipped the concierge as he walked into the foyer of the Intercontinental Hotel in Sydney. The guy had helped him carry his bags, cameras and tripod from the taxi earlier in the afternoon when Graysen had arrived from the airport. The young man had ensured that the equipment was safely sent to his room while Graysen went for a walk to Circular Quay. After eight hours confined in a plane on his connecting flight from Singapore, he needed fresh air and exercise. Even driving through the city from Mascot made him claustrophobic. He could have picked up a flight straight to Alice Springs, but he needed a couple of new lenses and filters for this photo shoot in the outback; it was much easier to pick them up directly from his supplier in Sydney.

'Thank you. I didn't have any Aussie cash before,' Graysen said as he slipped a fifty dollar note into the young man's hand.

'Thank you, sir. There was no need to worry.'

Being called sir made Graysen feel every one of his fifty-seven years.

'Where have you travelled from?' The concierge walked across the large foyer with him as Graysen headed for the lift.

'I've been in Nepal for a few months.'

'Good to be home?'

Not really, Graysen thought, but he nodded. 'Yes, it is. Thanks again for your help.'

'Anything else you need, sir, just call down.'

Graysen paused as the lift door opened. 'Actually, there is. I need secure storage for some of my luggage and most of my photographic equipment for a couple of weeks. I'm going on a trek in Central Australia, and I'm travelling lightly.'

Even though it was work, the trip to the centre was going to be the closest thing Graysen had had to a holiday since Marion passed away. There was no contract to fulfil, but he knew there would be a market for the photos he took as he trekked the Larapinta Trail. For the past five years, he'd worked nonstop in an attempt to bury his grief; he'd taken on back-to-back contracts and travelled the world, shooting from Antarctica to Africa. He and Marion had been together for thirty years, and it still felt as though part of him was missing.

He suspected that feeling would never leave him.

He'd spent the last few weeks in Kathmandu recovering from altitude sickness after an embarrassing evacuation.

'I think you need an Everest taxi,' the guide had told him when he'd begun to feel breathless at three and a half thousand metres.

'A what?' Graysen had asked crossly. His head was pounding and he felt like he was going to throw up.

'A helicopter. Don't worry, it won't be long. There's twenty-five companies that do the evacuations up here in our mountains. Altitude sickness is a common thing, even for the fit.'

'What are the symptoms again?' Graysen had read the literature and taken out the insurance, but his head was fuzzy.

'Headaches. Dizziness. Feeling sick. Not being hungry. Not sleeping. Grumpiness.' The guide had shot him a look at the last word.

Graysen was certainly fit, and he had rarely been sick apart from the odd head cold. Being medi-vacced from Namche

Bazaar had made him realise that he had been pushing himself too hard for too long. Physically and emotionally.

In her last days Marion had made him promise not to grieve too hard and too long.

'We've had a wonderful life together, my darling. We weren't blessed with children, and that worries me for you when I'm gone. You'll be lonely. I want you to promise that you'll go off and keep seeing the world. Visit new places, and only think of me when you see places that we visited together. Focus on being happy and appreciating the years we've had. Appreciate the beautiful things you see, embrace life and realise how precious it is.'

Graysen had held her close, the fragility of her bones breaking his heart.

'Go on, promise me.' Marion's smile was sweet, but he could see she was in pain when he touched her.

'I promise.'

He had carried her out to the small porch of the cottage they had rented on the east side of Lake Macquarie in Newcastle so she could see her beloved sunset. It wasn't far from the private hospital where she had had her treatment. The treatment that had failed.

There had only been three more sunsets before his wife had drawn her last breath in his arms.

'Mr Hughes?'

He frowned and looked at the concierge.

'The hotel can provide that service for you. We have secure short-term storage for up to eight weeks. Would you like me to organise that?'

'Thank you'—Graysen looked at the guy's name tag for the first time— 'Craig. I'd appreciate that. I fly out on Sunday and I'll be gone three weeks.'

'Leave it with me, sir. I'll arrange it for you.'

'Thank you.' As much as he hated being in the city, Graysen's mood lifted a bit. His walk to the harbour had been invigorating, thanks to the stiff southerly buster that had come through when they'd landed at the international airport. The plane had been buffeted by the wind as the pilots had brought the jet in to land, and for a brief moment he'd gone to reach for Marion's hand.

Sydney held sad memories of visits to the oncologist, and to surgeons. The quicker he got out of the city, the happier he'd be.

Not that *happy* was a feeling he knew these days.

He existed.

##

'Good to see you, Graysen!' Phillip Smythe, his friend and owner of PS Photographic Equipment and Supplies in Kent Street shook his hand the next morning. 'You should have said you were coming to town. It's been a long time, mate. Have you got time to come over for dinner one night or are you on your usual rushed schedule?'

'I'm on a schedule but I'd like that. I'm here until Sunday.'

'We're having a bit of a do tomorrow night. Just family. They'd all love to see you. It's Katy's thirtieth.'

'I don't want to intrude.'

'Mate, she's your goddaughter.'

'I haven't been much of a godfather to her.'

'Please come. In fact, I'll call Janette now.'

As Phillip called his wife, Graysen browsed through the locked cabinets; he knew what he wanted and there was stock on display.

'So, we'll see you at six-thirty tomorrow night. Don't bring anything, and if you'd like a bed, we've got plenty of room now that the kids have all left home.'

'Thanks, Phil. I'll see what the night brings.'

'Well, the offer's there. We've got a lot of catching up to do. It's been a long time, mate. Too long.'

The following night, a different concierge called a taxi for Graysen. He'd picked up a pretty silver bracelet for Katy in the hotel gift shop, and once he was in the taxi, he asked the driver to call in at a bottle shop where he bought a bottle of Glenfiddich for Phillip, and a bottle of Bollinger for Janette.

He didn't plan on staying too long, even though he hadn't seen his friends since Marion's funeral.

Janette wrapped her arms around him, and the sharp floral fragrance of her perfume hit Graysen hard. It was the same one Marion had always worn—Issey Miyake—and he knew straight away he'd made a mistake coming over.

'Oh, Gray, it's so good to see you.' Janette blinked away tears. 'I was so happy when Phil said you were in town. I've made the guest room up for you and I won't take no for an answer.' She reached up and put a hand to his face. 'I know what you're like.'

Graysen managed a smile. 'I'm paying top dollar for the Intercontinental.'

'I don't care. I'm not letting you go back to a lonely hotel room. You and Phil can sit and have a yarn. I'm sure the young ones will be heading out to a nightclub after dinner. It gives me a chance to babysit.'

'Babysit?'

'You'll see.'

In the end, Graysen stayed, and enjoyed himself. Sitting back and being cocooned in the warmth of the family—Phil and Janette had two sons and Katy. They all had partners and he was surprised to see two grandchildren.

'Yes, Uncle Graysen. We've grown since we last saw you.' Katy took his arm after he had greeted her with a kiss to her cheek. 'Come and sit down with your favourite goddaughter and tell me all the places you've been. David and I are going to travel before we settle down, so I'm going to pick your brains tonight.' She squeezed his hand, and her voice was gentle. 'It's so good to see you. We've missed you and Aunty Marion.'

'Thanks, Katy. It's nice to hear her name spoken. I've been a bit of a loner since I left Australia after the funeral.'

'We know. The only way we ever know where you are is to see you credited as the photographer in magazine articles and blogs these days.'

He chuckled. 'So, if you're reading them, you know where I've been.'

'Some of the places. Now tell me why you're home? Are you going to stay in Sydney? Are you going to retire? Dad's talking about it. David and I have been learning a lot about the business. My two useless brothers couldn't tell the difference between a camera and a Smart Watch.'

'Your dad's got a good five years on me. But no, I'm not thinking of retiring. I love the travel and I love the places that I get to see and photograph.'

'So, you're just here to buy more equipment? That was a top-class lens you bought today. Where's your next shoot?'

'It's good to know that you're interested in the business. And to answer your question, I'm heading to Central Australia.

Would you believe in all my travels, it's one place I've never seen or photographed?'

'Uluru at sunset? Overdone.' She pulled a face.

'No, the Larapinta Trail.'

'Really! David and I did that a couple of winters ago. It will be really good for you.'

'Good for me?'

'You'll see. The whole landscape is a very spiritual place. Sacred sites, Indigenous artworks and several archaeological sites. Are you doing the full walk?'

'I am.'

'The track is also home to what they call "song lines" or you might have heard of dreaming tracks. The one near Mt Sonder was incredible. Trust me, Uncle Gray, it will touch you.' She held his eyes. 'And it will heal you.'

Three days later, Graysen's gear was sorted and placed in storage at the hotel. His luggage for Central Australia consisted of a backpack, his laptop, a large, and a small camera bag, and an extendable tripod.

'You sure do travel light, Mr Hughes,' Craig said as he walked out and summoned one of the taxis waiting across from the gracious sandstone building.

'Best way to travel.' Graysen nodded.

'You enjoy your Larapinta trek. We'll see you in a few weeks.'

'Thanks, mate. You've been a great help.'

'I'll be interested to hear all about it. That trek's on my bucket list.'

'I'll show you some photos when I get back.'

'You like taking photos?' Craig nodded at the two camera bags as the taxi pulled up beside them. 'A great hobby.'

'I do.' Graysen nodded, seeing no need to tell the young guy that he was generally regarded as one of the top five landscape photographers in the world. That hobby had given him and Marion a good life. Unlimited travel, a cottage in the English countryside, and a beachside house at Palm Cove near Cairns. But Marion had always been a Newcastle girl and had wanted to spend her last months on the lake, even though she had no family left there.

'I'll look forward to seeing them. Have a great trip, sir.'

An hour later, Graysen was settled in the business class lounge at the domestic airport terminal. His flight had been delayed due to the strong winds and he shivered as he watched the rain running down the window beside him. He glanced at his watch.

Was it too early for a whisky?

It was past noon, and from the information that had flashed up on the departures board all flights had been delayed a couple of hours. He stood and crossed to the bar and soon had a tumbler of Glenfiddich and ice in hand as he chose a magazine from those on offer. Taking his seat in the circular lounge, Graysen sat back and flicked through the glossy magazine, picking straight away who'd taken the photographs of the African bushveld.

'I don't think I want to do this anymore, Paul. This is not a good omen.' The cultured English voice belonged to a very attractive blonde woman who was about to take a seat opposite him.

'Is it okay to sit here?' the man with her asked.

Graysen looked around, not particularly keen on having his solitude interrupted. The business lounge had filled up and there were very few seats left.

'Sure.' He put his head back down.

'Thank you. We appreciate it, don't we, Paul?' The woman was staring at him when Graysen lifted his head and he nodded.

'Looks like we could be here a while,' the guy called Paul said. 'We just heard our flight to Alice Springs has been put back to three-thirty. I'm Paul Dunn, and this is my wife, Cecily.' He leaned over and kissed her cheek. 'I love saying that, sweetheart.

Graysen tried not to groan as he realised he would have company for at least three hours. Newly-married company. He knew it would be rude to ignore them, so he stood and held his hand out. 'Graysen.'

'I hate flying enough without the delays. Like Paul said, we're going to the Red Centre for our honeymoon. Where are you off to?'

'Same,' he answered shortly.

'Business or pleasure?' Paul asked as he sat across from Graysen.

'A holiday trek.'

'You're an Aussie?' Cecily was slow to take the hint as she reached over and squeezed Paul's hand. 'Paul booked a trek for our honeymoon as a surprise. You know I think I would have much rather gone to the islands. And now with this delay, I think it's the universe telling us we shouldn't be going. We can still change our mind, honey. There were lots of flights to Cairns on the board when I looked.'

'Sweetie, now come on, you'll have a ball. It's supposed to be really pretty. How many people get to go trekking on a luxury tour for their honeymoon? Five-star service in an incredible location.' Paul looked over at Graysen as he lifted the glass and drained his whisky. 'I'm going to get a drink, what's your poison, buddy?'

For the first time, Graysen picked the American twang.

'Glenfiddich. Thanks. With ice.' If he had to sit and listen to Cecily's prattle, and sweetie and honey, for the next couple of hours it wouldn't hurt to anaesthetise himself.

'Wine for you, my precious?'

My precious?

Cecily nodded, Paul headed for the bar and Graysen wondered if they'd seen *Lord of the Rings*.

'So, you're travelling alone?' Cecily said as Graysen opened the magazine and tried to show her he did not want to talk. His breath caught, and his breathing shallowed as that familiar dull feeling began to unfurl from his gut and settle in his chest. He was pissed off he'd let this couple get under his skin.

'Yes, I prefer my own company.' Maybe it was rude, but he didn't really care. She might be beautiful, but she wasn't very intuitive.

'Yes, we do too. Paul works really hard and I'm left at home by myself most of the time. We've been living together for five years. His proposal was a shock to me, but we had the most incredible wedding in the Cotswolds near Mummy and Daddy's manor. Ten bridesmaids, and we had the most amazing pink theme. Would you like to see some photos?'

Graysen grunted and shook his head without looking up.

Give me strength.

'Paul's an investment banker and we lived in New York for a while before he agreed I needed to live back in England. At least we were near his family there. Mummy said I'd be bored with him at work, but I managed to fill in my days. Paul says another couple of years and he'll have made enough for us to retire. I have a lot of friends in London but most of them work, so I go to the gym, and I read a lot. I subscribe to that travel magazine you're reading too. I love walking too, but this trek? I'm still not sure. Where do you live, Graysen?'

For fuck's sake.

'I don't,' he said shortly. He blinked as his vision blurred. 'I travel.'

'Oooh, how exciting. But don't you get bored not having a home to go to? I thought when we came to Australia, I'd really, really hate it, but you know what I've discovered since we spent a week in Sydney?' Cecily spread her manicured hands in front of her.

She stared at him and he was obviously supposed to ask.

'No, I don't. And Cecily? I'm not really interested. May I read my magazine? I have work to do.'

She drew in a deep breath and let out a sigh, 'I'm really sorry. Paul tells me I talk too much, but you know what? I'm just interested in people and what makes them tick.'

Graysen nodded and opened to the spread of the giraffes in the Serengeti National Park. The text was jumping all over the page and he focused on breathing his way through his stress. How stupid to let a ditz like this give him grief. 'Admirable.'

'Are you okay?'

He reached up and wiped the sweat off his forehead. 'I'm fine.'

'What makes you tick, Graysen? Why are you going on the trek?' He looked up as her voice changed. Maybe she wasn't the ditz he'd thought she was. There was a hardness to her voice and her gaze was cold as she stared at him.

'Not a lot. I'm a pretty ordinary guy.'

'An ordinary guy who travels the world and doesn't have a home? You sound pretty interesting to me.'

He stared at her for a moment and then turned back to his magazine.

The next thing he knew, a fresh glass of whisky was in front of him.

'There you go,' Paul said.

'Thank you. Appreciate it.' He picked up the glass and took a deep swig as Paul took the seat closest to him.

'Paul.' The little girl voice was back. 'Take me down to the concourse please. I want to look at the shops. I might buy some more shoes. And I don't think I have enough warm clothes packed. I need some more nail polish too.'

'Aw, honey. I was going to sit and have a drink and chat to Graysen here.'

Her eyes widened and she shook her head. 'No. Shopping, please. Now.'

Relief filled Graysen as Cecily stood, and grabbed her husband's arm, and dragged him away.

Graysen couldn't help the smile as her loud whisper reached him. 'Look for somewhere else to sit. He is *such* a rude man.'

I'll save you the bother, sweetheart, he thought as they disappeared past the restrooms. Graysen picked up his drink and drained it. Gathering his laptop and camera bags, he left the business lounge. He'd fill in the time in the glassed-in area of the observation deck. Two whiskies were enough; they'd warmed him and taken the edge off his anxiety. It had been a few months since that tight feeling had gripped his chest, and he didn't like it.

Chapter 3

Darwin Airport - Sunday, June 7

Sandra's three daughters and James had gathered at the airport to see her off. Once they—especially Ellie—had accepted that she was determined to do this trip—and do it alone—they'd all pitched in and helped her get organised.

Shopping trips to buy the gear she needed, and coffee meetings in Darwin to consider the different companies running the glamping treks available, had filled in the last three weeks and Sandra had seen more of the girls all together than she had all year.

'Remember that school holiday when we stayed at the caravan park near the showground and we all came shopping here at Casuarina?' Emma said one afternoon as they were having a coffee break. They'd just spent an hour choosing the best hiking boots for Sandra to wear.

'I remember dropping you off and then I went to visit Susan Sordina.'

Ellie flinched. 'Susan was a lovely woman, but that name, Sordina still sends a shiver down my spine.'

'She made some poor choices.' Sandra reached out and squeezed Ellie's hand. 'Let it go, love. I have.'

'Yes, Mum. I can ninety percent of the time.'

'And she had a beautiful son. Kane is a wonderful son-in-law too.'

'She did, Mum. And he is a beautiful man. Nothing like that cranky pilot I thought he was the first time I saw him. And

Susan would have loved James. Bloody breast cancer,' Ellie said.

They were all quiet for a while. The year Ellie had met Susan's son, Kane, had been tough. Susan had passed away, her second husband, Panos Sordina, who had been involved in the supposed suicide of Sandra's husband, Peter, had been murdered too. Ellie had been attacked by Russell Fairweather, an industrialist who had been blackmailing the Chief Magistrate.

Emma chuckled to break the tension. 'We bought magazines, and makeup with money Dad slipped to me before we left the farm.'

'And we had lunch right here in this food court,' Dru said with a smile. She nudged Ellie beside her. 'Em and I had milkshakes and you decided you were going to be grown up—'

'Yeah, Miss Tomboy Ellie,' Emma interrupted.

'And you ordered a cappuccino and spat it all over the table,' Dru continued.

'I did not. I spat it in a tissue,' Ellie said.

It had been a wonderful afternoon, and when Ellie dropped Sandra back to her apartment, Sandra wondered why on earth she was going off to "find herself". Things were pretty good, and she'd seen so much of the girls these past couple of weeks.

'Did you pack your phone charger, Mum?' Ellie asked as Sandra nursed James on her lap in the coffee lounge at the airport as they waited for her flight to be called.

'There'll be nowhere to charge that in the West McDonnells,' Dru said.

'No, we got Mum a battery pack. Remember?' Emma said.

'Just more weight to carry.' Dru shook her head.

'Once I get in the hotel and talk to the guide, I'll see what they offer. I forgot to ask that when I called the company.'

'Anyway,' Emma said. 'There won't be much service out there.'

'But Mum'll still want her phone charged for taking photos.'

'That's true, Els.'

'Hey you girls. I know you're just trying to help, but I'm a big girl now. I have a small camera and two cards to store the photos.'

'And a spare battery?' Dru asked.

'Yes, three.' Sandra looked up as an announcement came over the loudspeaker.

'Passengers travelling to Alice Springs on Air North, Flight 200, please make your way to Gate Seven. Your aircraft is ready to board.'

Sandra stood holding James, and Dru picked up her carry-on luggage. 'You be a good boy for Mummy while Nan's away, won't you?'

'I'm always a good boy, Nanny.'

'I wish,' Ellie said with a chuckle. 'If you'd just sleep in your own bed at night, you'd be a perfect child, my Jimmy boy.'

'You make sure you get lots of rest, Ellie.' Sandra handed James over to his mother and took her bag from Dru when they reached the entrance to the air bridge. 'And Emma, you're working too hard, you look tired. Try to get some time off.'

'What about me, Ma?' Dru held her arms open for a hug. 'What are my instructions?'

'You, my baby child? You never do as you're told. So, I won't waste my breath.' Sandra laughed as she hugged her six-foot daughter.

'You have a great time, and stay safe, Mum.'

Sandra blinked away the tears that threatened. 'And you, my lovely girls, you all take care of yourselves.'

Ellie rolled her eyes. 'You'll be back in three weeks, Mum.'

'Ring us before you leave on the trek. What day was it again?' Emma asked.

'I have three days in Alice Springs at Lasseter's Resort and then I join the trek on Wednesday. It's all in the itinerary that I emailed to each of you. Print it out and put it on your fridge. Phone numbers, contact people, plus the emergency satellite phone number for the guide if you have an emergency. But only in a dire emergency. I'll call you as soon as I get back to the hotel after the trek.'

Emma lined up for her hug, and then Ellie.

'Take care, Mum, and have a wonderful time.'

When Sandra reached the air bridge, she turned and smiled at her girls and her grandson. 'Love you all,' she mouthed.

She would miss them all so much, but she was determined to have a wonderful time.

***

Graysen hurried across the tarmac to the terminal at Alice Springs. He'd managed to avoid that couple in Sydney, but he'd heard her and that plummy accent a couple of seats behind him on the short flight. Rude and demanding, and as hard as nails.

He slid his backpack off his shoulder as he waited for a box of camera gear to come onto the carousel. He'd left the new lenses in the boxes for the trip; Phil and David had packed it very carefully for him. The flight had been full and there was a crowd three deep beside the baggage conveyor belt. Eventually, with a loud jerking noise. the carousel began to move and luggage came through the rubber flaps. A pair of hot pink suitcases were the first to appear and Graysen was not a bit surprised when Paul stepped forward and swung them off the carousel. He put them over next to his wife, and then moved back to wait for more.

Probably full of her designer clothes and nail polish and new shoes, Graysen thought uncharitably.

He shook the thought off. He didn't usually let people bother him.

Live and let live had been Marion's mantra. She would have been surprised at his reaction to the obnoxious woman.

'Excuse me.' A quiet voice came from behind as a petite woman tried to get through the crowd to get her luggage.

'Sorry.' Graysen stepped to the side and watched as she tried to reach a large suitcase on the moving conveyor belt. It was wedged behind another suitcase on the inside of the carousel, and just out of her reach.

He stepped forward. 'Let me.'

'Thank you.' Her smile was warm. 'I'm not used to this.'

The suitcase wasn't heavy and he placed it on the tiles beside her, keeping an eye out for his camera gear.

'Many more?' he asked.

'Just one small, soft bag to come through. I'll be fine now. Thanks very much for your help.'

'My pleasure,' he said.

She smiled shyly and stepped back with her case beside her. He glanced at her curiously. She was a total opposite to the English woman who'd pushed his buttons.

Quiet and polite, she was an attractive woman. Middle-aged, but her skin was flawless and even in the short interaction they'd had, her eyes had sparkled with warmth. She reminded him a little of Janette. Not in looks, but with her kind and unassuming personality.

A good person.

She was obviously alone, and like him, not being met by anyone. Chatter filled the terminal as passengers were met by family and friends.

He spotted his box come through the flaps and waited until it came around to his side before he stepped forward to retrieve it. At the same time, the woman beside him stepped forward, but their collision was gentle.

'I'm so sorry,' she said as she moved away from Graysen and he picked up his box. 'I told you I'm not experienced at this. I guess there's a carousel etiquette.'

He nodded but tempered his lack of response with a smile. By the time he had picked up his box and backpack, she'd gone.

The dry heat hit Graysen as he wheeled a luggage trolley ahead of him through the main sliding doors. His eyes felt gritty immediately and he dug in his pocket for his sunglasses. There was a small queue at the taxi rank and the woman he'd assisted was at the end near the terminal entry. He carefully placed his trolley to the side and she turned to him.

'I guess there's taxi queue etiquette as well?' Her smile was rueful.

'The same all over the world.' He smiled at her again. She had a very calming demeanour. 'First in, best dressed.' He looked to the head of the queue, unsurprised to see a tower of hot pink suitcases there.

'I can't remember the last time I took a taxi,' she said. 'Even though I live in the city, I think I'd still qualify for the country bumpkin tag.'

'Which city?' Graysen surprised himself as he asked the question.

'Not far. I'm afraid I'm not very adventurous. Darwin.'

He nodded. 'A nice city. Almost a big country town the last time I was there, but it's been a while.'

'Still much the same, although the tourist numbers seem to increase every winter.'

'Everyone loves the warmth,' he said.

She was quiet as they waited for the taxis to arrive, and Graysen was pleased he wasn't next to someone who had to talk constantly. He could hear Cecily, at the front of the queue, giving her opinion on the heat, the flies, and the lack of taxis.

As her voice rose, the woman turned to him and grimaced. 'Maybe she should have stayed at home.'

'I think she'd be the same wherever she was. I had to share a lounge with them in Sydney.'

'You've had a long flight then. From Sydney, I mean.'

'Yes. Although not so much the time in the air. We were delayed because of wind and storms in Sydney.'

Four taxis arrived and they moved closer to the front of the queue.

'Not long now,' he said. A couple of the taxis were vans and the drivers were trying to fill them. The driver of the van that Cecily and Paul had boarded called along the queue. 'Anyone else for the city?'

'No, thank goodness,' Graysen said quietly. 'Sorry, that was a bit rude.'

She shook her head. 'Didn't bother me.'

Two couples ahead of them on the queue moved forward, and soon they reached the head of the queue.

A small sedan pulled up and the driver stepped out and approached them. 'Where to, sir and madam?'

'We're not together,' she replied. 'But I'm going to Lasseter's, I mean the Crowne Plaza.'

'I am too, if you'd like to share,' Graysen said.

'Of course. We don't have much luggage between us.'

'We don't.'

As the driver loaded their bags and his box into the boot, Graysen held out his hand. 'I'm Graysen Hughes.'

'Sandra Porter,' she replied, taking his hand. Her fingers were warm and soft.

'A pleasure, Sandra.' He climbed into the back seat beside her.

The trip to the hotel from the airport only took ten minutes, but Graysen noticed how Sandra took everything in as they drove along the Stuart Highway. Eventually when they turned right onto South Terrace and across the dry Todd River, she spoke.

'It's so different to what I expected. I was imagining something like Darwin.'

'You haven't been to the Alice before?'

Her smile was self-conscious. 'I haven't really been anywhere before.'

'It's been a while since I was here. Probably twenty-five years ago.'

Marion had wanted to see Ayers Rock back in the days before it was Uluru, and they'd hired a car and driven down from Alice Springs, and then continued down to Adelaide. That had been his first calendar contracted trip, and when his career had really taken off.

The taxi turned into the resort and pulled up outside the building that housed reception. The driver turned around, and Graysen handed over his business credit card before Sandra could reach for her purse.

'Thank you for letting me share,' he said. 'This can go on my business tab.'

'Thank you. That's very kind of you.'

As the concierge wheeled a luggage trolley out to collect their luggage, they stood together, and for the first time, the silence was awkward. They'd exhausted all the social chit chat. When they walked into reception, the three receptionists were free.

Graysen turned to Sandra. 'Thanks for the company. I hope you enjoy your stay in Alice Springs.'

'Thank you, Graysen. You too. You made my arrival that little bit easier. It's the first time I've travelled alone, and I'll admit I was a bit nervous.'

'Well, you're here safely now. Enjoy your sightseeing.' He couldn't believe it when he winked at her. 'And don't bet too much on the tables.'

Her laugh was warm. 'I won't be betting anything.'

He lifted his hand in a wave as they each moved to a different end of the reception counter.

Chapter 4

Crowne Plaza Hotel, Alice Springs - Monday, June 8

Sandra deliberated over her choice of clothing for the Larapinta Luxury Trek welcome function. Finally, she slipped on the simple navy sheath that fell to just below her knees and added simple gold earrings and a gold chain around her neck. Dabbing on a splash of perfume, and checking her hair she'd put up in a French roll, she looked in the mirror for a final check.

'You don't look too bad for an old chook and a grandma,' she said to her reflection. Since she'd been going to the gym, walking and eating well, she'd shed a few kilos and toned up. Her skin was clear and her eyes were bright, and despite her nerves about going to a function with a group of people she didn't know, she thought she could hold her own. Picking up the small navy bag that matched her shoes, she made her way out of the room to the elevator.

Sandra was pleased that the function was being held at the hotel where she was staying. If she felt too out of place, once she had the information she needed, she could go back to her room and have a room-service dinner. She knew nothing yet about the rest of the group on the trek; only that there were nine people including her, and a couple of guides. She hoped she wasn't the only single person; perhaps there would be another solo woman she could pair up with. Her nerves about undertaking a walk through a harsh environment were beginning to kick in. She'd been doing a lot of reading of the tourist brochures in her room, and it sounded challenging.

Maybe Ellie had been right. Maybe she should be lying beside a pool in a resort somewhere.

Pulling herself up straight, she waited for the elevator.

The doors dinged and opened and Sandra's eyes widened as they settled on Graysen Hughes; it was hard to ignore her increased heartbeat.

Just nerves.

He was a good-looking man, and she had warmed to him yesterday.

'Hello,' she said.

'Good evening, Sandra.' The admiration in his eyes made her glad she'd made an effort to dress up. 'You look very elegant.'

'Thank you.'

'Heading out for dinner?' he asked.

'No. I have a function to attend here.'

For a moment, his eyes narrowed, and she sensed a slight withdrawal.

'A function?'

'Yes, a meet and greet for a tour I'm doing.'

'What sort of tour?' His withdrawal was more obvious now.

She lifted her chin. 'Larapinta Luxury Treks. Why do you ask?'

'Ah,' he said. 'Interesting. Have you just booked it? Since you arrived?'

'No, why do you ask?'

'Because I'm going to the same function as you.'

Sandra was confused. 'Why would you think I just booked it? Because I found out you were going on that tour?'

'So, you did know?' His voice was cold.

'No.' Sandra felt like stamping her foot. Who was this guy? 'Of course I didn't know. How would I? Are you famous or something?'

'No, I'm not. I just value my privacy.'

'Well, I'm sorry, Graysen, but you seem to have an almighty chip on your shoulder. I didn't know you were in the tour, but perhaps if I had known I wouldn't have booked it.' She folded her arms and stared ahead. The numbers on the panel beside the door flashed down to the first floor where the function rooms were. She waited for an apology, but there was none forthcoming. He stood straight and silent beside her.

The door opened and she stepped out without a backward glance.

How rude. And how *arrogant.*

In such a small group it was going to be very difficult to avoid him. Sandra bit her lip.

What should I do?

She couldn't drop out; the girls had paid for over half the tour. She'd baulked at the amount when they'd shown her the brochure, but they had insisted.

As she approached the door of the Namatjira Function Room she finally smiled. Imagine filling out a travel insurance claim.

One of the guests was rude to me so I decided not to go!

Well, she'd "pull on her big girl panties"—one of Dru's favourite expressions—go on the tour and ignore Mr High and Mighty Hughes. At least she had one of the trek guests picked before they started.

A buzz of conversation met Sandra as she pushed the door open; there was no sign of *him* behind her. Who was he anyway? Should she have recognised him? Was he someone famous? She'd get Mr Google working later.

'Mrs Porter?' A tall man in a khaki shirt was waiting by the door beside a woman whose shirt had the same logo on the pocket. Larapinta Luxury Tours.

'Yes, hello, I'm Sandra Porter.'

'Welcome. I'm Andrew Hill from Larapinta Luxury Tours, and this is my colleague, Jodie Wright. May we call you Sandra?'

'Of course, Andrew. It's nice to meet you both.'

'I'll be your leading guide for the tour and Jodie is our hostess and chef,' Andrew said. He was a young man, tanned and rugged looking with light blue eyes fringed with fair lashes.

'We're just waiting for one more guest and we can get started,' Jodie said.

'If that's Mr Hughes, he came down in the lift with me.'

'Good, we can get started as soon as he arrives. What would you like to drink?' Jodie asked.

'Champagne?' *I might as well start the tour with a bang,* Sandra thought.

'Of course.' As Jodie headed off to the small bar, Andrew gestured for Sandra to follow him. 'Come and meet the others.'

Before he could start the introductions, the door opened and Graysen stepped into the room.

'Excuse me a moment,' Andrew said. 'We might as well introduce you both at the same time.'

Sandra stood to the side of the group who were chatting while Andrew walked over to Graysen. They shook hands, and she swallowed as they walked back over to her.

***

Graysen paused before they reached the group near the window. 'Excuse me, Andrew, do you mind if I have a quick word with Sandra before we start?'

'Not a problem, Graysen. I'll get you a drink. What would you like?'

'A light beer would be fine, thank you.'

Graysen walked over to Sandra—her back was turned to him. He touched her elbow gently and she looked around at him, her expression bland.

'Sandra,' he said quietly. 'I'd like to apologise for my behaviour in the elevator. It was extremely rude of me, and you did nothing to deserve it. I'm very sorry.'

She stood back and regarded him for a long time. So long, Graysen began to feel uncomfortable. Shit, he'd blown it, and upset a lovely woman who hadn't deserved one word of what had spewed from his insecurities. As they looked at each other, the conversation of the group beside them came to a sudden stop.

'Oh, fun. Look who's here,' said a familiar voice. 'Mr Personality himself.'

Sandra looked from him to the speaker and then back again. 'We'll talk later, but yes, I accept your apology,' she said. 'Thank you.'

Andrew stepped forward and it was easy to see his smile was forced. The next twelve days would prove to be very interesting unless the dynamics of this group were settled. Graysen knew he could take the blame for most of it.

Shit, why did I ever decide on a group tour? He should have walked the bloody trail himself.

But he knew he was getting soft. The comfort of an eco-tent that someone else had set up, rather than a swag he would have had to carry, and a hot shower at the end of the day, not to mention a three-course meal had enticed him. Now he had to make up for the angst he'd caused.

'Sounds like a few of you are already acquainted, folks, but we'll do the whole introduction spiel,' Andrew said.

Jodie came back with a tray of drinks and when everyone had a drink in hand, she nodded at Andrew. 'While you do the intro, mate, I'll get the hot canapes.'

Andrew ushered them all into a circle. Graysen avoided looking at Cecily, but he suspected he deserved everything she gave. That didn't bother him, but he couldn't believe how rude he'd been to Sandra. It had just come out without him thinking before he spoke. He'd regretted it as soon as she'd walked out of the lift. He'd gone for a walk around the lawn outside to calm down.

You have to stop being such a selfish and cranky shit. Marion's voice filled his head.

'Okay, guys, we're all about team work on our trek, and you're about to meet the rest of your team. I'll start on my left.'

Graysen swallowed his pride. 'Before we get going with the formal introductions, I'd like to apologise to Cecily and Paul for my rude behaviour in Sydney. It's no excuse but I'd just come off a twenty-hour flight after being medi-vacced out of Nepal. I was rude to you when you were simply trying to make conversation, I'm sorry.'

'Sorry to hear you were crook, Graysen. You're recovered now?' Paul said glancing at Cecily. Her arms were folded and he guessed he'd done his dash there.

'I am.' He forced a rueful smile; he had to get on with these people for the next twelve days. 'My mood has recovered too, I'm sure you'll be pleased to hear.'

Sandra was watching him and knew his apology needed more work.

'Okay, we've got a lot to get through tonight,' Andrew said. 'After we get to know each other and have some dinner, we're going to run through the itinerary, and the safety briefing. That way, we can start the trek as soon as we go to the drop off point tomorrow.' Andrew turned to the couple on the left. 'First off, this is Cecily and Paul from London.'

Graysen kept his expression bland as Cecily dropped a curtsy.

'Then we have Miska and Zed, also from the UK. Welcome, guys.' The young couple gave a wave and Zed smiled.

'Next to our UK visitors we have Clive and Jenny from Sydney, and then Sandra Porter, almost a local from Darwin.'

'Hi, Sandy, is it okay if we call you that?' The other woman standing alone raised a languid hand.

Sandra smiled. 'That's fine. It's a long time since I was called Sandy. Takes me right back.'

'Sandy, it is! *Please* don't introduce me as Margaret, Andrew. I'm Maggie, and I'm from Sydney.' Her flaming red hair and the rings on each finger caught the light. She certainly didn't look the type to be heading off on a two-hundred-kilometre trek.

'Welcome, Maggie,' Andrew corrected. 'And then last but not least, I'm sure many of you are familiar with the work of Graysen Hughes, world-renowned landscape photographer.'

Graysen bit back the groan and felt like leaving; Sandra's eyes were still on him.

'So, chat amongst yourselves, get to know each other, and enjoy a taste of the cuisine you'll be sampling over the next twelve days. We're proud of our company, and with our luxury accommodation, top class meals, and private treks, we can guarantee you a five-star experience on your trek on the famous Larapinta Trail.'

Jodie came out with a tray of hot canapes, followed by a young waiter holding a tray of small plates and napkins. Soon everyone held a plate of food and a drink, and the mood relaxed. Graysen made the effort to go over to Paul and Cecily.

'How are you enjoying the Red Centre so far?' he asked, injecting brightness into his voice.

Paul grinned at him. 'Wow, it's awesome. We took a tour out to Hermannsburg to look at the indigenous art today. It was great.'

'I'm very pleased to hear you've recovered,' Cecily said. 'We've checked out the west, and it's obvious the trek's not for the unfit or the fainthearted.' She looked at Graysen and then past him to Sandra. 'Do you think you're fit enough to get to the end?'

He was about to answer, but Sandra beat him to it. 'I've been training for three months, and I'm really excited. How about you, Cecily?'

'I'm young and fit. I don't need to train. Even though it looks very, very hard, it won't be a problem.'

Graysen raised his eyebrows and took Sandra's arm. 'Let's go meet the rest of our "team".'

Miska was standing beside the bar; her dark hair and tanned skin gave her an exotic appearance. Her skin-tight black dress showed off a fit and lithe figure.

'Where are you from, Miska?' Sandra asked when there was a lull in the conversation.

Miska looked at her partner.

'I'm from New York, but Mis and I have been living in London for a couple of years,' Zed answered.

Miska leaned into him with a smile. 'We're on our honeymoon too.'

'Congratulations,' Sandra said. 'Wow, two newly-married couples. Adventurous honeymoons.'

'This is pretty tame for us.' Zed put his arm around Miska, and Sandra thought how good they looked together. 'We usually try to push ourselves. Eco-tents and hot showers is a bonus for us this trip.'

'Paul and Cecily said you've been in Nepal, Graysen,' Miska said. 'We spent a few months there working in the villages after the earthquake.'

'So newly married, but you've been together a long time?' Sandra commented.

Miska smiled up at Zed. 'We have. Nine years. Zed's proposed about ten times, and I finally gave in. It's only a piece of paper to me, but his family is pretty traditional.'

'And we had a fabulous wedding in Tahiti.'

How the other half lives, Sandra thought. Dru had been her traveller, living in Dubai for a few years, but she'd settled in Darwin with Connor now.

The last couple, Clive and Jenny Clark from Sydney, came over from the bar and joined them, and Maggie followed them over. The three were closer to retirement age than the millennials in the group.

'Hey, great to meet you all. Looks like a good group we've got here,' Clive said.

'Good to see some other "mature" walkers on the trek.' Maggie's voice was husky, and Graysen was aware of her checking him out over the rim of her champagne glass.

More food and drink appeared, and after a few minutes, Andrew invited them all to sit in the chairs grouped in front of a wide screen while he dimmed the lights.

'This will save us time in the morning, team'—Graysen flinched every time he heard the word "team". Usually a loner, he was starting to wonder if he'd made a very wrong choice. He pushed his doubt away. Once they were on the trail, he could set his own pace and only socialise with the group at mealtimes. He hadn't chosen this trek to be sociable and make new acquaintances. Looking across at Maggie and Sandra, he wondered about the other two older women, and their motivation for doing the trek alone. Mrs Porter, Andrew had introduced Sandra. He wondered where Mr Porter was.

Graysen's eyelids began to droop, and he closed his eyes as the safety briefing continued. He'd heard it all before in Nepal, and on many of his other treks. The grades of this walk might be classed as difficult on some sections, but it was a safe walk from what he'd seen on the topological maps. Graysen was more interested in the sunrises and sunsets and trying to capture the landscape in the ethereal light at certain times of the day. He lifted his hand to his mouth and covered the yawn that threatened as Andrew's voice droned on, and was pleased when the lights came back on when the presentation finished.

There were a few general questions and he considered getting up and leaving but made himself sit there for a while. He'd been rude enough already.

'If there's no more questions, we'll see you all in the morning in the foyer. Seven a.m. sharp. Sleep well.' Andrew finally wound up the session.

Paul and Cecily headed over to the bar, followed by Maggie, but Graysen escaped before he had to talk to anyone.

Chapter 5

The Old Telegraph Station, Alice Springs - Tuesday, June 9.

Sandra stood in the shade under the awning at the Trail Station at The Old Telegraph Station and listened carefully as Andrew pointed to the large map on the wall. Her face and the exposed skin on her arms and legs were covered with fifty-plus sun cream, and her new sunglasses and cap fitted snugly. Her fly net was safely in her shorts pocket for when she needed it. She was worried that her lack of sleep last night would slow her down today, so she'd had a second cup of strong coffee when she'd gone back to her room after the five-thirty a.m. breakfast in the hotel dining room. The last thing she wanted was to lag behind the younger members of the group.

'A solid start this morning,' Andrew continued. 'An hour and a half easy walk to the Geoff Moss bridge that passes under the Stuart Highway and then a steady climb for over seven kilometres. Everyone feeling good this morning?'

There were nods and murmurs of assent all round.

'Our first three days are the most important in terms of getting acclimatised to the conditions. How you condition yourself and treat your body from here to our third day at Standley Chasm will set your performance for the rest of our trek.' He looked around. 'Any specific questions from what I've outlined this morning?'

Paul raised his hand. 'So, the first three days sorts out our hydration, boot issues, and gets our mindset in the right zone? But how much water *should* we actually drink?'

'It varies depending on your body weight and your energy output, but you do need to keep your hydration level high because it's hard to get it back up once it drops.'

'But how *much* should we drink?' Cecily's whining voice was annoying Sandra already.

'The best advice on our trek, which is moderate output rather than intensive exercise, is to drink to thirst. And be sensible about it. Drinking too much can also cause problems.'

Cecily turned away and muttered something to her husband.

'As far as our safety goes . . . you said last night you had a satellite phone.' Zed stepped forward, Miska hanging onto his arm. Sandra wondered how she'd go on the trek. She was quiet and seemed a bit nervous. 'I guess it's reliable? I mean is there service everywhere if we have a problem?'

'One hundred percent coverage on the Iridium network. If we have any problems—which I'm sure we won't—we can get a helicopter in fast. There's limited places where you'll have service with your phones—mainly Telstra—for making calls and uploading images to your social media accounts. Our hashtag—we really appreciate being tagged—is *#LarapintaLuxury*. Two capitals. You'll have some service tonight at Simpsons Gap.'

'Thanks.' Zed nodded.

Excitement bubbled up in Sandra's chest as Andrew gestured to the west. The biggest thing she had ever done by herself was about to start and she was feeling confident, more so after listening to Andrew last night.

'Jodie will meet us at Wallaby Gap campsite with lunch, just after noon. So, pace yourselves and keep an eye on the time. We've got just under fourteen kilometres to walk this morning, and as I said last night, this first section is a moderate to difficult walk. The track is rough in parts. Remember to stay fairly close to your partner. If you could make your way to the gate, I'll be with you shortly to lead the way.' As the group began to make their way to the western gate, Andrew caught up to Sandra and waited for Graysen to reach them. He was at the back of the group.

'I meant to talk to you both last night, but I didn't catch you before you left.'

'Is there a problem?' Graysen frowned. He was kitted out in khaki shorts and long-sleeved shirt, and his backpack was three times the size of anyone else's. A retractable tripod hung off his belt. Sandra had been a bit embarrassed last night when Andrew had introduced him as a world-famous photographer. That must have been what he'd meant when he'd had a go at her in the lift.

She'd never heard of him; then again, the only photographer she'd ever heard of was Annie Leibovitz. The girls had given her a coffee table book with her photographs one birthday a few years back.

'No, not at all. I just wanted to pair you and Sandy up.'

Heat rose up Sandra's neck, despite the chill wind.

'For walking, I assume you mean,' Graysen said. His lips twitched as he looked at Sandra.

'Yes, I don't mean you have to walk together, but just keep a buddy eye on each other. The others are all couples, and I've paired up with Maggie, so you're the only ones left.' He chuckled. 'Some groups I've led have been all singles, and it takes some working out, let me tell you. Are you both comfortable with that?'

Sandra nodded keeping her voice brisk. 'Good idea. Not a problem for me. The only thing is, I might slow Graysen down.' Even though she wasn't impressed, she could see the sense in the idea. She could have had Dru—or God forbid, Frank—along, but she'd really wanted to prove that she could do this away from her support network at home.

'Not at all,' Graysen replied. 'I'll be stopping frequently to set up my tripod and take photos.'

'Okay, guys, that's great. Right, let's get going.'

The trail started at the Old Telegraph Station, and Sandra looked with interest at the Pioneer Cemetery as they walked past. She had a few days in Alice Springs after the trek, and she'd make sure she came back to visit.

She looked ahead, excitement fuelling her steps. Already the frontrunners of the group were disappearing over the slight rise ahead of them. Beneath her boots was pebbly clay, and from the brochure she'd studied she could identify stunted mulga and casuarina trees in the scattered bush beside the trail. Above, the sky was almost clear, with an occasional wisp of white cloud drifting across the blue. Despite the arduous day ahead, serenity settled in her. Sandra smiled and knew she'd made the right decision to walk the Larapinta Trail. She would even forgive Graysen and forget his rudeness of last night. Who knew what others carried in their hearts?

***

If he had to be paired off with anyone, Graysen could cope with Sandra Porter. She was quiet and since he'd been rude to her last night, she'd kept her distance. Although not just with him; she'd kept herself apart from the whole group this morning. She'd sat at a single table for their early breakfast, and had stood alone as Andrew delivered the morning briefing.

Guilt stabbed at him; he hoped he wasn't responsible for her being a loner. With a shrug he stepped out. He'd been on numerous treks in many locations, most alone and some guided; on the group treks, people relaxed and got to know each other after a few days of walking and eating together at night.

Despite that, he did feel a bit responsible and decided he would be sociable and chat to Sandra when they stopped for the midday break. She certainly wasn't one for inane social chat like Maggie had shown when she'd shared his table at breakfast.

'My husband suggested this trip, the love.' Her laugh was loud. 'He was coming too, but had to go on a business trip to Europe at the last minute. Not my usual, but the luxury tags got me in. What about you?'

'Work,' he'd answered briefly, but she hadn't got the hint, talking nonstop as he quickly finished his cereal, and then toast. Finally, he'd swilled his coffee down, wiped his mouth and nodded before he left the table.

As they set off on the walk, Graysen slowed his pace to stay at the rear. The first few kilometres of the landscape were uninspiring, but he did snap some shots of the few remaining telegraph poles at the beginning of the track. Andrew was leading, and if there were any problems in the group, bringing up the rear meant Graysen could help deal with them. Plus, he'd keep an eye on Sandra, his designated partner. She'd set off at a good pace, and he noted her firm and muscular calves as she strode ahead. She was obviously a walker and had prepared for the trek.

After a few hundred metres, he caught up to Clive and Jenny. They were standing beside one of the telegraph poles. Clive's ruddy complexion was even redder than it had been at the Telegraph Station and he mopped at his brow with a handkerchief.

'Everything okay?' Graysen enquired, keeping his voice upbeat.

The new me, he thought. Marion would have been proud.

'Yes, all good. We're just looking at the poles.'

'I was surprised to see them on the trail. I didn't know the wrought iron poles were still here,' Graysen said. 'Apparently they're part of the Overland Telegraph Line.'

'Yes, completed in 1872, the line connected Darwin and Port Augusta.'

Graysen nodded. 'Not a bad feat for the conditions of the time.'

'It was one of the great engineering feats of nineteenth century Australia,' Clive said.

His wife stepped out of the shade of a low casuarina tree and fanned herself. 'It's part of the reason we came on this trek. Clive was a professor of engineering at Sydney Uni.'

'And my research focus was the engineering history of Australia.'

'Thus,' Jenny added, and there was a hint of acerbity in her tone, 'we are trekking the Larapinta Trail because of these telegraph poles. With a bit of research, we may not have had to spend thirteen thousand dollars to walk two hundred kilometres. We could have gone to the museum and seen them for the cost of an admission fee.'

'I told you, you didn't have to come. I was quite happy to do it myself, Jenny,' Clive snapped. 'Anyway, come on, we're falling behind. I've got enough photos.'

Before Graysen could respond they took off ahead of him, almost at a run. Just over an hour later, he passed beneath the Geoff Moss bridge, the highway so high above he could barely discern the traffic noise. After he crossed the Ghan railway a short time later, the trail began to climb but he didn't come across Jenny and Clive again. As the elevation of the track got steeper, he spotted Sandra ahead. She was sitting on a rock looking back over the landscape. As he reached her, he looked to the west. On the ridge ahead, he could just make out some of the group on the red, dusty track.

Sandra stood and he followed her gaze.

'In the distance you can just make out Alice Springs,' she said.

'Stopped to enjoy the view? All good?' He walked across and stood beside her.

'I am, but I actually stopped to wait for my partner. I wondered where you'd got to.'

'Sorry, I'd better pick up the pace,' he said with a grin.

'Have you been taking photos?' she asked.

'No, just enjoying the scenery, and I had a chat to Jenny and Clive. They must have passed you.'

Sandra shook her head. 'No, I passed them not long after we set off. They haven't caught up to me yet.'

Graysen frowned. 'I wonder where they are. They were ahead of me before I went under the bridge, and I haven't seen them again.'

Sandra turned and looked back along the track. 'At this rate, they won't get to Wallaby Gap in time for lunch. I was worried I was going too slow. I'm going to try to step out a bit from now on.'

'The morning walk is longer than the afternoon leg, so we should be right, I think.' He stared back across the red landscape dotted with green mulga. 'I wonder—' Graysen tapped his fingers against his thigh.

'You wonder?' Sandra looked up at him, her forehead creased in a slight frown.

'I wonder if I should go back and find them. Or is that intrusive? Clive's probably walked along the Ghan railway to have a look. He told me he's an engineering historian.'

'Maybe so early on the first day, it would be intrusive. It's not as though it's one person by themselves.'

'You're right, and ultimately Andrew makes the call, and everyone holds their own responsibility for getting to each stop on time. Okay, we'll just focus on our walk until we get to Wallaby Gap. Are you happy to wait while I take a couple of quick shots? Or'—he looked at her carefully— 'would you rather keep walking alone?'

It was hard to read her expression behind the big sunglasses.

'I'm happy to have some company. I'll sit here and have another drink while you take your photos.'

'Good. I won't be long.'

Sandra chatted to him as he set up his tripod and unwrapped one of the new wide-angled lenses he'd bought from Phillip.

'As different as it is in colour, this landscape reminds me of a Monet painting. How he used small dabs and strokes of paint as part of his technique,' she said.

'That was a well-known technique of the Impressionists,' Graysen said as he clicked the lens onto his Nikon. 'The Pointillism movement took it further. Are you familiar with the work of Georges Seurat?' He straightened and looked at her, taken aback to see her surprise on her face. 'What's wrong?

Sandra's lips spread in a wide smile, and it hit him what a pretty woman she was. Last night she'd looked elegant and aloof in her plain dress and gold jewellery. Today her cheeks held a natural pink glow. Her blonde hair had slipped from the ponytail she'd tied it back in, and she looked vibrant and alive.

'Nothing,' she said. 'Nothing at all. It's just a pleasure to have someone know what I'm talking about And, yes, I am familiar with Pointillism and Seurat, *and* Signac.'

Graysen crouched a little and squared the shot, adjusting the depth of the lens slightly. He quickly snapped off half a dozen shots of the valley landscape. '*A Sunday Afternoon on the Island of La Grande Jatte* is a great example of his work.'

As he packed up the tripod, Sandra stood, reached up and tightened the band on her hair. 'One of my favourites.'

She waited until Graysen was packed up and they began to walk along the ridge together. 'My girls always know to give me art books for birthdays and Christmas, but unfortunately none of them inherited my love of art. They take after their father,' she said.

'How many do you have?'

'Books?'

'No, girls,' he said with a laugh.

'I have three daughters and a stepson.'

'A good-sized family.'

'You?'

'Just me, now. My wife and I were never blessed with kids.' Graysen didn't want to continue with the personal stuff. He pointed down as the path narrowed. 'Look at that.'

Below them, the jagged cliffs of Euro Ridge plunged down a precipitous drop to the valley below. To the east, their conversation lulled as sweeping views of Alice Springs and the McDonnell Range took their attention.

Chapter 6

Wallaby Gap

An hour later, Andrew walked over to meet Graysen and Sandra as they entered the Wallaby Gap campsite. Sandra was pleased they'd arrived at the rest area; her heavy-duty hiking boots had held up well and her feet weren't blistered, but her legs were aching from the steep climb up the ridge. Once they'd reached the top, she'd been fine. It had been pleasant talking to Graysen, but when they'd started down towards the campsite—just over a kilometre walk—they'd both focused on negotiating the decline.

'Good timing, guys,' Andrew said. 'Jodie just called. She's about ten minutes out with our lunch.' He looked past them. 'Are Clive and Jenny far behind?'

'I haven't seen them since just after we started out. They fell back before we got to the bridge. I couldn't see them from Euro Ridge either,' Graysen said.

Andrew didn't look particularly worried. 'They'll be setting their own pace. As long as we're away from here by one-thirty, we're on schedule.'

Sandra walked over to a picnic table in the sun and sat opposite Cecily and Paul. Not her choice of company, but she needed to get off her feet for a while. She pulled out her water bottle and took a deep drink. When she'd finished, she put her head back and closed her eyes.

A few minutes later her breathing had evened out. She opened her eyes as the tyres of a vehicle crunched on the gritty track. She turned to speak to Cecily and Paul, but to her surprise, Graysen was sitting at the end of the table.

Cecily and Paul had moved to a large undercover area with bench seats along three sides and were sitting with Zed and Miska and Maggie. Jodie had parked a four-wheel drive vehicle with the Larapinta Luxury Treks logo beside them. She and Andrew were setting up a trestle table in the middle of the covered area.

'Sorry, I guess I'm not Cecily's favourite person. You looked like you were having a bit of a breather, so I stayed quiet.' Graysen looked up from the lens he was cleaning. The wind was stronger here and a fine layer of dust covered the table.

'Just resting my eyes . . . and legs. Not to worry, they're probably hungry and keen to get lunch as soon as it's out,' she replied. 'I found Cecily hard work last night, but hey, live and let live. We can't all get on with everyone all the time.'

'A good philosophy.' Graysen nodded to behind Sandra. 'Here's that other pair now.'

She turned. Clive and Jenny had just entered the campsite. 'That's a relief.'

'Are you hungry? They've just about got lunch set up.'

'I am. I'll just use the facilities and have a wash.' She couldn't help shooting him a cheeky grin. 'Don't worry. It's not the company I'm leaving. Nature calls.'

She got a big smile in return. Graysen Hughes wasn't so bad after all. She'd enjoyed his company on the ridge, but it was clear that he was a private person, and she would respect that.

The facilities were basic but clean, and Sandra rinsed her face and neck in the cool water. Feeling refreshed, she headed back out but there was no sign of Graysen and the other older couple, so she made her way to the undercover area where there was a selection of cold meats, salad, and pre-made baguettes laid out under a small wired net. Best of all was the smell of brewing coffee.

At the far end of the table, white crockery plates and mugs sat beneath a sheer white cloth. Sandra took a mug and poured herself a coffee before collecting a ham and salad baguette and an apple.

The only spare seat was beside Cecily, and Sandra made her way over. She sat down and began to eat, enjoying every mouthful of the fresh roll.

Once she'd finished eating, she dabbed at her mouth with the napkin. 'How did you go this morning?' she asked the young woman.

'It was much easier than I expected. How about you? Did you find it too much?' Despite Cecily's innocent words, true to form, there was a sting in the tail.

'No, it was great, although I must admit to my leg muscles protesting on that climb up the ridge.'

'You'll be sore tomorrow.'

'We probably all will be,' Sandra said with a smile.

'Only you oldies will be, *Sandy*. I can't believe you're doing it at your age. My mother would have more sense.'

God, what a rude little bitch.

'My daughters encouraged me to come. They took me shopping and got me kitted up for the trek. Very supportive.' Sandra was determined not to let this young woman push her buttons. It had been a good day so far, and she wanted to keep the calm mood she was in.

'Mad rather than supportive. What would they do if you fell and broke your hip?'

'The same as your family would do, I imagine, if you fell and broke yours. Oh, here's Graysen back. Enjoy your walk this afternoon, and be careful.'

Getting the last word in was very satisfying. Sandra was proud of herself. Once she would have curled up and taken whatever was dished out. After Peter's death her confidence had hit rock bottom. Placing the sandwich wrapping in the bin provided, and the empty coffee mug in the plastic tray, she walked across to Graysen and the Clarks as they stepped off the path from Wallaby Gap.

'Lunch is out over there. Very nice catering.'

'Thanks, do yourself a favour and head down the path and have a look at Wallaby Gap itself,' Graysen said.

'It's worth the short walk,' Jenny said. 'Unless you've had enough walking.'

'No, I want to see everything I can on this trail. Crazy to walk so far and miss out on the scenery. Enjoy your lunch.' Sandra bit into her apple as she headed off along the path to Wallaby Gap. The further she moved away from the lunch area, the quieter it became. Eventually, the only sound was the wind whistling through the gap ahead. At least the wind brought the benefit of fewer flies.

Only a couple of hundred metres along the track, she drew a quick breath as the stunning landscape opened out in front of her. A bare-footed rock wallaby sat on a rock above the trail looking down at her for a moment before it hopped away. Ahead of her the silence was suddenly broken by the unique squealing of zebra finches.

Looking for a secluded spot, she spied a large rock and walked slowly towards it as a variety of birdlife sang around her. Another wallaby jumped along the path, and Sandra slipped behind the rock out of the wind, and sat quietly, her back against the warm stone, watching the scene unfold in front of her. She'd read up about the birds and wildlife that could be spotted at each stop on the trail, and was pleased that she could identify the white-plumed honey eaters that skimmed over the water and dipped in for a drink. She recognised the crested pigeons that strutted around the edge of the water, the bright iridescence of their wings glowing in the midday sun. Glancing at her watch, she knew she had time to rest here and enjoy the sights and sounds for a while before they set off for Simpsons Gap and their overnight stay.

Calm stole over Sandra as she enjoyed her solitary view of nature's performance. But the quiet was soon interrupted.

'No. I can't do it!' The loud voice made her jump. 'I know I agreed, but I can't. It's too risky. And the group's too small. I've got a bad feeling about this.'

Cecily? Sandra hoped they hadn't followed her. She'd had enough of Cecily's attitude today. *Maybe they'll drop out?* Sandra hoped, wondering how many dropped out of the treks.

'Don't be stupid.'

'Don't speak to me like that, Paul.'

'Listen to me. You are not going to pull out.'

'I'll think about it, but I had no idea it was going to be this hard. I'm putting on a tough front but the whole thing is shit.'

'You're being too rude. You're going over the top with that old biddy. Tone it down. You're drawing attention to us.'

Sandra widened her eyes. *Old biddy!*

'I don't like any of them.'

'Jesus Christ, Cecily. You don't have to like any of them.'

'Let go of me. You're hurting me.'

Sandra froze; any hint of violence took her back to Peter's death. She still couldn't even watch television shows. Last time she'd picked a movie on Netflix, not knowing it was about a suicide, she'd had a panic attack. A sick feeling gripped her stomach and she put a hand to her mouth.

'Okay, so the group is smaller than we expected. Not a problem.'

Sandra felt guilty eavesdropping and was terrified they'd come around and see her sitting here listening to them. There was a long silence, and for a while she thought they'd moved on.

Cecily moaned and Sandra closed her eyes. She couldn't cope with this. Paul's voice broke the silence. 'You're turning me on, babe.'

'No, not here, Paul. Anyone could walk down the track.'

'Better here than in the camp tonight when we've only got tent walls between us and the others.'

Sandra wasn't game to move; holding her breath, she wondered if she could back out and leave without them seeing her. What an awful man he was.

'Stop it. Do my shirt up. I can hear someone coming down the path.' Cecily's voice was low and angry.

'Sandy?' Graysen's voice boomed around the clearing. 'Andrew's ready for us to head off.'

Sandra pushed herself against the rock, her eyes closed, trying to get her breathing under control. She knew she was overreacting. Since Peter's murder, her imagination was unfettered, and she imagined the worst in every scenario. She should have stepped out as soon as she heard them speaking and made her presence known.

'It's only us here, mate. We were just down looking at the wallabies,' Paul called out loudly. 'Haven't seen her.'

'Okay, thanks. She must have taken the loop walk back to the campsite. I'll go that way in case she's gone further.'

'We'll head back this way. See you there.'

'Okay, tell Andrew we won't be long.' Graysen's voice came from close by.

Sandra strained to hear but there was only the receding footsteps and the low voices of the young couple. Not the sort of relationship of a couple on a honeymoon. She cursed herself for her over-the-top reaction, and wondered what to do. Maybe she could wait ten minutes and go back the same way and if she was asked, pretend she'd started on the loop track and then turned around.

She hadn't even seen a sign to a loop track. Sandra pressed her palms flat on the rock, lowered her head and took another deep breath trying to calm herself. Suddenly the light was blocked as a shadow fell over her.

'Sandy?' Graysen squeezed into the narrow space beside her. His hand touched hers. 'What's wrong? Are you hurt? Are you feeling faint?'

She realised she was trembling as she tried to lift her hands. Her chin shook as she dragged in another deep breath.

Or tried to.

Warm hands held her shoulders. 'Sandy, look at me. Look at me and focus on your breathing. Don't worry about anything, let's just get you feeling better. Now, breathe slow and even.'

She did as he asked, and her eyes fixed on a pair of deep brown eyes. She hadn't noticed his long eyelashes before. Gradually her breathing calmed, and she managed to get air into her lungs.

Finally, she let out a shuddering breath. 'I'm okay. Thank you.'

'What happened?' Graysen's voice was worried. 'Did you see a snake? What scared you?'

She shook her head, but her thoughts skittered around. She didn't want to say she'd been eavesdropping.

Heat ran up her neck. Thank goodness Graysen had interrupted them.

'Very occasionally when I get tired or stressed, I have a bit of a panic attack. I guess I overexerted myself a bit, and I've overdone it. I'm fine now. Thank you.'

He looked at her as though he didn't believe her. 'How about we go back and you can get a lift to Simpsons Gap with Jodie?'

'No, I'm fine to walk.' As they made their way out from behind the rock, she put her hand on his arm. 'Graysen?'

His expression held concern. 'Yes?'

'Please don't tell Paul and Cecily I was there. Before they arrived, I was watching the wallabies and the birds and then . . . then . . . um—'

'And then?'

'They were um . . . about to get, shall I say . . . up close and personal, and I'd hate them to know I was there. I'm so embarrassed.'

'Of course I won't. Young love, hey?' His smile was wide and she forced a smile back. Her stomach was still churning and her heart rate was up.

'I guess. Those memories are long gone for me.'

He nodded slowly. 'Shame how we forget the good things and the bad memories take over, isn't it?'

Sandra held his gaze. 'Yes, you can certainly say that again. But I guess if you can remember some of them, it helps to cope with the grief. My memories and my girls have been my rock.'

She shook her head as she realised she was saying too much; Graysen had shown he wanted to keep his privacy and although he'd started this conversation, she knew he wouldn't want to turn it into a "let's share our stories" session. Sandra didn't want to think of the past. Not while she was here anyway, so she nodded briskly.

'Yes, let's focus on good memories. Come on, we'd better get back and find out the plan for this afternoon's leg. We don't want to get left behind.'

Graysen chuckled 'Or even worse. Get stuck with Cecily!'

Sandra held back a giggle but it came out as a snort. 'You're terrible, Muriel!'

Graysen's loud laugh made her smile. She was thoughtful as they walked back along the trail. Despite first impressions, and his gruff exterior, Graysen Hughes was a very kind man. And he had a sense of humour.

Chapter 7

Simpsons Gap

Wallaby Gap to Simpsons Gap was just over ten kilometres and Sandra and Graysen completed the walk in just over four hours, with a couple of breathers along the way at Scorpion Pool and Fairy Springs. The public campsite at Simpsons Gap was full of tents and swags. A large group of young people sat in a circle around a campfire.

'Hey, guys, welcome. Feel free to join us.'

'No packs,' one of the girls said with a smile 'You're at the posh camp in the bush. Half your luck.'

'When you're our age,' Graysen called with a smile and a wave.

Graysen and Sandra continued to the private eco camp. The Larapinta Luxury staff had set up seven tall tents in the scrub and an outdoor area covered with a canopy sat in the middle of a mostly-cleared area. Their campsite was far enough away from the National Park campsite that the noise of the large group didn't travel across.

'Looks good,' Sandra said. 'I have no regrets about taking this tour.'

'I feel as though I've gone a bit soft, but I have to agree. It will be a pleasure to have a hot shower. That wind's cold.'

Despite the cold, the walk west to Simpsons Gap had been easy, a flat walk on a narrow track through magnificent bloodwoods and tall ironwoods that shaded the track from the afternoon sun. The wildlife—more wallabies and many birds— had been active as the strong light faded into late afternoon.

Graysen had been attentive and had stayed by her side for the whole distance, and Sandra knew he'd been concerned about her. She was cross with herself that Paul and Cecily had set her off; it was the first panic attack she'd had for a couple of years. When she called the girls tonight—if there was phone service—she wouldn't mention it. There was no point in worrying them; she knew they were worried enough about her being on a two-hundred-kilometre trek with a group of strangers. A diverse group of strangers, and despite all the reading that she'd done about the camaraderie that developed in these groups, Sandra had no sense of that yet, apart from Graysen's kindness.

With a shrug, she kept walking and glanced across at Graysen. It was only early days yet, but she'd keep her distance from Paul.

Different to this morning's trek, this afternoon they'd stayed near the front of the group, and Andrew and Maggie had taken up the rear. Jodie was in the camp to greet them with a different guide.

'Sandy, Graysen, this is P.D. He set up the campsite for you.'

'Hey, there,' the young indigenous guide nodded at them as he carried a tub of food across to the area under the canopy.

'Set up? Isn't it permanent?' Sandra asked.

'No, we set it up for each trek. That's the truck over there in the scrub. Tomorrow after you leave, P.D. and I will pull the camp down, take all our rubbish and restore the bush to its natural state.'

'You're a true eco camp then,' Graysen commented.

'Yes, enjoy this one. We can get in here easily; there's a road all the way in, so there's more facilities.'

'So, we're not really remote?' Sandra asked as she looked around. Four double padded swing seats hung from triangular frames.

'Not yet, but you will be in a few days, so enjoy the luxury tonight. Seeing you've arrived first I'll show you to your tents and the showers. They'll be hot by now.'

'Sounds divine,' Sandra said.

'Two buckets per shower,' Jodie said.

Jodie walked with them over to the tents that were spaced far enough from each other to give the occupants privacy.

That'll make Paul happy, Sandra couldn't help thinking, and then pushed the thought away. She was not going to let anyone spoil her trek and take over her thoughts.

Jodie opened the flap of the first tent. 'This is you, Sandy. Even in the single tents, you have a double bed with a comfy chair to sit in and look out at the view.' Jodie walked across to the back side of the tent and lifted the flap. 'If you'd like to roll it up and look at the stars as you sleep, ask Andrew or P.D. and they'll put it up for you after dinner.'

'Dinner smells good,' Graysen commented as Jodie pointed out his tent two along from Sandra's and then led them across to the temporary shower block.

'A camp roast tonight with baked yams and potatoes, and steamed greens,' Jodie replied. 'And caramel dumplings with custard.' She must have seen the look on Sandra's face. 'Don't worry you'll walk it off tomorrow. Also, one thing you need to be very aware of is keeping everything away and secure in camp. No food scraps or wrappers. And make sure your tent is zipped up when you're in there or when you leave it.'

'Not leaving a footprint?' Graysen commented.

'No, dingoes.'

Graysen looked sceptical, and Sandra wondered if it was just a standard warning. There'd been no sign of dingoes on the trail today.

Jodie quickly showed them the bathroom setup, a shower with two buckets and a pull cord, and a couple of hooks in a narrow tent for hanging towels and clothes. Sandra decided to have a quick shower first up and change into some warmer clothes. The temperature was dropping quickly.

'You're welcome to come and join P.D. and Andrew and I in the communal area, or have a rest before dinner. If you've prepaid for drinks, they're in the fridge in the truck. Just let P.D. know what's yours and he'll get them out. He's got a list of who's paid for what. After dinner, he'll be giving a talk about the local indigenous culture and customs. So, relax while you can, we have a busy night ahead.'

Sandra caught Graysen's eye as Jodie walked away. 'Definitely a five-star resort this one,' she commented.

'We're being very well looked after. How are you feeling now?' he asked quietly as the two young couples walked into camp together. Paul and Zed were deep in conversation and Cecily and Miska walked behind them.

'I'm fine. Don't worry about me please,' Sandra answered. 'And thank you for your company this afternoon, but please don't feel as though you have to look after me. I came on this trek to prove I can be independent, and I will prove it.'

'Who to?' he asked.

'To me.'

'Okay, but if you ever feel like company, I'm happy to oblige.'

'Thank you.' Sandra went to her tent and was pleased to find that the kit bag she'd handed over as they'd left the hotel in the passenger four-wheel drive truck this morning was now safely beside the bed. She pulled out a clean set of clothes and a warm jumper, then her toiletries bag and made her way to the shower. First there, she quickly stripped off and was soon standing beneath a bucket of steaming hot water. Conscious of preserving the water, she quickly soaped up and washed off with the second bucket.

As she stepped out onto a fluffy bath mat—talk about a luxury camp—her thoughts went to the afternoon leg of the trek. Graysen had stayed by her side; his conversation had been sporadic, but he'd insisted on detouring with her to the two scenic spots on their route, where they'd stopped for a short rest. Fairy Springs and Scorpion Creek had been disappointing because there wasn't much water in them, and there wasn't much wildlife. When they were almost to camp, Graysen had stopped suddenly and she'd heard his camera click on. Sandra's eyes had been on the trail beneath her boots and she'd gasped when she looked up.

'Oh wow, how beautiful.'

The saddle known as Hat Hill was illuminated by the setting sun and defined by the dramatic colour of the rocks against the soft sky. Shafts of golden light were back lit by pink and purple; it was one of the most beautiful sunsets Sandra had ever seen.

'This is what it's all about.' Graysen's voice was soft and his mouth was set as his shutter clicked a dozen times.

She'd glanced at Graysen, but had sensed his words had been more to himself, so she didn't reply. The more time she spent with him, she was appreciating what a good man he was.

Kind and thoughtful, but still an enigma. She wondered what his background was. All she knew was he was a photographer who had no children. *'Just me, now. My wife and I were never blessed with kids,'* he'd said.

Just him.

By the time Sandra headed back to her tent from the shower, everyone had arrived at camp, and Jodie called out. 'Twenty minutes until hors d'oeuvres and drinks around the campfire while dinner cooks, guys. Don't forget to tell P.D. what you want in the way of drinks.'

Sandra stayed in her tent and pulled her phone out from her backpack and turned it on, pleased to see three bars of service. She lay back on the bed, and appreciated the softness of the pillows behind her.

The first number she dialled was Ellie's, hoping to catch James before he went to bed.

'Mum! Hi, great to hear from you. Kane and I were just talking about you.'

'Saying nice things I hope, and not what a silly mother you have.'

'Always nice things. How are you? How did you go today? Is it what you expected?'

'Really well. All that training paid off. My legs are a bit sore, and I'll probably feel it more in the morning, but our guide said tomorrow's walk is much flatter than today's. What's all that background noise? Are you out?'

'So, the tour company's good? How many on it?' Ellie was much more talkative than usual. Sandra was hard pressed to get a word in. 'Are they a good group? Is it cold?'

'It's excellent. There's nine of us plus the guides. Some interesting people. The other support staff, the cook and those who set up camp drive in and meet us. But apparently not every day, when there's no access to some of the more isolated spots.'

'Have to go, Mum. You take care and I'll talk to you later. Bye—'

'Hang on, Ellie can I talk to James. Is he still awake?'

'Sorry, Mum, he's asleep. I have to go.' Ellie's voice shook and Sandra knew her middle daughter well enough to know she was on the verge of tears.

As the call disconnected a couple of loud voices spoke in the background, and Sandra waited a few minutes before she dialled the number again, a niggle of worry settling in her stomach. The call went straight to voicemail, as did Emma and Dru's numbers when she tried to call them.

Sandra put the phone down and frowned. There was no point worrying. If there was anything wrong, the girls would have been in touch with her. She lay back on the pillows and did the breathing exercises the clinical psychologist had taught her when she'd been recovering. It had taken a long time for the truth to come out about Peter's death.

She lay there in an unfamiliar tent in the middle of the bush, and a pang of loneliness hit.

What am I doing here? What am I trying to prove? I should be home with my girls where I belong.

Maybe Dee had gone into labour? Maybe she'd had the babies, and there was something wrong?

A single tear escaped and rolled down Sandra's cheek.

One day on the trail and I'm losing it.

The rasping screech of a barn owl jerked her from her introspection.

Stop it!

She swung her legs over the side of the bed, stood straight and ran her fingers through her now loose hair.

She would not give in to worry and have another panic attack. Worrying about her girls achieved nothing, neither here or at home.

Reaching into her toiletries bag, Sandra ran a touch of lipstick around her lips, grabbed her puffer jacket and stepped outside.

***

Graysen grabbed Sandy's arms with both hands when they collided as she came around the front of her tent.

'Woops, sorry,' she said. 'I wasn't watching where I was going.'

'I was just coming to see if you'd gone to sleep. Jodie's about to serve dinner up.'

'I had a quick lie down and tried to make some calls while we have service. I only got through to one of my girls though.'

Graysen fell into step beside her, and shone the small torch on the ground ahead of them. 'Did you zip your tent right up when you left it?'

'I did. I took note of what Andrew said about critters last night. Oh my God.'

Graysen hesitated as Sandy came to a sudden stop. Her mouth was open and her eyes were wide. Voices and laughter came from the group underneath the canopy ahead, but he knew exactly why she was wide-eyed. He lifted his ever-present camera and quickly took a photo of the scene ahead.

'I thought the sunset was beautiful, but look at that.' Her voice held awe.

'Yes, it's the first of many beautiful night skies I think we'll experience.'

Ahead of them, the group were gathered around a campfire and the firelight lit up a graceful gum tree and the golden brown of the canopy which rose in peaks like a small circus tent. But it was the stunning backdrop that had Sandra staring in wonder.

The clear sky was a deep purple and the arch of the Milky Way glowed sharp and bright in the heavens.

'That alone has made the trip worthwhile,' Sandra whispered and a shiver ran down Graysen's spine as she moved closer to him. 'It puts everything in perspective and makes everything seem so insignificant, doesn't it? In the scheme of the universe, what's gone before and what will come in the future doesn't really matter. It does make you wonder why we're here, doesn't it? We have to appreciate the beauty in the world, and ignore the ugliness.'

Graysen's throat closed. Sandy's words were almost identical to what Marion had said to him the night before she passed. 'Appreciate the beautiful things you see, embrace life and realise how precious it is.'

He took a deep breath. 'Yes,' he said simply unable to say more.

'Come on you, pair, we're all starving.' Paul's yell broke the mood. 'You can go stargazing later. They'll be there all night. And for the next eleven nights.'

'We hope,' Andrew said. 'It has been known to rain in June.'

He was met with a chorus of disbelief.

Without thinking, Graysen held his hand out to Sandra and she took it. When he realised what he'd done, it was too late to let go, so he enjoyed the feel of her hand in his as they walked across to the group. Before they stepped into the light, Sandra slipped her hand out of his and moved away.

'Right, dinnertime,' Jodie called from the undercover area. 'Grab a plate and come and help yourselves.'

Graysen stood back beside Clive until the women and the two younger men had filled their plates and gone to sit back down. As soon as he'd eaten, he'd excuse himself before the evening's talk and go back to his tent. The hours since last night were the most he'd spent in company for months and he needed some space.

And he knew he was spending way too much time thinking about a woman he'd only met twenty-four hours ago.

Chapter 8

Royal Darwin Hospital

'I should have told Mum I was in hospital.' Ellie's eyes filled with tears and she looked at Kane through a blurred haze.

'And what could she have done, love? There's no point interrupting her holiday and making her worry. The doctor said you're going to be fine. As long as you do what he says.'

'He did seem confident that the baby was okay, didn't he?'

'He did.' Kane reached for her hand. 'We both saw her strong little heartbeat, didn't we? As well as resting up, you need to stop worrying. Dru and Connor are looking after James until I collect him.'

'Will we tell him he's having a little sister?'

'If we decide to, we'll wait until you're home.'

'Dr Mitcham said I can go home as soon as the canula comes out. At least the bleeding's stopped.' Ellie would never forget the feeling when she had started to bleed yesterday morning.

'And bed rest for a couple of days.'

'Don't you worry, I'll be doing exactly as he said. Four months of taking it easy, no exercise.' She pulled a face at Kane. 'No sex.'

He grinned at her and a surge of love for her husband warmed her heart. 'That's okay. I'll be so busy doing the housework and looking after James, I'll be too tired anyway.'

'The doctor said the placenta can still move away from the cervix, so I might not have to have a Caesarean.'

Kane leaned over and brushed his lips across hers. 'We'll take one day at a time. Dru said she'll come and stay with you through the day, and I can take care of everything else. I'll work shorter days until the harvest. I'm sure when your mum gets home, she'd be happy to come and stay for the last three months of your pregnancy.'

'What a day it's been. Dee in here with pre-eclampsia too!'

'But she's in good hands and in the right place. Ryan said she won't be going home before the babies are born. They're trying to see if they can get her blood pressure down and try to hold the birth off for at least another three weeks.'

'I should have told Mum. I know she knew there was something wrong because I was babbling so much.'

'Els?'

'What?'

'Do you know how much like your mother you are? You're turning into a worrier. All worrying will do is make you sick.'

She nodded. 'I'm sorry. Okay. Let's take one day at a time and trust everything will be right.' She chuckled. 'At least I've stopped worrying about Mum on her trek. She sounded really good when she rang.'

Kane stepped aside as the nurse came into the room. 'You're right to go home, Mrs McLaren. I'll just take that canula out for you.'

'My sister-in-law is in here too. Would it be okay if I called in to see her before we leave?'

'What's her name?'

'Dee Porter-Carey.'

'That should be fine. I've just come from her room. She's along the corridor and to the left. Bed Six.'

A few minutes later, the wardsman had brought a wheelchair and Kane was pushing Ellie towards Dee's room. As they approached the elevator, the door opened and Emma and Jeremy stepped into the corridor.

'Ellie! What's happened? Are you okay?' Emma grabbed her hand.

'I'm fine. A bit of a scare, but we're on the way home. Placenta praevia.'

Emma put a hand to her chest. 'Oh no. You know you'll have to take it really easy, and you might have to have a Caesarean.'

Ellie pulled a face. 'Yes, Doctor Langford. It's handy having doctors for a sister and brother-in-law.'

'You feeling okay now, Ellie?' Jeremy asked. 'I assume you're heading home?'

'I am now. It gave me a shock, but I'm fine now that I know what it is.' She turned to Emma. 'I tried to call you, Em, but your phone went to voicemail. I didn't leave a message. I didn't want to worry you. Ryan obviously got through to you.'

Emma frowned and looked at her.

'He didn't?'

'No, what's happened? Is Dee okay?'

'I thought you were here to see her too. We're just on our way to her ward. Are you both working? I didn't think you were in obstetrics.'

Emma's face coloured and she bit her lip as she looked up at Jeremy. For the first time, Ellie noticed he was carrying a small overnight bag.

'What's going on, Em?' Ellie asked.

Emma hesitated for a moment before answering. 'I'm just having a minor procedure this afternoon. Nothing to worry about.'

'What sort of procedure?'

'Just an exploratory thing.'

Ellie stared. 'More specific please.'

'Ellie, it's nothing. Don't worry. I'm just having a laparoscopy to remove a cyst from my left ovary. No big deal.'

'Is that why you've been so quiet lately?'

Emma nodded.

'So, for you to be quiet, you must be concerned. I've missed your bubbly self. Jeez, everything is awful lately.'

'The doctor thinks it's okay.'

'Thinks?'

Emma nodded.

'I wish you'd told us. You obviously didn't tell Mum. She's going to be really cross at us when she gets home. She called last night, and she picked up something in my voice. She's so intuitive.'

Emma finally smiled. 'That's why my phone's switched off. I sent her a text when I saw her missed call and said I hoped she was having a good time, and all was good.'

'Fibber,' Ellie said. 'But I know why you did it. Mum deserves a break.'

Jeremy touched Emma's arm 'We'd better get a move on if you want to call in and see Dee, Em. Otherwise, you'll be late for your admission.'

Ellie put a hand on Kane's arm. 'We'll let Em and Jeremy go first.'

'Thanks, we'll be quick.'

'Bed Six. We'll wait in the waiting room until you come out. We don't want to overwhelm Dee.'

Emma leaned down and kissed Ellie's cheek. 'You take care, Ellie. Rest up.'

'And you let me know as soon as you get results.'

'I will.'

Ellie put her hand over her face as Emma and Jeremy headed for Dee's room.

'All we need now is for something to happen to Dru!'

Kane pushed the wheelchair into the waiting room. 'Don't tempt fate, Els.'

Chapter 9

Simpsons Gap to Jay Creek

Sandra slept really well and managed to put her worries aside; she was ready to face whatever challenges the day brought. She'd only woken once. An eerie howl had filled the silence, and for a moment she'd wondered where she was. But she'd gone back to sleep quickly and slept deeply.

She reached for her phone to try the girls again, but the service had dropped out overnight, so there was no chance of calling them this morning. Wincing as her muscles pulled in her thighs and calves, Sandra dressed and walked over to the fire to stay warm.

'Was that a dingo I heard howling through the night, Andrew?'

'It was. I'll show you all something interesting after breakfast,' he replied.

Jodie had laid out cereal and fruit, and P.D. was cooking eggs and pancakes on the hot plate over the fire.

Once they'd eaten and Jodie was clearing away, Andrew gathered the group together near the board displaying the map of the track.

'Even though the terrain is only a little bit steeper than yesterday morning's climb up Euro Ridge, it's going to feel more challenging to you as we move further away into the wilderness. We'll be walking twenty-six kilometres today.'

Sandra focused on his words. She wanted to be prepared, and listened carefully.

'Maggie's chosen to miss today's trek. She'll go in the truck. At the end of the day, Jodie and P.D. will pick us up in the Isuzu truck and we'll meet up with Maggie at the old Hamilton Downs Homestead for dinner. Then we'll use their facilities, and tonight we'll be camping under the stars in swags. But before we split up, follow me.' He led them all back to the camp fire and pointed to the ground. 'Who else heard the dingo howling through the night?'

There were a couple of nods, but Cecily squealed. 'A dingo? I thought you were teasing when you mentioned them last night.'

Andrew had repeated Jodie's warning as they all headed for their tents last night.

'Most certainly not,' he replied. 'Follow me and I'll show you the tracks. The visitor to our camp came in to the campfire first. See where he circled it?'

Paul and Cecily leaned forward, and their eyes were wide. Sandra was really interested to see the tracks. She'd always been fascinated by dingoes. When she and Peter had first been on their mango farm, they'd soon learned not to leave any food out. Even though Emma had been born about eight years after the incident with the dingo and the baby at Ayers Rock, Sandra had been hesitant to have the girls outside when they were tiny. The Azaria Chamberlain incident had stayed with her for years.

'Now come with me and I'll show you how he visited each of you.' From the fire, Andrew led them to and around each tent before following the barely discernible tracks to the scrub where the dingo had headed back into the wild.

Cecily squealed again as they saw the tracks at the entrance of the tent she'd shared with Paul. 'Oh my God, what if we meet one on the track?'

'There's not much chance of that,' Andrew said. 'But take heed and learn not to leave anything out at all. They're very intelligent creatures.'

'I also think they look like they're thinking. Their eyes,' Sandra commented.

Sandra was surprised when Graysen spoke. 'I'm impressed, Andrew. Those tracks are very hard to see. Did you look because you heard the howl?'

'Yes, I did hear the howl, but I'm always aware of tracks. I wanted to be sure he was a young adult. Young adults have a solitary existence during non-mating seasons. This guy was a loner.'

'How do you know all this?' Miska rubbed her arms to keep warm.

Andrew picked up his hat and placed it on his head. 'My parents worked for the government and I spent most of my childhood in indigenous communities. I ran wild with the Aboriginal kids and I learned a lot about tracking.' He spread his hands wide. 'I love it out here. This is my spiritual place.'

'It shows,' Sandra said quietly to Graysen as the group moved to collect their packs for the day.

'Have fun, everyone. See you tonight.' Maggie's husky voice hung in the morning air.

Cecily narrowed her eyes as Maggie headed for the truck. 'Why trek if you're going to pull out after the first day.'

Sandra couldn't help defending Maggie. 'We all have that option every day. Some of us want to see different parts of the country.'

Cecily smiled. 'How long do you reckon you'll last, Sandra? I mean, *Sandy*?'

'Three hours to Bond Gap, team,' Andrew interrupted, his voice brisk again, but the look he shot Cecily wasn't impressed.

'Make sure you fill your water bottles and stay near your buddy, and we'll have a cuppa when we get there. You'll see the sign with the track that heads to Bond Gap itself. This section of the track is well signposted because a few day-walks join in. For those of you who are energetic, there's a swimming hole at Bond Gap, so feel free to have a dip, although I don't think the temperature's going to get up very high today. They've only forecast twenty degrees. I'll boil the billy where the track heads north and wait for you.'

The rest of the group set off straight away; confidence was building, and they were adept at discerning the trail now without Andrew's assistance. It had been an extremely cold night and Sandra kept her puffer jacket on as they started out. It wouldn't be too heavy to cram into her backpack when she warmed up.

As they set off with the cold wind at their backs, winter was in full voice. Birdsong surrounded them as finches and budgerigars welcomed the morning. Sandra hummed to herself as she walked along, feeling good. Despite the cold, it was a crystal-clear morning, promising a cooler walk and clear views as they climbed. She smiled when she noticed Graysen had two cameras hanging around his neck today.

'Double the photos?' she asked.

'There's supposed to be some good vantage points on today's section,' Graysen replied. 'And the atmosphere is so clear today, I'm sure to get some good wide-angle landscapes. I'm going to head a little way off the track for a while. I'll catch you guys up.'

'Be careful,' Sandra said and then regretted it straight away.

Andrew walked with her for the first hour.

'So far, so good, Sandy?' he asked as they passed the point where the Woodland Trail—one of the day walks—joined the Larapinta Trail. 'You're setting a good pace.'

'Yes, I feel good, even after that climb up the ridge yesterday.' The clarity of the air and the stillness of the day was adding to her calm. She'd managed to forget about the things that had worried her yesterday, and was determined to enjoy the day.

'The path from here to the Bond Gap trail is undulating and not particularly challenging. You'll see mulga and witchetty bush and there's a couple of spots with good views back to Simpsons Gap.'

'I enjoyed looking back over where we walked yesterday. It adds to my sense of accomplishment. I must remember to take some photos today, to show my kids where I walked. I was too focused on settling into the walk yesterday, and I'll admit to a bit of trepidation, but after a day on the trail, I love it. Your company runs a great tour and you guys have been great. I enjoyed P.D.'s talk last night too.'

Graysen had excused himself politely and disappointment had settled in Sandra as he headed to his tent before the indigenous guide started speaking. Maggie had come over and sat beside her when he'd left last night.

'We need to hook up, lovely. Two single women on the tour.'

Sandra smiled politely; she was quite happy the way things were going. Maggie was a little bit hard for her. As they'd sat around the fire last night, Maggie had talked about all the real estate she owned, and how hard it was to decide where to live.

'I think the house on the cliff at Portsea is the one I'll decide on, but Alan says it's too far from Sydney. It's time he retired.'

'He didn't want to come on the trek with you?' Cecily asked as she sipped her wine.

'I chose this one and he booked for both of us, but the business intruded as usual, and you know what I said?'

No one asked.

'I said, "stuff you, Alan. You work. I'll go on the trip." It's a relief to be away from him actually. All work and no play make him a dull boy. Our investments are all my family money, so he does as I say.' Maggie called P.D. over and held up her empty glass. 'Mine is the Bolly please, gorgeous boy. Maybe grab the second bottle.'

P.D. nodded and walked across to the fridge in the Isuzu. Sandra flinched as Maggie turned to them and said, 'Isn't P.D. a gorgeous looking man? I could do with a honey like that to clean my pool.'

Maggie winked at P.D. when he came back with the bottle. 'I pay well, my lovely.'

Miska looked at Sandra and pulled a face, obviously trying to change the subject.

'What about you, Sandy? Do you have a partner at home?'

'No.' Sandra shook her head. 'But I have three wonderful daughters—a helicopter pilot, a doctor, and an engineer. And a stepson with a huge cattle property, and a beautiful grandson, plus another grandchild on the way.'

'A lovely full life,' Miska said with a smile.

'Yes, I am blessed.'

Maggie leaned over and clinked her glass against Sandra's coffee cup. 'Divorced, Sandy? I'll have to get some tips.'

Sandra straightened in her seat. 'Actually no. I was widowed almost ten years ago.'

Miska reached over and squeezed her hand. 'I'm so sorry to hear that, Sandra.' Her voice was soft and her English accent had a pretty lilt to it.

'Good on you, Sandra, for leaving all the family and doing something for yourself,' Cecily said.

It was an interesting evening, and by the time she went to bed, Sandra was feeling a bit more settled. Hard to believe even Cecily had said something kind.

##

Sandra had told herself she was getting too reliant on Graysen, so as she lay in bed the next morning, resisting stepping out into the cold, she vowed to walk the trail alone today. Andrew starting off with her had given her an excuse.

'I was surprised when Maggie decided not to walk today. Although she told me last night she was a bit sore,' Sandra commented once they had covered half the distance to the first stop.

'She probably would have been better to push herself, but we can only make suggestions. Everyone has a different goal, and different ways of approaching the trek. And we do provide the option to only walk sections of the trail for that reason. Are you right if I leave you to it? I'll go on ahead and get the fire going and the billy on.'

Sandra looked at the big pack on his back. 'You're carrying everything for morning tea in there?'

'And lunch. There's no access for Jodie to reach us on this section.'

Sandra shook her head. 'I don't know how hikers walk the track carrying their tents and food and water.'

'It takes dedication and fitness, but there's water on the way, plus food drop points, so a well-organised hiker can do it easily.'

'I've learned so much already in a day and a bit.'

Andrew gave her a wave and, despite the heavy pack on his back, he set off at a light jog. 'See you at the trail.'

Sandra warmed up quickly so she stopped and removed her puffer jacket. Unzipping her pack, she took out her phone and put it in her shorts pocket, and crammed her jacket into the pack. She set off and walked through a grove of witchety bush. The bright yellow brushes glowed in the strong morning sunlight and as she watched a tiny bird flew in and hung upside down drinking the nectar from the flowers. She quietly reached for her phone and switched it on and zoomed in for a close up. The number of small birds was many more than what she had expected.

Footsteps crunched on the pebbly rock of the path and she ignored the jump in her heartbeat as Graysen caught up to her. His camera was up to his eye and she stayed quiet and still as he completed his shot of the tiny bird.

'Thank you for not spooking it,' he said as he lowered the camera. 'Enjoying the walk so far?'

'I am. It's been pretty easy today.'

'Want some company?'

'Sure.'

They walked along; their conversation desultory as the track began to climb.

'I think that's Bond Gap over there.' Graysen pointed to a red outcrop a kilometre or so ahead and to the north. 'Do you want to walk in and look at the swimming hole?' He lifted the camera and the shutter clicked.

'I do, but no swimming for me today. It's not warm enough.'

'The water will be cold too—what the hell is he doing?' Graysen stopped dead in the middle of the track and Sandra turned with a frown. There was no one else in sight, so she followed his gaze to the rocky outcrop in the distance.

'Who? I can't see anyone.'

'I think it's Paul. Or it could be Zed?'

'No. Zed and Miska are behind us. What's happening?'

Graysen quickly slipped his backpack off and opened the camera bag inside the larger pack. He took out a huge lens and handed the one he took off the camera to Sandra while he replaced it with a bigger zoom lens. He quickly handed her a lens cover.

'Just screw that on the exposed end please, to keep the dust out.'

She did as he asked and she followed his gaze again as he rotated the lens and peered through the camera.

'Bloody hell. It's Paul. He's got hold of Cecily and he's shaking her. They're right on the edge of the cliff. He's holding her arms and she's leaning backwards right over the edge.'

'Oh my God. What should we do?'

Graysen kept the camera focused on the outcrop. 'We can't do anything. They're too far away. It'll take us a good ten to fifteen minutes to get there. Hopefully they're just mucking around, but it's stupid behaviour. Reckless.'

'Maybe they've had a disagreement.'

'Where was Andrew heading to?' Graysen asked. 'I saw him leave you.'

'He went to set up morning tea where the trail splits to Bond Gap. So, they're probably ahead of him, and Clive and Jenny and Zed and Miska are behind us.'

'He's gone now. I can't see either of them anymore.'

'I hope she's all right.'

'So do I.' Graysen unscrewed the lens and replaced it with the one Sandra had held for him. His brown eyes held hers calmly, but he shook his head. 'As much as I hate to say it, if the worst comes to the worst, and she's fallen, I have photos of him holding her over the edge.'

'Maybe she was mucking around and he was trying to hold her back?'

'I don't know. He looked pretty angry, and he seemed to be shaking her, but you're right, I shouldn't make assumptions. At this distance it's too hard to see.'

Graysen repacked his bag and turned back to Sandra. 'Are you up to a faster pace?'

'I am. We'd better get there and check she's okay.'

By the time they reached the fork in the trail where Andrew had the fire going and the billy hanging above it from a tripod, Sandra's calf muscles were burning and her breath was ragged. From the fork there was no clear view to the outcrop where Graysen had witnessed the altercation, if it had been one.

Sandra slipped her pack off and sank to the ground as Graysen hurried over to Andrew. She focused on getting her breath back while they had an intense conversation.

After a moment Andrew ran across to her. 'Sandy, you look knackered. I'd prefer you didn't come with us, in case there has been an "accident". Are you happy to wait here for

Clive and Jenny and keep an eye on the fire? There's no wind in this gorge, but if one does come up, there's a bucket of sand beside the fire pit to douse the flames.'

She nodded, still unable to speak, her chest was hurting each time she dragged a breath in.

'Wait until you get your breath back and then sip your water slowly.'

She nodded again and watched as Andrew pulled the satellite phone out of his pack and then he and Graysen disappeared down the track. Even though Cecily was a difficult person, she couldn't imagine her husband hurting her. Then again, she'd never imagined anyone hurting Peter either. From tragic personal experience, Sandra knew some people were inherently evil.

Finally able to breathe, she uncapped her water bottle and sipped it slowly as Andrew had advised.

It didn't take long before she began to feel better, and Sandra walked over to the fire and waited for the others to catch up to them.

***

Graysen and Andrew reached the top of the outcrop together.

'Here, I'm pretty sure this is where they were.' Graysen had taken note of the shape of the knoll where he'd seen them.

Andrew looked at the ground and frowned. 'There's a lot of scuff marks in the red dust. And solid footprints.' He walked to the edge and peered over as Graysen took out his camera.

'I'll take some shots. Just in case.'

'Bloody hell,' Andrew said. 'I've never had anything like this before on my tours. I've been working for Larapinta

Luxury for four years. I've had a few drunk young blokes, but they were harmless and slept it off after a verbal altercation. And I had a couple from Europe who decided they were going to get divorced halfway along—not far from here actually—and she refused to stay on the trail. He wanted her out too, so he paid for a helicopter to pick her up, and he kept walking. And not long ago, everyone lost their wallets and phones, but we never found out who took them. The company reimbursed the customers if they signed a non-disclosure agreement. They didn't want it all over social media. Jodie and I, and the other guides, keep a pretty good watch now. One bad experience, and you learn not to trust.'

'Takes all kinds, Andrew. I learned that a long time ago,' Graysen said. He walked to the edge of the precipice. 'Any sign of anyone down there?'

'No, thank God. But there is an overhang halfway down that would block our view if there was. Come on, we'll go down to the pool. Shit, Graysen, if something has happened this will be the end of my contract.'

'They can't blame you.'

'They can and they will.' Andrew nodded. 'Duty of care.'

As they scrambled down the steep track to the pool at Bond Gap, voices floated up on the air and they looked at each other. Just as they reached the bottom a high-pitched scream greeted them. Andrew met Graysen's eyes and took off, with Graysen not far behind. As they ran along the last small section, the scree slipped beneath Graysen's hiking boots and his cameras bounced on his chest. He reached up and held them steady as he and Andrew ran to the end of the track where it reached the waterhole.

'No, Paul, no!' Cecily's scream echoed around the gully.
What the hell was he doing?

The last fifty metres of the track down to the swimming hole were steep, but gave a view of the sheer red rock walls that dropped into the deep pool. The easiest way to enter the water was from a narrow rocky beach at the far end. Paul was chasing Cecily across the beach.

'No,' she screamed again.

Graysen slithered down the last bit of the slope close behind Andrew as another scream rent the air.

But this time it was followed by Cecily's laughter, and then a splash. 'No, Paul. It's bloody freezing cold.' She disappeared beneath the surface of the narrow waterway before she surfaced, flicked her wet hair and swam towards Andrew and Graysen.

When she was close to the edge, Cecily turned around and pointed to her husband who was treading water in the middle of the pool. 'You are so going to pay for that, Paul Dunn.'

He laughed at her. 'I owed you for making me scuba dive in Cairns. That Moray eel frightened the crap out of me that day.'

Cecily walked onto the narrow beach where Andrew and Graysen were standing. Her brief red bikini showed off a super-fit muscular figure and lily-white skin.

'Don't be tempted. It's colder than the North Sea.' Cecily flung her head back and water drops flicked onto Andrew and Graysen.

Graysen looked over at Paul and shrugged when Paul swam for the side and Cecily picked up her towel and passed it to him.

'Where's the rest of them?' Cecily asked, squeezing her hair dry.

'We're over at the beginning of the track. Came to tell you the billy's boiled,' Andrew said weakly, but Graysen could see the relief on his face.

Graysen couldn't resist adding, 'There was so much screaming, we thought one of you was in trouble.'

'No, just my darling husband, who is so going to pay for throwing me in that bloody cold water.'

Andrew and Graysen climbed slowly back to the top of the hill. When they reached the top, Graysen looked at the scuff marks in the dirt.

'I didn't like her before, and my opinion hasn't changed at all.'

Andrew looked back at him, and the relief on his face was obvious. 'As you said before, mate. Takes all kinds.'

'I'm sorry I caused you to worry.'

'I'd rather that than an accident. Thanks for being on the ball. I'll do another safety briefing after lunch before we head off again.'

Graysen headed back to the fork in the track, determined to keep to himself for the rest of the day. He'd created a situation with his vivid imagination, and that was enough excitement to do him for a while.

Sandy was standing by the fire warming her hands and she turned to him as they came back into camp, her face a picture of worry.

'They're fine.' Graysen shook his head. 'Just some tomfoolery. All good.'

She put one hand to her chest. 'Thank goodness. That's a relief. My imagination was running overtime.'

Andrew looked around. 'No Clive and Jenny yet?'

'No, although I thought I heard some voices coming from the track a few minutes ago.'

On cue, the older couple appeared at the end of the track with Zed and Miska, and at the same time Paul and Cecily came from the direction of the waterhole, arms around each other and smiling.

Andrew's smile was tight, and Graysen could see the tic in his cheek.

'Cup of tea, team?' he asked.

Chapter 10

Darwin

Emma's colleague and gynaecologist, Geoff Jennings sat on the other side of the desk, and read over the report. As he raised his head and looked at her, cold ran through her veins.

'The pathology is still not conclusive from the sample we took,' he said.

She managed to keep her voice calm. 'Not conclusive in terms of what?'

'It's a dermoid cyst, but I want to take a wider sample under a full anaesthetic. Although they have very similar imaging appearances, there is a fundamental histological difference: a dermoid is composed only of dermal and epidermal elements and a teratomas has mesodermal and endodermal elements.'

'So, you're thinking?'

'Emma, I'm not thinking anything. I just want to take a larger sample to make sure, okay?'

'When?'

'As soon as possible.' He lifted one hand. 'Not because of any sinister reason, but because I know you, and how you'll worry. A doctor makes the worst patient. So, let's get this sorted as soon as possible. I've added you to my list for first thing tomorrow morning. So, fasting from now.'

Emma nodded but knew her chin and lips were shaking. Geoff and his wife, Lucy, had been friends to Emma and Jeremy since they'd moved to Darwin. He reached across the desk and took her hand.

'And Emma? In the unlikely event that it is cancerous, it's early days, and the treatment is successful.'

Emma blinked back tears as she stood. 'Thanks, Geoff. I'll see you tomorrow.'

As she crossed the hospital corridor to go back to Geriatrics where she was undertaking a specialisation, Emma paused. Jeremy would probably be in the wards, and she needed some time to compose herself before she talked to him.

She turned to the elevator and pressed the button for the third floor. Spending some time with Dee would take her mind off things, and she knew Dee would appreciate some company. She was going stir crazy stuck in bed. Ryan came in as much as he could, but he was waiting for his cousin, Cy, to come home from Western Australia so he could take over the management of the cattle station, so Ryan could stay in town.

Emma stood outside Dee's room for a moment; she smoothed her hands over her hair, composing herself. Fixing a smile on her face, she walked into the ward.

'Hey, Dee. I was going past and I thought I'd call in.'

'Hi, Emma. It's good to see you.'

'How are you feeling?' Emma tried not to look concerned as she looked at Dee and then picked up the OBS chart from the end of the bed. Dee's blood pressure readings had been increasing all day.

'Pretty yuck.'

'Have you seen your doctor yet today?'

'No, apparently he got an emergency call to theatre.' Dee lifted her hand and rubbed her shoulder. 'Do you think you could chase up some paracetamol for me. My headache's back.'

'What's wrong with your shoulder?

'I've had a pain there for a couple of hours.'

Emma reached for the trolley with the blood pressure monitor and pressed the button to call the nurse as she did.

'I think you might be ready for theatre,' she said. 'How long since you've eaten?'

Dee's eyes widened. 'I didn't eat my lunch. I was feeling nauseous.'

'So, morning tea?'

'No, I had a Weetbix about seven, but it didn't stay down.'

Emma's own worries fled as she looked at Dee's blood pressure. It was way too high. If it wasn't addressed by taking the babies, there was a likelihood of damage to her liver and kidneys. 'Where's Ryan today? Is he coming in?'

Dee looked up at the clock on the wall. 'He'll be on his way in now.'

The nurse came to the door of the ward and looked in. 'Do you need me, Mrs Porter-Carey?'

Emma squeezed Dee's hand before she walked to the end of the bed to speak to the nurse privately. 'I'll give Ryan a call and tell him to hurry up, Dee, and I'm going to go and find another obstetrician if your doctor's in theatre.'

She turned to the nurse. 'Nil by mouth, and no painkillers until Dr Jennings gets here.' Emma was not impressed that the nursing staff hadn't called another doctor. It was lucky she'd called in when she did.

'Yes, Dr. Langford.'

The next half hour passed in a blur. Emma met Geoff Jennings in the corridor outside the ward. After a quick examination of Dee, he agreed that the babies needed to be taken. As Dee was prepped for theatre, Emma called Ryan and told him to get to the hospital as quickly as he could.

'You're going to be a dad today, Ryan.'

Her next calls were to Ellie and Dru, and then Emma went down to Geriatrics to find Jeremy.

Even though she'd spent the past hour sorting Dee's situation, as soon as she saw Jeremy her fears came rushing back and her tears spilled over.

'Em?' He led her into the office and closed the door. 'What is it? Have you been to see Geoff?'

She nodded and her throat clogged. 'I have. I'm back in surgery tomorrow for more tests.'

His arms went around her and he rested his head on the top of hers.

Emma leaned against her husband. 'Oh, Jem, what if it's the worst? What if he takes my ovaries while he's in there? What if we can't have children?'

'We won't worry about that until it happens. But it won't, Em.'

Her voice broke. 'Will you still love me if we can't have a family?'

Jeremy pulled her closer. 'I won't even acknowledge that you said that. Em, I love you, and whatever happens, we'll face this together. *You* are my life.'

Chapter 11

Old Hamilton Downs Homestead

They stopped at Mulga Camp for lunch, a simple meal of premade bread rolls and fruit. The camp was a no-frills campsite, with only a water tank to refill their bottles and a drop toilet, and no shelter shed. Sandra didn't mind as the wind still held an element of chill, so she was happy to sit in the sunshine.

Andrew insisted the group stayed together on the last leg of the day through the Chewings Range at Spring Gap. He'd given a safety briefing before they'd headed off for the afternoon trek.

'The final seven kilometres of the day takes us along a low ridgeline covered in mulga scrub, on the north side of the range. The trail can get confusing through this section, and I don't fancy losing any of you this afternoon, so please stay close and don't take any detours. We've been a bit scattered over the past couple of days, and we're on a schedule today. The only time schedule for the next ten days, but we need to be aware of pick-up time.'

Graysen and Sandra exchanged a look. Andrew had been a bit tense since the episode before morning tea.

'Please stay within sight of each other until we reach the gate where Jodie will pick us up in the truck.'

This section of the walk was the most scenic of the day and the chirping of a huge flock of blue and gold budgerigars surrounded them as they walked beneath the river red gums.

Andrew perked up a bit as they got closer to the meeting point. Sandra felt sorry for him; he was obviously keen to share the burden of the group with another guide after the events of the day.

'This is one of the most historic parts of the track,' he said as they approached a sign indicating a trail to a place called Fish Hole. 'Above Fish Hole the trail follows a route used by camel trains travelling between Hermannsburg and Hamilton Downs station. That's where we'll have dinner tonight.' He switched back into the guide patter for the first time this afternoon. 'You've all seen the buffel grass along the side of the track. It's an invasive weed introduced by the Afghan camel drivers who used it as saddle padding and then after that it was used for cattle feed. Tomorrow before we set off, I'll take you down to Fish Hole. It's a beautiful place; a sacred site to the local indigenous people, so no swimming; we can only walk the creek bed.'

'Cecily and I want to go down there for a swim this afternoon,' Paul said.

'I'm sorry, but we don't have time. You mustn't have heard me clearly, there's no swimming allowed there,' Andrew replied. 'Jodie's picking us up shortly and we're booked into the Homestead for dinner.'

Cecily interrupted. 'We've paid for this trek and paid very well. We'd like to go there this afternoon. And swim.'

Sandra straightened and glanced at Graysen. He was staring at Paul and looked as though he was about to interrupt. He obviously thought better of it and walked away as Andrew replied.

'The choice is yours, but if you do choose to go down now, you'll have to hike to Hamilton Downs yourselves. Plus, if you choose to break the rules, it may put your place in the trek at risk. The indigenous owners of this land allow us to walk it; we then reciprocate by showing respect for their culture.'

'No-one would see us.'

'If you want to go to Fish Hole today to have a *walk,* you'll have to trek back to the station, and you'll miss dinner.'

Sandra was embarrassed to be witnessing this and she walked away to where Graysen was sitting on a log. He was wiping his camera down with a soft blue cloth.

'Gosh, they're difficult people, aren't they?'

Graysen nodded. 'Very selfish. If I was Andrew, I'd put them in the truck and take them back to Alice Springs. The bottom line is, the guide has the final say. He's responsible for the safety of the group.'

Miska broke away from the others and strolled over to them. She pulled a face. 'I do hate confrontation. I certainly didn't think we'd encounter that on our trip. We chose the Larapinta Trek for our honeymoon because of the quiet and the spirituality of the landscape. We've been looking forward to it for ages. This really takes away from it.'

Graysen put the cleaning cloth on his knee and slipped the camera into the small bag. 'Just ignore them. Andrew will handle it, I'm sure.'

'It's almost as though they're trying to get the rest of us to side with them and discredit Andrew,' Miska said. Her hair had come away from her hairband and fell in dark ringlets against her olive skin. Sandra thought what a beautiful looking woman she was. Miska was lithe and fit, and had a sweet personality too.

'I'll be reporting you to your company for that remark.' Paul's voice was getting louder.

From where they stood, they could see Andrew's shrug, but couldn't hear his reply.

LARAPINTA

'Poor guy,' Miska said. 'If they do anything I'll put in a good word for him.'

'Me too,' Sandra said.

Zed walked across and joined them. 'Graysen? Got a moment?'

Graysen nodded and he and Zed walked a short distance away.

Miska smiled. 'That's my man. He has a heart of gold. I'd say he's asking Graysen to back him up while he has a quiet word to Paul.'

***

Graysen secured his camera in his kit bag and zipped it up before he headed to the shower block at the back of the old homestead. In the end, Cecily and Paul had reluctantly got into the truck with the rest of the group.

Zed had spoken quietly to Graysen before they'd boarded the truck, and they planned to speak to Paul before dinner. He looked around as he walked to the shower; there was no sign of anyone else. The old homestead had been left in its original state and the rooms he and Sandy had had a brief look into when they arrived were furnished with old furniture. Not antiques, but maybe nineteen fifties vintage.

The shower block was empty and Graysen was pleased to have some solitude as he showered and shaved. As he picked up his toiletries bag and towel to leave, the door opened and Paul walked in followed closely by Zed. Graysen hesitated as Zed gave him a brief nod.

Graysen put his towel back on the bench. 'Paul?'

Paul was about to step into the second shower stall and he turned with a scowl. 'Yes?'

110

'A quick word, mate.'

'Mate? I don't think so. It was you who dobbed to our guide this morning wasn't it? You both looked like idiots when you came running down to the pool. I don't know why you're trying to cause trouble, Graysen, but I'd appreciate it if you'd just fuck off and leave Cecily and I to do the trek like we want.'

Zed stepped forward and his words were quiet. 'Paul, your attitude is making it hard for the others in the team.'

'Team? I didn't sign up for any fucking team.'

'That may be so, but you're in a group. If you'd wanted to do it your way, you shouldn't have picked this trekking company, but you would still have had to respect the local culture. But you chose this one and there's others on this trek, and we'd all appreciate it if you'd pull your head in.' Zed was a tall, well-built guy and when he walked closer to the shower stall, Paul took a step back.

'One more thing too,' Graysen added. 'Andrew and the others are excellent guides. If you make a report about the problems you're creating, I won't hesitate to support them. To be frank, *mate*, you and your wife have been pains in the arse. So how about you focus on enjoying your holiday—your honeymoon. Let Andrew do his job and let the rest of us appreciate the experience too.'

Paul threw them both a filthy look and slammed the door of the shower.

Zed walked to the door with Graysen. 'Thanks, I think we made ourselves quite clear. I'll see you at dinner.'

When he got back to his swag, Graysen took out a clean pair of jeans and a long-sleeved shirt. They were in the dining room of the homestead for dinner, and it wouldn't hurt to make an effort. He removed the battery from his camera and slipped it and the battery charger in his pocket to charge at a power point in the homestead.

He hesitated and looked at his camera bag, and then decided it would be safe enough in the swag. They were the only trekkers on site tonight and the homestead was too far off the main trail for any hikers to come over from the public camps. As soon as they'd eaten, he planned on an early night anyway.

When they'd arrived at the homestead Andrew told them tomorrow was one of the biggest days. The trek would take them to Standley Chasm where there was a campground, and a café. 'Swags for a few days for those of you who choose to walk each leg.'

'Hmph, a luxury tour they said,' Paul muttered, but no one paid him any attention.

With one last glance back at the swag, Graysen decided his gear would be safe and he headed for the dining room.

Soft music and candlelight met him as he looked through the door from the veranda into the bar where Jodie had asked them to meet before dinner.

Disappointing in a way; it wasn't the sort of thing he wanted on a trek. But he had to keep in mind he'd paid for the luxury tour—the top end of the market. The bar was empty; he scouted around and on finding a power point, he slipped the battery into the charger and plugged it in.

He turned as footsteps came along the veranda and was taken aback when Maggie stepped into the bar in a long dress more suited to a ballroom than a trek. The candlelight glinted on the rings on her fingers, and when she came up to him and pressed a kiss to his cheek, he realised she already had a few drinks under her belt.

'I missed you today, Gray. There wasn't a lot to do here, but at least it gave me a chance to have a long hot shower and tidy up a bit for dinner. Not even a pool.'

"Tidy up" wasn't the word he'd use for the long red dress with the plunging neckline and the gold jewellery.

Holding back a sigh, he nodded and headed to the bar in the corner and poured himself a glass of water. 'You missed a good trek today, Maggie. Some excellent views.'

'Did you get many photos?' She walked over and was standing too close for comfort.

'I did.'

'Perhaps I could come to your swag later, and you could show me.' Her hand went up to his chest, and he put his hand over hers, and lifted it away.

'I don't think so, Maggie. I'm flattered, but no.'

Heat ran up his neck as Sandy appeared at the door, and hesitated in the doorway when she saw them standing together.

Graysen stepped away from Maggie and crossed the room to Sandy. She was wearing a pair of denim jeans and a long-sleeved dark blue T-shirt. Her hair was pulled back in her usual ponytail, and the only "tidying up" she'd done was put on some pretty pink lipstick.

'Would you like a glass of iced water, Sandy?' he offered, holding up the glass he'd just poured.

'Or a glass of bubbles?' Maggie had followed him over.

'Water, thank you. I want a totally clear head for tomorrow.' She took the glass he held out and as Graysen headed back to the water cooler, the door at the other side of the room opened. Zed and Miska walked in, both also dressed in jeans and T-shirts. Graysen bit back a grin when Miska's eyes widened as her gaze settled on Maggie. It was a bit hard to miss that red dress.

Clive and Jenny came in from the veranda followed by Paul and Cecily.

'So, no dinner yet?' Paul said loudly. 'And no barman?'

Maggie lifted her glass. 'We had to tell P.D. what we wanted from our order. Did you forget?'

Paul shook his head. 'No, we didn't forget.'

'My bubbles were in the fridge over there. Perhaps your drinks are in there too.'

Paul walked over to the bar fridge and took out two cans of beer. Conversations started up around the room as the others took their drinks from the fridge.

Sandy was still beside Graysen, and he felt a gentle nudge in his side. 'Maggie seems to enjoy goading Paul. That's the last thing we need,' she whispered.

Graysen looked down at Sandy and rolled his eyes. 'It reminds me of one of those dinner parties where everyone plays a character.'

'Where you have to guess the murderer. I'll pass on that, thanks,' she said with a smile.

'Yes, me too. Anyway, I'm going to have a quick dinner and then an early night.'

'So will I. I want to be fresh tomorrow. And this is the only night in a dining room. I really enjoyed last night around the campfire. I'm looking forward to more of that.'

'So am I. More water?'

'Thanks.' Sandy passed her glass to him.

A few minutes later, Jodie walked in with a tray of canapes. 'Sorry I'm late, guys. A slight drama in the kitchen. The stove ran out of gas and we had to transfer everything to the electric ovens. You found your drinks okay?'

'We did, thanks,' Zed said.

'After you have some canapes, grab your drinks and head into the main dining room. We're just about ready to serve up.'

***

Sandra was pleased when Graysen took the seat beside her at the dining room table. She must tell him later that she valued his friendship. She'd ignore the little sparks of attraction that fired every time she was near him; she was too old for that sort of thing. But she knew he'd make a good friend.

Seeing Maggie come on to him in the bar had sent a spurt of jealousy surfacing, and she'd been taken aback at the strength of the feeling. Maggie was almost as difficult as Paul in her own way; she wanted to be the centre of attention. Sandra was sick of hearing how rich she was.

Maggie had taken the seat between Zed and Miska while Zed had slipped outside for a moment. She was in full flight to anyone who'd listen.

'I'm supposed to be meeting Alan in Darwin after the trek, but it's not a city that appeals to me. More of a country town from what I've heard.'

Sandra bit her lip; she wasn't impressed hearing her home town disparaged.

'He wants to buy a couple of hotels.' She turned to Sandra on the other side of the table. 'You're from Darwin aren't you, Sandy?'

'I am.'

'What do you think are the best places there, in terms of going to restaurants or upmarket bars? Alan can't buy anything without my approval—it's my money—so I want to be well informed.'

'I'm sorry I can't help you there. I don't go out much.'

'My God! What do you do at night?'

'My apartment complex has a pool, and some social activities at night, plus I spend a lot of time with my girls.'

'God, darling, you're too young for that. With a bit of help in the makeup and clothes department, you could easily hook yourself a rich fella.'

Sandra didn't know what to say, but when Miska winked at her across the table, she stifled a laugh that came out half between a snort and a cough.

'Thank you, Maggie. I'll keep that in mind,' she said demurely.

The pressure of Graysen's thigh against hers surprised Sandra, and when she looked up at him, he leaned down and whispered in her ear.

'You're perfectly fine as you are. Don't let her bother you.'

Sandra's smile was wide as she whispered back. 'She's not.'

'Good.'

Graysen's leg stayed against hers as two young waitresses brought their entrees out. Sandra's heart thumped and she reached for her water.

'So, I think we need to get to know each other a bit more tonight.' Maggie seemed to have taken on the role of host, and talked over the quiet conversations taking place around the large table. 'We heard everyone's brief background back at the resort the other night, but now we've got to know each other a bit better, we'll have a question-and-answer session. I'll ask the questions. I'm good at this sort of thing.'

No one objected, but Sandra suspected it was because surprise had kicked in. Maggie started before anyone could say no.

'Zed and Miska, we'll start with you. Where do you live and what jobs do you do?'

Miska's face coloured and she looked to Zed.

'At the moment we're in Aberdeen in Scotland. We're both doctors and we do locum work around the United Kingdom. We move often,' he said.

'We lived in Aberdeen for a while.' Clive's voice boomed around the table. 'I did a research year in the engineering faculty at the university. Where do you live?'

'Um, we haven't found anywhere yet,' Miska said. 'We're starting work after our honeymoon.'

'We had university accommodation. You might be able to get some of that. The hospital is a university hospital, or it was when we were there.'

'Thirty years ago,' Jenny added drily.

Zed and Miska looked at each other and smiled. 'We'll be fine.'

'Where are you both from?' Maggie persisted. 'That's a pretty posh accent, Miska. Any lords or earls in your closet? Related to Harry?'

Miska's laugh was pretty. 'Sorry to disappoint you, Maggie. Just a normal childhood in a council flat in London.'

'Zed?'

'Born in Cornwall, but we moved to the States when I was a kid. I went back to the UK, and Miska and I met at uni. We've been together eight years. No children. No plans to have any. Both career people. That's us done.' Zed reached for his glass.

'Okay, that's enough, thanks,' Maggie continued. 'Clive and Jenny? Scotland, then?'

Jenny spoke as if by rote. 'Only for a year. Married thirty-five years. Two kids. No grandkids. We're both retired.'

'Clive was an engineer. What about you, Jenny?'

'I was in the police force. I was a detective when I retired.'

'Ooh, we'd better all behave,' Maggie said. 'Speaking of which, Paul and Cecily, your turn.'

Paul had had a couple of drinks and his recent sullen expression had relaxed.

'I'm an investment banker, and Cecily is a kept woman.' His wife squealed and punched him lightly on the arm.

That explained a lot about Cecily's spoiled attitude, Sandra thought.

'And you live in the US or England?'

They looked at each other before Paul answered. 'I'm about to retire. We haven't decided yet.'

'Ooh, lucky lovebirds. Honeymoon and then retirement.'

Sandra swallowed, getting her response ready.

Maggie turned to her and her expression was crafty. 'So, a widow, Sandy?'

'Yes.'

'You must have been young.'

Sandra lifted her chin, determined not to give in to the anxiety that was uncurling in her stomach. 'I was forty-five. But I had three wonderful girls to look after, and they became my rocks. Got me through a very hard time.'

Every head at the table was turned to Sandra and listening.

Miska smiled at her as if in support. 'Was your husband ill? Did you nurse him?'

'Perhaps it would be easier if we moved on and didn't probe into private lives,' Graysen said.

Sandra looked at him. 'No. It's fine.' She was proud of how calm her voice was. 'I'm not the boring person you seem to think, Maggie. You see, my husband, Peter, was murdered. It was a contract murder, set up by an industrialist who was trying to get the borders of Kakadu National Park changed. The wife of the Chief Magistrate of the Territory was kidnapped at the same time as part of a blackmail attempt, and my daughter crashed her helicopter when it was sabotaged. She was involved in the rescue operation.'

Sandra looked around the table; there was shock and sympathy on most of the faces staring at her. Her gaze finally settled on Maggie. 'It took a long time for the truth to come out, and even longer for me to recover. I am doing this trek to prove to myself that I can.'

'Bravo, Sandy.' Miska's voice was soft.

Cecily and Paul were looking at each other, and Jenny, who was sitting on her other side, reached over and squeezed Sandra's hand.

Maggie went to speak, but Graysen interrupted her. 'Thank you for sharing that, Sandy. I lost my wife a few years ago, but it was simply illness. Or I shouldn't say, simply. I can still hear Marion telling me there's nothing simple about breast cancer.'

Andrew had been standing at the door, and he gestured to someone outside. 'Thanks for sharing your personal stories, everyone. Jodie has a fabulous curry ready for you. So, top up your water glasses. I'm used to Jodie's curries, and you'll need a drink. If you're not a fan of spicy food, there's an alternative out there. So, grab a bowl from the servery and make your way up to the veranda where it's all set up for you.'

Chairs pushed back as the group made their way outside.

Sandra hesitated, waiting for the rest to go, but Graysen stayed beside her.

'Are you okay?' he asked. 'Maggie shouldn't have pushed everyone.'

'She's a strong-willed woman,' Sandra said as she finally pushed her chair back and stood.

'Actually, I don't think she is. I think the clothes and jewellery and the brashness might cover a lack of self-confidence.'

Sandra chuckled as Graysen stood. She pointed to herself. 'This is what a lack of self-confidence looks like.'

He shook his head slowly. 'No. I think you're very wrong. After dinner, would you sit outside with me and have a nightcap? Or a coffee?'

Sandra met his gaze steadily. 'I'd like that very much.'

Chapter 12

Royal Darwin Hospital

'I'm fine, Kane. I'm allowed to walk.' Ellie stabbed at the elevator button on the ground floor of the hospital.

'It's a long way along the corridor,' her husband said.

'And it's a bloody long time until the baby's due,' she said shortly. 'I'm sorry. I didn't mean to snap. This is a happy day, and I won't spoil it by being cranky. You have to trust me. I know what I have to do and I won't do anything to put our child in jeopardy.'

'I'm sorry, love. I know you won't. Just a nervous husband and father.'

'Kane? Over the past week I can't stop thinking about Gina and how she must have felt when she was kidnapped and locked in that house.'

'Thanks to you and her strength, she survived, so stop dwelling on it. Look at them now.'

'Living in a Tuscan villa. I had an email from them the other day. Gina and David said congratulations on our pregnancy, and they invited us to go over and visit after the baby arrives.'

'Would you like that?'

'I don't know. I'm an outback girl, but I guess I should broaden my horizons.'

'We'll pick a time next year. Something to look forward to.'

Ellie touched her growing stomach. 'I think we've got plenty to look forward to.'

'When can we see the babies, Mummy?' James leaned over Kane's shoulder as the elevator door finally dinged open.

'Maybe today. They'll probably be in their special cribs, but you can say hello to your cousins. We'll go and see Aunty Dee first.'

'Can they play with me when they get out of their cribs?'

'They have to grow a little bit first, sweetie, but I'm sure you'll play with them lots of times when they grow bigger.'

Kane put his free arm around Ellie's shoulder. 'Love you, Els.'

'Love you too.' She reached up and kissed him. 'Ignore me when I'm cranky.'

'I always do.' Her husband's smile was cheeky.

Ryan was standing outside the door to Dee's room, looking down at his phone. Ellie walked over and put her arms around him. 'Congratulations, big brother.'

Kane shook Ryan's hand. 'Way to go, mate. James, hold Mummy's hand for me. I'll be back in a minute.'

Ryan gestured towards the private room. 'The doctor's in there. Everything's good, though. I stepped out to make some calls. What do you think we should do about Sandra?'

Ellie frowned and she pulled a face at Kane when he came back with a plastic chair.

'Sit.'

'Yes, boss. And, Kane, I don't know. We looked at her itinerary when you rang to tell us about the twins last night. She's out of range today, but she'll be at Standley Chasm tomorrow. I'm not sure if there'll be service there.'

'The problem is, knowing Sandra, she'll pull the pin on her trip and come straight back to help out,' Kane added.

'And if I tell her about my issue, and also that Emma's going through a bit of a tough time, she'll feel as though she's needed, and she'll be home before we know it. She was so looking forward to this trip, and she wanted to prove to herself that she was capable of doing it.'

'I know. Dee and I are thinking that we'll keep it quiet and off social media until she gets home. The boys are going to be in the hospital for at least three weeks and Sandra will be home by then.'

'And I'm fine. And Emma won't have her results for about ten days, she said.'

'Your mum will be upset,' Kane warned. 'She'll think you don't need her.'

'Well, we do, and we'll make that clear to her, but she also needs to know that she has her own life to live. I want her to finish her trip. It's only two weeks until she's home. Dee and the boys will be in hospital, and she can't do anything to change Emma's results. I say we don't tell her anything until we meet her off the plane.'

'Let's run it by Emma and Dru, and then make it a family decision and no one cops the flack,' Kane suggested.

Ellie chuckled. 'Mum won't have a go at anyone. She's too sweet.'

'And we love her for it,' Ryan said.

The doctor came outside and stood beside Ryan. 'All's good. Dee's going well. I told her she can go home in a few days if she wants to.'

Ryan frowned. 'Can she stay in the hospital? We live on a property a long drive out. Plus, the road is rough.'

'In that case she can stay. If we need the bed, we can organise some accommodation in the parents' wing in paediatrics.'

'Thank you.' Ryan waited as the doctor headed towards the nursery. 'I'll go and see if Dee's ready for visitors and then

I'll take you down to the neonatal nursery on your way out. You can look through the glass window.'

As Kane helped Ellie out of the chair, the elevator door opened, and James took off along the corridor. 'Aunty Dru!'

Dru and Connor each took one of his hands as they walked towards the private room.

'Great timing. We might call Em, and see if she's in the hospital, and we can all make a decision about what to tell Mum,' Ellie said.

'Tell Mum what?' Dru asked.

'About me, about the twins coming, about Emma.'

Dru looked at Connor and he nodded. She reached out for Ellie's hand and put it on her own stomach. 'And me. I've just passed twelve weeks.'

Ellie squealed and threw her arms around Dru. 'Oh my God, our babies will only be a few months apart.'

Dru nodded but her expression was serious. 'Connor and I talked about it last night. We'll wait to tell Mum until she gets home, because I also don't want Emma to know yet. So just for you and Kane at this stage, Ellie.'

'Oh God, Dru. What if Emma's not okay?'

Dru shook her head. 'We'll be there for her.'

Chapter 13

Old Hamilton Downs Homestead

Sandra took her empty bowl back to the servery table and waited to speak to Andrew; Maggie had him bailed up at the door.

'We didn't hear about you, Andrew.' Her words drifted across to Sandra. 'Are you married or do you just live out here on the trail?'

He laughed. 'I don't think my wife would be very impressed if I did that. Yes, we live in Alice Springs and I have two little boys.'

'Lovely. What are their names?'

'Beau and Cooper.'

Sandra waited as Maggie peppered Andrew with more questions. She suspected that Graysen was right. Not only was Maggie's self-confidence low—despite her wealth—Sandra suspected she was lonely. She promised herself that she'd try to talk more to Maggie over the next few days. Finally, Andrew looked over and saw her waiting.

'Excuse me, Maggie.' He came over to Sandra. 'A question for me?'

'Yes, thanks, Andrew, I didn't mean to interrupt. I was just wondering if there'll be phone service at Standley Chasm.'

'There should be. A new tower's just gone in thanks to a funding grant.'

'Excellent. I'll be able to call home.'

Andrew touched her arm lightly. 'I was at the door when Maggie grilled you. I was working in a community at Kakadu when that all happened. I worked with Bill Jarragah for a while. He was devastated by the whole thing.'

Sandra blinked back tears. 'Bill worked on our mango farm, and he and my husband were good mates for a long time. He was a lovely man.'

'Was?' Andrew frowned.

'Yes, sadly Bill passed away last year. His daughter, Heather rang to let me know, but we'd lost touch with her over the years. She was another casualty of what happened. Her mental health isn't good.'

'Greed is a terrible thing, isn't it?' Andrew said.

'It certainly is.'

'I'm pleased to see how well you're handling the trek. It's a pleasure to have you with us, Sandy.'

Sandra smiled. She was getting used to being called Sandy; strangely it made her feel younger. 'Thank you. I'll leave you in peace now.'

Andrew smiled. 'Any time you want to chat, feel free. Also, if you ever need to call home and there's no service, see me and you can use the sat phone. It works wherever we are.'

Graysen was waiting for her at the end of the veranda. He held two mugs of coffee and Sandra leaned over to see what was in the bottle under his arm.

'Whisky?' she asked.

'I ordered one bottle for the trek.' He looked sheepish. 'In case it was cold at night. I must be getting soft in my old age. I was going to offer you a splash for your coffee.'

'Why not?' she said. 'But just a splash.'

'Are you warm enough?' He looked down at the jacket she'd worn across to dinner. 'I thought it'd be nice to sit out under the stars.'

'I'm warm.' She chuckled. 'Don't tell anyone. I've got thermals on underneath.'

Graysen's grin was wide. 'Don't you tell anyone either, but so have I. I know how cold it'll get through the night.'

As they strolled across the grass to a seating area near the fence, Sandra looked up at the sky. 'We had no outside lights at our farm and I thought the stars were beautiful there'—she spread her arms wide— 'but this is incredible, the sky is so big.'

'It is. The best night skies I've ever photographed are here in Central Australia. Marion and I came to Alice Springs twenty-five years ago. I haven't been back since.' Graysen gestured to the double swing seat. 'Happy to share?'

'Of course.' Once she was settled, he passed her one of the coffees and put the whisky bottle on the grass. The seat swung a little as he sat beside her.

'Thanks for the company.'

'Thanks for the invitation. I was going to catch you anyway.' Sandra held out her coffee as he held up the bottle.

'Just a splash,' he said.

She nodded and then took a sip once he'd poured the whisky into her mug. She swallowed. 'Nice. Warming.'

'What did you want to talk to me about?' he asked.

'Nothing major. I just wanted to say thanks for the friendship and for looking out for me. I appreciate it. You're a kind man.'

'My pleasure. I enjoy your company, Sandy. I'll be honest with you. There are very few people who fall into that category.' Graysen put his head back and rested against the high cushion. 'Since Marion died, I've been a loner. I've travelled the world, and I've kept to myself.'

'You said the other night you had no children.'

'No. There was just us, and when she died, I had no family to turn to.'

'My girls have been my life, but recently I began to realise that I need to let them live their own lives. They were incredibly patient with me after Peter died. I was pretty hopeless for a few years.' For the first time her voice cracked a little. 'It was set up to look like a suicide, but I knew my Peter would never have taken his own life. I persevered and I researched, and I read government reports and then I finally convinced the girls something had happened, that it wasn't me looking for spooks in the corner. It was a massive corrupt scheme to get our land that backed onto the national park. So many innocent people were hurt before it was all sorted.'

'You're a strong woman. You remind me of Marion. Not in looks but in your attitude.'

'Thank you. I'll take that as a compliment. Coming on the trek has created a good distance from the girls for me. I can't be there for them forever. They need to make their own choices and their own decisions without my input. They each have lovely partners, as does my stepson.'

'Your husband had an earlier marriage?'

'No, Peter never knew about his son, so neither did I. That's another long sad story for a rainy night. Ryan found us a couple of years ago, and he's become part of our family. He and his wife, Dee, are having twins in a couple of months. That was one of the reasons I was a bit hesitant to come away. Plus, my middle daughter is pregnant too.'

'Even if you let them lead their own lives, it sounds as though you'll have a rich and full life.' He sounded wistful. 'I envy you.'

'Well, if you're ever in Darwin, come and visit. I'd love you to meet my family.'

'I'd like that. It would be nice to have a friend too. It's a date.'

'Where are you going after the trek? Or where is home?'

'There isn't one. We lived in Sydney for a while and I do have good friends there. I don't want to sound like Maggie, but we had two homes. One in England and one on the beach in Cairns. When Marion died, I sold them both. I didn't even go back. Sold them furnished.' Graysen reached into the V at the neck of his T-shirt and pulled out a fine gold chain. This is the only thing of Marion's I kept. I wear her wedding ring around my neck. And lots of photographs, of course. But I still find it hard to look at them.'

His jaw was tight as he stared ahead. 'I guess I'll have to find a place to put down roots. I can't travel forever.'

'You've been lots of places?' she asked.

'More than a hundred countries over my lifetime.'

'I haven't been to one. We planned that for when the girls grew up and we sold the farm. But—'

'But life happens,' Graysen said. He reached for her hand and it felt right. 'Don't leave it too long, Sandy.'

'Once Ellie's baby is past the newborn stage, I'm going to look into some trips overseas. The thought of travel excites me. I've managed well by myself for a few days so far, I'm sure I could spread my wings.'

'I'm sure you could too.'

'What's your favourite country?'

Graysen replied immediately. 'Anywhere in the UK. The countryside, I mean. I always avoid big cities. I love the softness of the light and the green of the landscape. Marion always said it was genetic memory because my grandparents were all from the same area in Wales.'

'When I go, I'll make sure to ask you where to go.'

'Good.' Graysen glanced at his watch. 'We've got an early start and it's after ten. Maybe we should call it a night.'

He sounded as reluctant as Sandra felt. She'd enjoyed Graysen's company.

Very much. Maybe too much.

It was like a school camp. You were thrown into the wilderness and the people with you became an important part of your world until you went home again.

Her hand stayed in Graysen's as he walked her across to the campsite where the swags were set up. Either everyone was asleep or still over at the homestead; each swag was in darkness, and all was quiet.

In the distance the eerie howl of a dingo broke the silence and Sandra shivered.

'Zip up well,' Graysen said as he let go of her hand. 'Thanks for the company.'

'Thanks for the friendship.' Sandra stood on her toes and brushed a kiss across his cheek. 'Sleep well, Graysen.'

Once she was in the swag, Sandra closed her eyes and placed her fingers to her lips as happiness and calm filled her.

Yes, maybe too much.

Chapter 14

Old Hamilton Downs Homestead to Standley Chasm

Graysen put the newly-charged battery into his camera. He looked around the swag checking that he had everything before stepping outside. Another clear and cold morning greeted him. He couldn't help but look over at Sandra's swag; it was zipped up so she was either in there or had gone across to breakfast already.

Paul came out of the double swag, looked at Graysen for a brief moment and then dropped his gaze.

'With two sugars, babe,' Cecily called out.

Graysen grinned. Room service in a swag in a paddock.

Zed and Miska were sitting at a table in the sun with Sandra.

'Morning all,' Graysen said brightly, enjoying the warm smile from Sandy.

'Morning, Graysen. All ready for a big day?' Zed asked.

He patted the camera on his chest. 'Batteries are recharged. Both the camera's and mine.'

Gawd, first time anything like that had come from him for a long time. Maybe he did have a sense of humour buried in there somewhere.

'Please join us,' Miska said. 'We've all eaten but still have to get our coffee.'

'Thanks.' He put his camera on the table.

'Mind if I have a look at some of the photos you've taken?' Zed asked.

'Sure, go ahead. These are just for my pleasure. I'm not on a contract this trip.'

Zed picked up the camera and started scrolling through while Graysen went to the other end of the veranda where breakfast was laid out.

Clive was loading his plate. 'We can't complain about the food, hey, mate,' he said.

'You're right there. It's very good.'

'A good tip for the chef, I think.'

'They're all good.' Graysen made a note to make sure he had enough cash to give the three guides a decent tip at the end of the trek. He filled his bowl with granola and fruit and headed back to the table.

'Some fantastic shots, there, Graysen. What sort of lens do you use?'

'Most of those were taken with a Pentax 150-450 mm.'

'Great clarity.' Zed lowered his voice. 'What are the ones of Paul and Cecily? It looked like he was trying to push her over the cliff.'

'Just some stupid behaviour. They were mucking around yesterday and then he dunked her in the water at Bond Gap.'

Miska shook her head. 'It's sad, but I don't give that marriage long.'

'Hopefully he'll pull his head in after you guys spoke to him last night,' Sandy said. 'He just needs to do some growing up. Hopefully, they'll sort it.'

'Ever the romantic, Sandy?' Miska had a strange look on her face and her words held bitterness.

'Yes, I am. I believe in happy endings, don't you?'

'I'd like to, but there aren't many of them.'

Zed reached over and put his hand on top of Miska's. 'Mis has just finished a contract in paediatrics and you saw some pretty nasty stuff in there, didn't you, darling?'

Miska blinked and seemed to pull herself together. 'I'm sorry, Sandy, I don't usually let it get to me. Not the sort of stuff to bring on our holiday.' As she spoke, she and Zed stared at each other and Graysen liked what he saw. They seemed to be able to read each other's minds; his relationship with Marion had been the same.

'It's okay,' Sandy said. 'It's time I went and packed up. I was so hungry when I woke up, I came straight over for breakfast.' She looked at her watch. 'I'd better get my skates on, Andrew said to be ready at seven-thirty and it's almost that now.'

'I'll walk over with you. I have to get my kitbag out of the swag.'

Within fifteen minutes they were in the Larapinta Luxury Tours truck, their bags in the back, and the food and rubbish in the special compartments in the truck. When Graysen and Sandra returned with their bags, P.D. pulled the swags down, and they'd watched Jodie and Andrew load and pack the truck, and it was clear that they had an efficient and fast system in place.

'Right, let's start the next segment of our walk.' Andrew spread a map on the table near the truck. 'After we have a quick look at Fish Hole, Jodie will drive us to Tangentyere Junction, where you have a choice of routes through the magnificent Chewings Ranges. Your choice is the hard way or the "easier way". The hard way, the "alternate high route" will reward you with great views and scenery'—Andrew looked at Graysen— 'and photographs, but there are some difficult ascents and descents. The "low route" goes over and through rocky and narrow gorges and creek beds. And a warning. While it's not as hard as the high route, it's still pretty rough on your feet and ankles. And *without* the scenery.

'But the upside for those of you who decide to take the low route, it's an hour shorter and any views you miss today, you'll catch up with tomorrow from the amazing Brinkley's Bluff.'

'What are your thoughts, Sandy?' Graysen moved closer to her. She looked very attractive today. Her hair was pulled back in a high ponytail and her cheeks were pink.

'What do you think?' Her grin was cheeky.

'I'd have to guess the high?' He smiled back and found it hard to look away.

'Spot on.' Her skin was flawless, and despite the tragedy she'd suffered in her life, laughter lines fanned out from her eyes when she smiled. It was hard to believe she had grown up children.

Andrew continued. 'I'll guide those who take the high route, and P.D. will be walking through the gorges with those who choose the low. That is unless everyone decides to take the high? If you're taking the low, please go over to P.D.'

Maggie, and Clive and Jenny indicated that they'd take the low route and walked across to join the young indigenous guide. Cecily and Paul were arguing in low voices to one side. Zed and Miska came over to stand with Graysen and Sandra.

'Thanks, guys. Looks like we've got two groups today. P.D. and I have snacks and fruit for morning tea in our packs, and the billy, of course, but even with the difficult walk it's only five hours to Standley Chasm. There, Jodie will have our camp—and lunch—set up. Make sure your water bottles are topped up before we leave.' Andrew walked over to Paul and Cecily. 'No need to decide right now. It'll take us an hour or so in the truck to get to Fish Hole.'

Graysen stood back and let Sandy board the truck first. Once she'd taken a seat, he sat beside her. A small smile crossed her lips and he felt good. Being happy was an unfamiliar emotion and he let it wash over him as he looked over her head to the scenery flashing by.

It was going to be a good day.

***

The visit to Fish Hole was not marred by any bad behaviour from the usual suspects. Paul and Cecily had opted for the easy walk with P.D.

Sandra enjoyed the young guide's talk as they traversed the spectacular gorge. The bright red of the cliffs of the gorge, contrasted with the white sand at the end of the rugged drop. At the southern end was the deep permanent pool known as Fish Hole.

'Over there, guys. That's the first steep pinch of the high trail.' P.D. pointed out the short sharp climb on the western edge of the pool where they would begin the trek to the fork in the trail.

Maggie stood with her hands on her hips. 'So, I do have to climb too!'

'Just a short one, Maggie.' P.D. assured her. 'I'll walk behind you.'

It was still early, and cold, when they all began the climb.

Sandra was puffing before they reached the top, and wondered if she'd made the wrong choice choosing the high trail.

'You'll be fine, Sandy.' Graysen held out his hand to help her up the last steep pinch over a couple of large boulders the size of small trucks.

When she had her breath back, she managed to speak. 'Are you a mind reader too?'

'No.' He chuckled. 'I was starting to wonder if I'd made the right choice too. I was wondering if I should have saved my energy for Brinkley's Bluff tomorrow. Come on. We're at the fork now. I'll stay with you as we climb.'

Graysen and Sandra took the lead, Zed and Miska were between them and Andrew who was bringing up the rear today.

After three days of walking, Sandra fell into the swing of striding out. Zed and Miska had pulled out telescopic walking poles from the kit bag he carried on his back and she felt good that she was walking without the help of poles. It built her confidence. Plus, every few hundred meters, Graysen would hold his hand out, and the feel of his warm fingers was better than the best walking pole you could buy.

'Look.' Graysen stopped suddenly and lifted his camera. 'A diamond dove.'

'Aw, what a cutie.' The little fluffy bird seemed to be posing on the branch for them.

The track turned into a switchback to let them ascend the three hundred metres to the top more easily. Every fifty metres or so, Graysen would pause and lift his camera to capture the incredible views, and then ask Sandra to hold the lens and the caps as he switched over to his zoom wide angle lens.

'I hope I'm not holding you up,' he finally said.

'No, the opposite, it gives me a chance to take a breather and enjoy the view. It's absolutely awe-inspiring, isn't it?'

'It is. I have some amazing shots today.'

'Will you show them to me tonight?' Sandra burst out laughing. 'Oh dear, I don't mean in your tent, though.'

Andrew finally caught them up and waited for Zed and Miska to join them before he described the panoramic view, giving them a three-hundred-and-sixty-degree vista.

'South of us is the Heavitree Range and further ahead you can see along the Chewings Range to the west. The highest peak over there is Brinkley Bluff that we'll all climb tomorrow.'

A huge gust of wind buffeted them on the razorback ridge, and for the first time on the trek Sandra was a little scared as adrenaline rushed through her body. She stepped back from the edge, automatically grabbing for Graysen.

'My God, that was a bit scary,' she said. Graysen stood behind her and his broad chest protected her from the next gust.

He put his big camera back in the camera bag as they began a steep descent down a small gully.

A variety of birds flitted in and out of the rocks, swooping into the occasional pool surrounded by lush vegetation.

Andrew called for a rest as a huge flock of budgerigars surrounded them, chattering and chirping, the movement of their wings disturbing the air as they flew past.

'The walking gets a bit easier now. You've done the hard yards,' he said.

'I think the descent was harder on my knees than the climb up,' Sandra commented. She and Graysen had fallen behind Zed and Miska and Andrew.

'One more little climb to Cycad Creek, but trust me, it's well worth it,' Andrew added.

By the time she and Graysen had reached Cycad Creek, the others had gone on ahead. More birds drank from the pools along the creek floor. Two more flocks of budgerigars swooped past, and Sandra looked up, widening her eyes as the wind from their wings lifted her hair.

'Sandy!'

She swivelled around as Graysen called her, wondering what was wrong, and then smiled as the shutter clicked on his camera.

He lowered it and walked over to her. Lifting a hand, he reached up and brushed the loose hair from her cheek.

'*That* is one of the best photographs I've ever taken,' he said, as his hand cupped her cheek gently.

'The budgerigars?'

'No, the expression on your face, the angle of your head, your hair around it like a halo. It's perfect.'

Sandra stared at him and her heart seemed to quiver. It seemed natural when Graysen lowered his head and slowly brushed his lips over hers. Her fingers tingled with the need to lift her hand and touch his face, but her lack of confidence held her back.

Finally, he moved away and lowered his hand from her face, and she raised hers to touch her lips, but her eyes remained on his.

'I should apologise,' he said softly. 'But I won't. It felt right. You looked like a wood nymph, with those delicate fronds framing your face. I couldn't help kissing you.'

Sandra stood still and didn't speak as a myriad of emotions ran through her. Uppermost was disbelief that she had just been kissed.

'Thank you. And no, I don't expect you to apologise. It was very nice. And that was a lovely thing to say.' Her lips were still tingling, and despite being alone with this man she had only known for a few days, she felt safe.

Graysen held his hand out to her. 'One more climb apparently up to the saddle and then all downhill to Standley Chasm.'

Their conversation was natural as they slowly picked their way along the course of the creek, past large boulders and dry waterfalls.

It was strange, Sandra thought, just how easy it was to be in Graysen's company after her first impression of him. She thought she'd be feeling self-conscious after he'd kissed her.

He kissed me! She couldn't help the smile that tugged at her lips. It was like being a teenager again. Not that she'd had many kisses before she'd met Peter at her uncle's store at Marrakai. Those days, the tennis afternoons at Hidden Valley, and her friendship with Ryan's mum, Suzanne, who had passed away a few years ago, seemed like another life.

'Going okay?' Graysen asked as they reached the end of the creek and started to climb to the saddle.

'Yes, going well,' she replied.

He dropped her hand and moved to the front to lead the way. The route was made easier by many flat slabs of rock positioned on the steep slope and Sandra sent up a thank you to the track workers who'd made this leg a bit easier.

The views from the saddle were amazing, as was the feel of Graysen's arm as he casually slung it over her shoulder when he'd finished taking photos. It was a clear winter's day, and the temperature had risen to the hottest day they'd had so far. As they stood on the saddle Graysen pointed below. They could just see the rest of the group stepping out of a tall gum forest on the south side of the chasm.

'They've made good time. It shouldn't take us long to reach them.'

##

Walking into the bitumen car park of the campground and café at Standley Chasm, and encountering a throng of tourists in cars and buses who had driven in to walk the one kilometre walk into the actual chasm, had been a little anti-climactic.

Graysen looked around. 'Hmm. Different.'

Sandra nodded. 'I've been really surprised how few trekkers we've seen so far. I thought we'd be passing walkers every day, but it's really isolated.'

Graysen was walking beside her, but it seemed to be unspoken that they kept their distance from each other when they were with the group. No matter what happened, or whether they stayed in touch, this interlude with Graysen had been wonderful for Sandra's self-confidence.

Plus, it makes me feel young again.

As they sat around camp after dinner with the rest of the group, Sandra knew the day and the night at Standley Chasm would stay in her mind forever. The walk had been difficult, but the scenery and the views magnificent, the stars filled the velvet sky with diamond brilliance. She'd been likened to a wood nymph and kissed by a very attractive man.

What on earth would the girls think?

This trek was touching her soul, even without Graysen's contribution, and she knew she'd go back a very different person.

The trek was working its magic on everyone, and Maggie's animation was more natural as she described the sights they'd seen on the low trail.

'The budgerigars!' she explained. 'I thought they were cage birds.'

'There must have been thousands of them that flew between us. It was so noisy.' Even Cecily and Paul were happy and smiling.

'I thought they were going to get tangled in my hair,' Cecily said with a shiver.

Graysen and Sandra exchanged a warm look and a pleasant shiver ran down her spine. The landscape was weaving its spell on everyone.

'We saw them at Cycad Creek at the end of the high trail,' Miska said. 'Absolutely amazing.'

Zed put his arm around her, pulled her closer and brushed a kiss on her cheek. 'You're amazing. Miska handled the climb today better than I did.'

'You're *all* amazing,' Andrew reinforced. 'It's been a top day. And if you thought the views were good today, wait until you walk the quartzite ridges along to Brinkley Bluff tomorrow. Breathtaking views in all directions. Make sure all your camera batteries and phones are charged.'

'How far tomorrow?' Maggie asked. 'I really enjoyed today. It was a long way but I managed.'

'You managed well,' P.D. chipped in. 'Very well.'

'And so did I,' Jenny said. 'I'm starting to surprise myself. How did you go on the high trail, Sandy?'

'It was wonderful. I had the best day, and we saw budgerigars too.'

Andrew waited until everyone was listening. 'Early start tomorrow. We've got a nine-hour trek, so we'll be up at dawn for breakfast, so set your phone alarms. Jodie will send P.D. along to the tents when breakfast is ready, so try to be packed up and ready to set off as soon as you've eaten.'

'God, it'll be cold that early,' Maggie said.

'It will. P.D. and I will lead you out tomorrow, and then when we get on the main trail, I'll lead the way and P.D. will bring up the rear. Jodie will meet us with the truck at Birthday Waterhole and when we get there, P.D. and I will help her set up camp.'

'Are we allowed to swim in that waterhole?' Paul asked, but he was grinning.

'You can. And you'll appreciate it after tomorrow's walk. Plus, our campsite is a kilometre from the public trail camp, but there's no phone service out there anywhere.'

Sandra gave a little gasp and her face heated when everyone looked at her.

'Sorry.' She shook her head. 'I just realised we have phone service here and I hadn't even thought of ringing home and checking in.'

'That's what we like to hear. The Red Centre has worked its magic on you.'

'It certainly has. Excuse me. I'll be back in a little while.'

As she stood to leave, she put her hand on Graysen's shoulder. 'Wait for me?'

Her answer was the squeeze of his hand on hers.

The café was closed but the tables and chairs were still out on the stone balcony undercover. There was no one else sitting there, so Sandra walked up the hill and pulled out a chair.

Who to call first?

Chapter 15

McLaren Mango Farm

'Here we go,' Ellie said as she looked down at the screen of her phone when it rang. 'Thank goodness James is in bed already. That's one thing I can be truthful about.'

'Your mum?'

Ellie nodded at Kane. 'Yep. Don't look at me or I'll sound unnatural.'

'I'll go and load the dishwasher and give you some privacy. Say hello from me.'

Ellie took a deep breath and answered the call. 'Hey, Mum. So good to hear from you. We've missed you!'

'Hi darling, it's good to hear your voice. I suppose I've missed James.'

'Yes, he's been in bed for a couple of hours. He went out to the trees with Kane this afternoon and came back filthy. So, early bath and tea and we've had some peace and quiet. Kane says hello.'

'Hello back to Kane, and give James a kiss from Nanny in the morning. How are you?'

'You'll be proud of me, Mum. I'm having a rest most afternoons. I'm enjoying this not going to work. Now enough about us, how are *you*?'

'Oh, darling, It's absolutely incredible here. I'm having the best time.'

Ellie smiled. She hadn't heard her mother so animated for ages.

'Our guides are fantastic and most of the group are lovely. They call me Sandy.'

'Uh oh, most?' Ellie said. 'That doesn't sound good. Most?'

'One young couple who took a while to settle in. They're on their honeymoon, but they're coming good.'

'Any other oldies?' Ellie teased.

'Half of the group are around my age,' her mother replied. 'Another couple, another woman on her own, and one other man. Graysen is a photographer and he's been my trekking buddy. We had the best walk today and I actually got my photo taken as a flock of budgerigars surrounded me. You've never heard anything like it.'

'I'm so pleased you're having a good time. The walk's not too hard?'

'It is. Very hard, but I'm getting fitter by the day. Google Brinkley's Bluff. That's what we're climbing tomorrow.'

Before Ellie could answer, her mother kept talking. 'I have to go. I couldn't get onto the others. Are they all okay?'

'I was talking to Dru yesterday. They're fine. Ryan called in to see Kane this morning, and Dee's good. Emma's probably at the hospital.'

'Okay, sweetie. Give everyone my love, tell them I'm having the best time. I'll talk to you all next time we have service. Probably another three or four days, I think. Love you. And a kiss for James.'

'Love you too, Mum. If you can send me that photo, I'd love to see it.'

'Will do. Bye.'

Ellie looked at the phone in disbelief. A call with Mum usually went for half an hour, and it was always Ellie who ended it.

Her phone pinged straight away with a text message.

I don't have the budgie photo yet LOL Graysen told me I looked like a wood nymph(!!!!) but here are some of the group. Some candid snaps I took around camp on our first night. Plus one of my luxury tent. Can you forward to the others pls?

Ta, Love Mum aka Sandy xx

'A wood nymph? Who is this guy?' Ellie chuckled as she scrolled through the photos.

'What?' Kane came out of the kitchen, a tea towel over his shoulder and a frown on his forehead. 'Is everything okay?'

Ellie nodded slowly. 'I think so. She had to rush off. She looks really happy. Half the group is around Mum's age. And the best part is, I didn't have to tell her one porky. Emma *is* at the hospital, and Dee is fine.'

'Have you talked to Emma today?'

'No, not since yesterday. She has to stay in a couple of days after her surgery.'

'Do you think she's doing okay?' Kane sat on the double sofa beside her.

Ellie took a deep breath. 'It's hard to know. She's trying to be upbeat. I know she doesn't want to bring the rest of us down. But shit, Kane, losing one of her ovaries and waiting for the biopsy results must be just awful for her.'

'How about we drive in and see her tomorrow while James is at kindy, and you can tell her about your mum's call.'

Ellie rested her head against her husband's shoulder. 'Thank you, I'd like that. And we can visit Dee and the bubs as well.'

'But we won't tell James!'

'Not that he'd probably care. He was most unimpressed at how little they were and they didn't look at him.' Ellie blinked back tears. 'Mum sounded so happy, and Dee and the babies are fine, Dru's news will send Mum over the moon. I just hope and pray that Emma's okay. It's so unfair.'

Kane's hand smoothed her hair. 'It is, love, but you worrying about it isn't going to make any difference. You need to try not to worry and keep resting. You've been good without me having to nag you.'

'I have. I love you, Kane.'

'Love you too.' His frown cleared as he leaned over to take her lips with his.

***

Standley Chasm 9.00p.m.

Sandra hurried back to the campsite and was pleased to see Graysen still sitting there talking to Clive and Jenny. Jodie was collecting coffee cups and there was no sign of Andrew or P.D. or Maggie. The campsite was on Aboriginal land and there was no alcohol permitted.

Zed and Miska, and Cecily and Paul seemed to have made up their differences and were walking towards the track to the chasm. Despite Paul and Cecily's turnaround, Sandra was still wary.

She had a long memory.

'Did you get onto your family?' Graysen asked as she sat in the same chair she'd vacated. The fire had died down and was now a pile of glowing coals. Most of the lights had gone out around the campsite, and the sky was even brighter.

'I did. Everyone's fine.'

'Good to hear.'

'I'm going to grab my tripod and my night lens and walk up to the chasm. Do you want to come for a walk, Sandra, or is it too cold for you?'

'I'd love to. I want to squeeze every minute and every sight I can out of this trek.'

'Make sure you take a flashlight,' Jenny said. 'I'd hate to see you break a leg or something.'

'Or a hip?' Sandra giggled. 'Cecily's already warned me about that. Sorry. I'm being naughty.'

'I have a memory like an elephant,' Jenny said. 'Anyone who does their dash with me, I don't forget.'

'Must be a female thing. I was just thinking the same, unfortunately,' Sandra said.

'Yep, we're intuitive. That's why women make the best detectives.' Jenny nudged Clive. 'No matter what the opposition says, hey, my dear? My intuition stood me in good stead in my career, and there's just something about that pair that's not quite right.'

'Now Jenny, we need to be tolerant,' Clive said.

'Takes all kinds,' Sandra agreed.

'Do you want to get another jacket, Sandra? I've got a good LED flashlight in my kit,' Graysen said. 'That'll light our way.'

'We went for a stroll down to the chasm before dinner,' Clive said. 'A flat easy walk, but we missed the best part of the day when the sun peeks through the narrow gap.'

'Yes, I've seen photos taken at noon, but not the real thing,' Graysen said. 'I might come back here after the trek and walk down in the middle of the day.'

'Sounds like a plan. We might hang around for a few days too. I know Clive wants to go to the museums in Alice. Okay, we're off to bed. See you both in the morning.' Jenny smiled at Sandra and her eyes held a twinkle.

Sandra waited by the fire and warmed her hands over the coals while Graysen went to get his photographic gear.

He was back quickly, carrying a tripod and a larger camera bag. 'I haven't done a lot of astrophotography so this is a practice run for me. It could take a while to get the settings right, so if you'd rather go to bed early—?'

'If you'd rather go by yourself, just say.'

He shook his head. 'I'd love you to keep me company.'

'Well then, I'd love to come.' Sandra stood and zipped up her hoodie and pulled the hood up over her hair.

'I'm pleased.' Graysen slung the bag over his right shoulder and held out his left hand. Her hand fit into his naturally.

'I'm going to stay around a few days after the trek too. If you'd like more company. . .' she ventured.

'Sounds like a good plan to me.'

As they walked along past the café to the beginning of the track, Graysen's hand tightened on hers a little. 'I hope you don't think I'm being a bit over-the-top saying this, but meeting you on the trek has really increased my enjoyment. You're excellent company.'

'Thank you, and ditto.' They walked along for a while and contentment stole over Sandra. Her limbs felt light and now that she knew her family were all fine, she could relax even more.

Halfway along the track to the chasm, Graysen directed the flashlight on a sign and a set of flat rocks that climbed the hill. 'That's our start tomorrow.'

Voices drifted down to them.

'Sounds like Paul and Cecily,' Sandra said.

Sure enough, within seconds the pair jumped down off the last step. 'Hello, we were just having a look at the track for tomorrow.'

'And the others too?'

'Zed and Miska kept going when we turned around.' Cecily giggled. 'I don't think the campsite is private enough for them, if you get my drift.'

Sandra smiled. 'Young love, how sweet it is.'

'We're off to take some photos, so see you in the morning,' Graysen said.

'Night,' the young couple called.

'They have mellowed a bit,' Sandra commented.

All was quiet as they completed the fifteen-minute walk to the three-metre gap in the high gorge.

Graysen stopped about fifty metres before the gap, set up his tripod and attached the camera to the top. 'Sandra, can you hold the flashlight over the top of the camera for me for a minute?'

'I can,' she said, doing as he asked. 'I'm enjoying this photographic assistant role.'

His teeth flashed white as he grinned at her. 'I'm enjoying having one.' He fiddled with the camera settings for another minute, and then pulled out his phone, and took the flashlight from Sandra.

'All set. All we have to do now is find a comfortable rock.'

'How does that work?' she asked as they walked over to the wall of the gorge.

'I have an app that lets me control the camera from my phone. It's great because it takes away any camera movement in the long exposure shots. I've got a few settings I want to try, so about ten photographs that will take up to two minutes each.'

Graysen found a flat rock tucked against the wall. 'If I was a gentleman, I'd take my jacket off and spread it on the rock for you. But it's too cold.'

He sat down and patted the rock beside him. 'God that's even colder than the air. It's going through my thermals.'

Before Sandra could sit, Graysen's hands were around her waist and he pulled her down onto his knee. 'A much warmer option.'

'Thank you,' she said shyly.

His arms went around her, and the screen of the phone lit up in his hands. A big red dot appeared in the centre and when Graysen pressed it, she heard the camera whirr over on the track.

'I'm impressed.'

'I'd like to take credit for it, but it's simple technology.'

'But *you* know how to do it. I don't know half the things my phone is capable of.' As he moved his hands a little to raise the phone, his arms brushed against her breasts and a long-forgotten shaft of exquisite sweetness went shooting into Sandra's lower belly. At the same time her cheeks burned.

'So,' he said softly as his face moved closer to her cheek and his breath warmed her already heated skin. 'I wonder how we should fill in a few minutes. The camera's doing its thing well. Any ideas?'

Sandra knew what followed was entirely up to her and she froze, her body as taut as a guide rope. Graysen took one hand from the phone and lifted it to her face. Ever so gently with the backs of his fingers, he brushed her mouth.

'Perhaps your lips need some warmth,' he murmured, his mouth so close to hers Sandra could feel the vibration of his words. Her lips parted in anticipation, and then his mouth opened over hers.

A shudder rocked her and the exquisiteness of a moment ago spread through her entire body. When he groaned against her lips and put the phone on the rock beside them, she was barely aware of anything except for Graysen's mouth seeking the warmth of hers. Their tongues met and moved into that age-old dance of need and wanting.

The camera clicked off and Sandra pulled away reluctantly. 'Your camera needs your attention.' Her words seemed blurred by her swollen lips.

'It'll only take a moment and I don't have to move. I'll be quick. Hold that pose,' he said, and she smiled at the joy in his voice. The joy that mirrored the feeling shooting to every nerve cell in her body.

Every one.

It was only a few seconds before the phone went back on the rock, and Graysen resumed doing what Sandra was fast discovering he was *very* skilled at.

Chapter 16

Standley Chasm to Bridle Path Lookout

When the alarm on Sandra's phone woke her the next morning, she snuggled into the warmth of her bed, reluctant to get out and put her feet on the cold floor. With a determined movement, she pushed back the soft doona on her bed and swung her legs over the side. Reaching for her socks, they were the first thing she pulled on in the faint dawn light.

Her dreams had been sensuous and a warm blush crept into her cheeks as she recalled them. Her heart beat faster and her fingers tingled against the woolly socks as she recalled the pleasant half hour she and Graysen had spent at the chasm.

On their return he'd walked her to her tent, and kissed her good night. 'Pleasant dreams,' he'd said, and she'd certainly had them.

Sandra warmed up quickly as she pulled her warm clothes over her trekking shorts and T-shirt before she made a dash to the facilities.

'Morning, Cecily.'

The young woman was in there putting her makeup on and by the time Sandra had washed her face, brushed her teeth and lathered sun cream on, Cecily was still outlining her lips with a lip pencil.

Whatever floats your boat, Sandra thought.

'See you at brekky,' she said as she left, and the rude grunt she got in return didn't bother her.

But nerves did quiver in her chest and tummy after she packed up her gear in the tent.

Damn, she'd forgotten to charge her phone after she'd texted the photos to Ellie last night. That would teach her to daydream like a teenager. Packing her flat phone into the soft bag that would go in the truck, Sandra took out her small digital camera and put it in her backpack. She grinned as she made her way to the breakfast area; her little camera would be a poor relation to Graysen's.

In her usual efficient fashion, Jodie had a continental feast laid out, and the coffee brewing.

'Oh, you're a sweetheart, Jodie,' Sandra said as she poured her first coffee. She'd had a quick look around but there was no sign of Graysen. A lump formed in her throat. Maybe he was sorry about their little interlude last night.

God, she thought, a few shared kisses shouldn't make him think she wanted a relationship or commitment surely?

Anyway, he'd been the one to start it.

Forcing herself to eat her cereal and fruit, and not make do with just the coffee which she would have preferred, Sandra tried to get her new-found self-confidence back.

Gradually the others drifted over to the breakfast area, but Graysen was the last one to emerge from his tent. Her stomach sank when she saw the straight line his lips were set in, and he looked like the cranky man she'd met in the elevator at the resort in Alice Springs.

She sat straight and stared ahead. If he said anything rude, she'd simply ignore him. Foolishly she'd placed her jacket on the back of the chair beside hers, saving it for Graysen, and now it was the only vacant chair.

Sandra buried her face in her mug and looked down at the table as he pulled the chair out and sat beside her. She almost spluttered in her coffee when a warm hand settled on her thigh, and Graysen leaned over so his face was next to hers.

'Good morning, sweet Sandy. I hope you slept well.' Her head flew up and she met his eyes.

Putting a hand to her chest, she whispered, 'I thought you were angry at me.'

'Of course not. I was angry, but never at you.'

She frowned. 'What's wrong?'

'Someone's been interfering with my camera, and I've got a fair idea who it was. But I don't know when he could have taken it.'

'He?' she whispered quietly.

'I'll tell you what happened when we start walking today. In the meantime, I'd better grab something to eat, because Andrew has got our packs over at the trail already. Are you packed up? I'm all set to go.'

'I am.' She nodded.

Breakfast was a quiet and quick meal. It appeared that everyone was focused on the big climb ahead today, and it wasn't long before Andrew appeared and asked them to put their kit bags out ready for Jodie to load in the truck, and to make use of the facilities and then head over to the trail head.

As the sky began to lighten before sunrise, with that apricot and pink tinge to the sky in the east, Clive and Jenny and Maggie were the last ones to make their way to the trail head where Andrew was going through the trek for the day ahead.

'Take note of the trail markers, and follow as close as you can behind P.D. I know that in conditions like this, you'll all have a different pace, but please don't leave the trail today.' Andrew's glance towards Paul and Cecily seemed to push their buttons and they both returned a sullen look.

'Any questions?'

'What is the name of the place we're stopping at tonight? I've forgotten,' Maggie asked.

'Jodie will meet us at Birthday Waterhole,' Andrew replied. 'Morning tea at Reveal Saddle after the opportunity to go to the Bridle Path lookout. Then we have a two and a half hour climb to Brinkley's Bluff where we'll have lunch and a long rest before a short afternoon leg down to Birthday Waterhole.'

'Thank you,' Maggie said.

The older woman looked tired this morning and Sandra made her way over to Maggie. Miska must have had the same idea.

'Are you feeling all right, Maggie?' Miska asked before Sandra could speak.

'Just a bit down. Had a few texts from Alan last night. Sometimes he manages to upset me.'

Sandra put her arm on Maggie's arm. 'I'm sure he didn't mean to.'

'Oh, he did. He always does. Told me I was too old and overweight to do this leg today—he's been looking at the itinerary—and I'm determined to do it, even though I didn't sleep well. Then again, maybe I should just get in the truck and go with Jodie.'

'Oh Maggie, you can't miss Brinkley Bluff. It's one of the highlights along with the sunrise at Mt Sonder. Walk with Zed and I. We'll help you.'

'Maggie, if I can do it, you can do it. We'll give you a hand too.' Sandra was sure that Graysen would agree.

Maggie bit her lip as she looked back at Miska and then to Sandra. 'I will. I can do it. If that's all I do, at least I'll get to see the view.'

'Great. Zed has some spare walking poles in his bag. You're quite welcome to use them.'

'Thank you. You're a lovely group of people.'

Miska hugged Maggie. 'And you're a sweetheart too, and we don't want you to miss out, do we, Sandy?'

'No, you'll be fine.' Sandra made her way back to the spot where she'd left Graysen with her small backpack. He'd moved to the edge of the campground and he and Paul were in an intense conversation.

As he watched, Paul raised both hands in a sort of shrug and shook his head.

Graysen strode back over to the trail head. 'Let's get started,' he said abruptly. He'd tell her what the problem was in his own good time, if he wanted her to know.

She slipped her pack onto her shoulders and waited until P.D. set off, followed by Zed and Miska and Maggie, and then Paul and Cecily. Graysen and Sandra began to climb the flat rock stairs they'd seen last night, and Andrew brought up the rear with Clive and Jenny.

The air was tight with tension, and Sandra wondered how the lovely night they'd all shared last night could have changed so quickly. For the first time in a few days, she felt a little homesick. She should have tried harder last night to call the girls again. Graysen was quiet and she was finding it hard to keep up with the pace he was setting.

It was a long slow climb up to the Bridle Path lookout and at the end of the two-hour climb, Sandra wondered what the hell she was doing here. Graysen had slowed down to her pace, but she'd been in no state or mood to have a conversation as they climbed.

Each time she looked up, the ominous cliffs seemed to be higher; it was the most sustained and steepest climb on the

Larapinta Trail so far, and she wondered how Maggie was going ahead of them, but there was no sign of the three.

They reached the Bridle Path lookout just after nine and the sun was climbing the morning sky, the heat bearing down on them relentlessly.

'Friggin' hell, how good was that!' Zed greeted them with a wide smile. 'This is more like it.'

Sandra simply shook her head and looked around for Maggie. She was sitting in the shade with Miska and smiling.

Sandra suddenly felt inadequate. She'd found the climb really hard and knew there was worse to come.

'Sandy?' A gentle hand touched her back and she turned around. 'Have a big, slow drink. I think you're a bit dehydrated. Have you got a headache?'

She frowned and nodded slightly as Graysen led her over to the shade. He opened her pack, took out her drink and passed it to her.

Gradually as the fluid hydrated her, she began to feel better. 'Thank you.'

'Andrew won't be far behind, and you can eat something too. I'll ask if we can have morning tea here. I think we're all in need of some food.'

'I'm sorry. I think it was my mood and my attitude that brought that on. I feel okay now. Much better.'

'Good.' Graysen touched her face gently. 'I thought I'd done something to upset you. Maybe overstepped the mark last night?'

'No. Not at all. I thought you'd regretted it.'

'Not one little bit.' His rugged face creased in a grin and Sandra's nerve endings jumped. 'In fact, I was hoping to try out some more star photography tonight.'

'Sounds good.' This time she smiled. 'If I get there before sunrise! Those cliffs ahead have put the fear of God in me.'

'One step at a time, Sandy.'

'What were you and Paul arguing about before we left?'

'I'm pretty sure it was Paul interfering with my camera.'

'Really? How rude.'

'He denied it, of course. I really don't like them. Speaking of which'—Graysen frowned—'where are they? Andrew asked us all to wait here.'

'P.D. must have gone ahead with them. He's not here either.'

'Have another drink. I'll go and ask Zed.'

***

Graysen had been worried about Sandy all morning. She wasn't her usual chirpy self, and he knew he'd walked too fast for the first kilometre; he'd been walking off the anger after the words he'd had with Paul.

Zed was lying on his back under the shade of a rocky overhang.

'Where did Paul and Cecily get to? Have they gone ahead with P.D.?'

Zed sat up and frowned. 'No, Cecily rolled her ankle about half an hour into the trek. P.D. and Paul made a carry chair with their hands and were taking her back to Standley Chasm to get help.'

Graysen stared at him. 'They didn't pass us.'

'They must have. They turned around and went back that way.'

'Shit. What if they've fallen?'

Zed pushed himself to his feet. 'They couldn't all fall.'

Graysen turned around and looked back along the ridge that led to the lookout. Andrew came into view followed closely by Clive and Jenny.

Graysen left Zed and hurried across to Andrew. 'Hey, did you guys pass P.D. and Paul and Cecily?'

'No, why?' Annoyance crossed Andrew's face as he folded his arms. 'Don't tell me they kept going?'

'Zed said Cecily rolled her ankle and they turned back that way.' Graysen pointed back to Standley Chasm in the distance.

'Turned back? This is the only track. They couldn't have. We would have passed them.'

Zed came over followed closely by Miska and Maggie. Sandy looked over at Graysen and frowned.

He gestured for her to stay where she was in the shade.

Andrew looked at Zed. 'Can you tell us exactly what happened?'

'About half an hour into the climb we—Miska and Maggie and I—came across them. Cecily was sitting on the ground and howling, Paul was swearing at her and poor P.D. was trying to keep the peace. She'd stepped on a loose rock and rolled her ankle, she said.'

'She said?'

Zed pulled a face. 'Miska and I had a look at it, and there was no sign of a sprain or swelling.'

'We tried to tell them to stay there and wait, but Paul insisted on going.' Maggie looked upset. 'He told Cecily she was useless and he was over this fucking trek, and they were going home.'

'P.D. said he'd help Paul until they got back to you, and that you could call for help.'

'Why didn't P.D. call me on his satellite phone?'

Zed shrugged. 'I got the impression he thought you'd only be a few minutes away.'

Andrew ran his hand through his hair. 'Well, where the bloody hell are they? They can't simply have disappeared into thin air.' He looked around and his eyes did a three-sixty sweep of the landscape. 'Can you guys take my pack and get the morning tea supplies out of it, please? I'll try and call P.D. and base and get some help out here.'

Andrew slipped the huge pack off his back and unzipped it. He reached down to the bottom and pulled out a square red phone with a thick antenna.

Andrew walked over to the edge of the drop and then looked up. 'I'll just climb up that knoll so I can get a clear signal to the Iridium satellite.'

Zed and Graysen carried the pack over to the shade where Zed had been lying.

'Excuse me a minute, mate,' Graysen said. 'I'll just let Sandy know what's going on.' He left Zed unpacking the supplies.

'What's wrong?' Sandy stood as Graysen walked across to her.

'Apparently P.D. and Paul were carrying Cecily back the way we came, but they appear to have gone missing. She said she'd hurt her ankle, but Zed and Miska seem to think there wasn't much wrong with it.'

'I suppose they'd know, being doctors.'

'And you never know what Paul and Cecily would get up to, to get their own way. Anyway, come on over and have something to eat. You're looking a lot better. You've got some colour back in your face.'

'I just want water,' Sandra said. 'If there's some fruit, I'll get an apple for later. Would you like one?'

'Yes, please.'

As Sandy walked across to the rest of the group, Andrew scrambled down the rocky cliff face and landed in front of Graysen. 'Graysen, can I have a word please. In private.'

'Did you see something from up there?' he asked quietly as he followed Andrew along the trail until they were out of sight.

'No, but, mate, I'm going out on a limb here. I know you're who you say you are. You've got a rep as a nature photographer and I've seen your photos in magazines.'

'So?'

'So, I don't trust anyone else on this trek. There's something going on and I don't know what it is.' Perspiration ran down Andrew's forehead and he brushed it out of his eyes impatiently.

'Did you get onto P.D.?'

'No, and that's another problem. Someone's taken the battery out of my phone. And I'm guessing the spare battery won't be in the pack either. I'll go and have a look now without making it obvious.'

'If it's not, what are you going to do?'

'I don't know. My gut tells me we should all go back to Standley Chasm, but if they're already back there, it means I'll have made the wrong call. Bloody hell, I don't know.'

'How about we all wait here while you go back and find them? Without your pack, and being downhill most of the way, it won't take long.'

Andrew stared past him, thinking. 'Yes, that makes sense. Then if I don't find them, I can report it in when I reach the Chasm, and we can get the company chopper in the air fast. If they are there, I'll get the chopper up anyway and it can drop me off up here back to you guys and we can carry on.' He looked relieved to have come to a decision. 'It's just got me beat where they've gone. P.D. has more sense than to go off the trail.'

'Okay, see if your spare battery's there and if not, tell the others you're heading back to look for them.'

Andrew nodded. 'I was just thinking about when I come back. There's a small helipad at the back of the bluff. If the rest of you set out for there, it'll save time when I come back. We can get to Birthday Waterhole a bit late, but I can call Jodie from the café at Standley Chasm and let her know we're behind schedule. God, that blasted Paul. I should have sent them back when he put on that performance at Fish Hole.'

'I just hope they're okay.' Graysen looked at him intently. 'I can't get out of my mind him holding Cecily over that cliff.'

'But the three of them couldn't go over. Unless one of them pushed the other two. What makes you so suspicious of Paul?' Andrew asked.

Graysen hesitated.

'Graysen? Why?'

'Because someone's wiped some photos off my memory card. The ones I took of Paul and Cecily at the edge of the cliff.

Chapter 17

Bridle Path Lookout to Brinkley Bluff

As Andrew had predicted, the battery was not in his pack. He rummaged through what was left in there after the morning tea supplies were taken out, on the pretext of looking for his wallet. 'I must have left it in the pack that went in the car with Jodie. All good.' His voice was upbeat. 'I'll probably be back before you guys finish morning tea. If not, I'll catch up to you at Brinkley Bluff.'

'Do you want a quick cuppa, Andrew?' Miska asked.

'Thanks, put a big splash of milk in for me. I'll chug it down and get going. Graysen, I'm going to make you honorary trek guide while I'm gone. I know you've had a lot of experience in Nepal.' Andrew forced a chuckle. 'Be kind to them and don't push them too hard.'

Miska tipped the tea from the billy and went across to get the milk, and then passed it to Andrew.

He drained the cup and set off at a jog, carrying a light pack with water in it. Graysen stared along the track after he was out of sight, worried about what he was going to find.

'A cuppa for you too, *boss*?' Zed called out with a grin.

'No, thanks, I'll stick with water.' Graysen frowned. Maybe he and Andrew were overreacting; no one else seemed to be terribly worried about the three missing.

Clive ambled over to Graysen and Sandy, his tea in one hand and a muesli bar in the other.

'I'm feeling a bit below par, since we stopped, so Jenny and I are going to head off now and take it really slow. I've read up on this leg and the trail is well signposted. If you don't catch us, we'll wait at the Bluff and won't go any further.

'Okay, mate, take care. We don't want any more sprained ankles.'

'Will do. See you guys up at the Bluff.'

Zed came over to Graysen and Sandra. 'What should we do with the pack, do you think? Andrew didn't say.' Zed had already put his own large pack on his back. 'I've got my stuff to carry, and you've got your cameras. Do you reckon it'll be okay if we leave it here?'

'I can't see a problem with that. Andrew'll come back this way.' Graysen decided not to mention the possibility of Andrew coming in by helicopter.

'Okay, I saw a bit of a cave a couple of hundred metres back. I'll take it back and put in in there.'

'I'm going to take some photos,' Graysen said. 'Sandy and I won't be far behind you.'

It was a while before Zed came back. 'Safely stowed.'

'Thanks, see you soon. Be careful, it's not been a good day.'

'We will. And don't worry, we'll take care of Maggie,' he called over his shoulder as he followed the trail along the razorback ridge.

'Stay in the shade, Sandy. I won't take long. I just want to climb up a bit higher and have a bit of a look around through my strongest zoom lens.'

'In case you can see Paul and Cecily and P.D.? You're not taking photos?'

'Yes and no. Something's off. Andrew's going for help. He's coming back in the company helicopter.'

Sandy's face lost its colour. 'Should I be worried?'

'No, but we will be careful. Wait over there for me.'

She followed him to the base of the rough track up the knoll, and waited while he pulled himself to the top. It was high enough to give Graysen a three-sixty view around the gorges and gullies.

Putting his eye to the view finder, Graysen did a slow sweep of the terrain. To the east, he got a clear view of the track back to Standley Chasm. He swept the lens from left to right and back again.

There was no sign of Andrew on the track, and there should have been. He couldn't have got that far yet.

Suspicion began to curl in his gut. He turned to the west and could make out the track along to Reveal Saddle, the next high point. There was no sign of Jenny and Clive on the track either, but he could see Maggie and Miska standing very close to the edge of the cliff.

He lifted the camera as a movement caught his eye on a rocky ledge above them.

'Oh, Christ. Sweet Jesus. No!'

In the wilds

Sandra froze as she heard Graysen's distressed cry. She looked up at him as he hurled himself down the low cliff, and she covered her face as small rocks fell from above.

'What is it?' she asked as he grabbed her arm. 'Graysen, you're hurting me? What's wrong?'

'Quickly.' The urgency in his voice frightened her. 'We have to get off the track and go bush. We have to hide. Zed's got a rifle. A high-powered rifle with a telescopic sight.'

'What?' Sandra kept her hands on her face as the landscape tilted and then spun around her. 'Why would he have that? Surely it's against the rules?'

'Don't go fainting on me, please, love. We have to move fast. Where's your pack and your water?'

'There.' She pointed to her bag a short distance away on a flat rock.

Graysen picked it up and slipped it over his back. 'Quick, take my hand. We'll go back along the track a short way where we can't be seen, and then we'll head into the scrub.'

'What about the others? I don't understand. What's he doing?'

'I don't know,' Graysen said as he pulled her along the path. 'And the others have disappeared too. Andrew, and Clive and Jenny. I should have been able to see them all from up there.' His voice cracked and Sandra knew Graysen had seen more than he was saying. Something that had frightened the life out of him.

Her legs were shaking as fear gripped her, but she trusted Graysen and she'd do her best to keep up with him. Fifty metres along there was a short bank off the path that led to a bare hill with only tufts of spinifex grass.

'The cliff face to the west is higher and should keep us out of sight until we get to that bush.' Sandra looked down off the track. Two hundred metres down was a gully with a thick stand of bush on each side.

'Stay with me, and do exactly as I say.'

Graysen gripped her hand firmly and they stepped down off the trail onto a steep slope. Sandra's feet slipped, but Graysen kept hold of her and she regained her balance. The ground was uneven and Sandra kept her eyes to the ground as they ran, dodging the large tufts of grass, and avoiding the furrows that were a trap for unwary feet. Halfway down, Graysen turned around and looked up the hill as the slope began to even out.

'There's no one up there yet. I think we're clear. Quick, we're almost there,' he panted.

'Watch where you're stepping,' she said, her voice ragged. 'There's a whole heap of channels in front of us.'

Graysen nodded and led her a little to the left, and soon they were almost to the trees. Digging for the last of her energy, Sandra took a deep breath and ran the last twenty metres. As they reached the cover of the bush, she stopped, but Graysen tugged at her hand.

'No. We need to get further in. The gully kicks to the south down there. I'll feel more secure if we can get cliffs between us and the ridge, and not just trees.'

Fear and confusion held Sandra in a terrifying grip. She fought the familiar feeling as panic threatened to take hold. That awful feeling of losing control—light weightless limbs and pressure on her bladder. It had been over two years since she had had a full-blown attack.

'I have to find a rock. I need to go.' Her words were ragged as she fought for breath.

'Only a couple more minutes. Come on.' Graysen gripped her hand firmly and pulled her along. 'We're almost there. We're safe now.'

His words reassured her slightly and she focused on the landscape around them, and away from her threatening anxiety. One of the things Sandra had had to fight when she was recovering, was not focusing on Peter's fear and distress when he had known he was going to die. The counsellor had taught her to focus on physical objects and she did that now.

'Stop it. Look at the trees. Look at the sky,' she muttered to herself. The stubby trees were covered with fluffy yellow balls of flowers and a couple of tiny birds chirped as they flitted in and out of the bush. Sunlight glinted on a small pool of water ahead of them, and the tight pressure on Sandra's chest began to ease. Her thoughts moved from her immediate fear, and she began to wonder what was happening up at the ridge, worrying about the safety of the others.

Finally, they turned into a narrow gorge, and Graysen stopped. He let go of her hand and bent over dragging in deep breaths. Sandra leaned against the rock wall behind them and closed her eyes. The pressure on her bladder had eased and her hands had stopped tingling. After a moment she opened her eyes and tipped her head back as she inhaled and exhaled evenly. Above, the sky was clear, and a single bird was riding the thermals above the top of the cliff.

Finally, she faced Graysen as he straightened.

'There's a break in the cliff over there that's private. Keep an eye out for snakes.'

'The urgency has passed,' she said. 'I can wait a while. It was more fear than anything.' She pushed herself away from the wall and walked over to him. Her legs were still shaking, but she'd managed to overcome the panic.

Graysen rubbed his face as Sandra stood beside him. When he looked at her, his expression scared her.

'What did you see?' she whispered. 'Tell me, please.'

His mouth was set as he stared at her, obviously weighing up his words.

'Please tell me the truth. I know it must be bad for you to feel as though we had to hide. What did you see?'

'I worry about you, Sandy. It wasn't a good thing. I don't want you to be upset. '

'It's too late for that, Graysen. I saw your face, and I heard your cry. I'm not going to lose it. I'll be more worried if you don't tell me what happened. You said Zed had a gun, are you sure? It wasn't his walking poles?'

Graysen reached out and his arms went around her. He held her close before he spoke; her head rested on his shoulder. His heart was still racing; she could feel his pulse against her cheek.

Slowly Graysen moved back, but kept his arms around her. His eyes were bleak as he held hers. 'It was a rifle. He was up higher on the ridge, out of sight of anyone on the track.'

'What was he doing?' she whispered.

'I followed his line of sight. He lifted the rifle and was looking through the scope so I knew he wasn't looking at me. Miska was right on the edge of the path and she was behind Maggie. Maggie had her arm out pointing at something.' His arms tightened around her. 'If it hadn't been for the rifle pointing at them, I wouldn't have thought anything of it, but Miska lifted her hand high and then stepped back. Then there was a small crack, and Maggie fell. Miska lunged forward and pushed her.'

Sandra gasped. 'Zed shot Maggie?'

'And then Miska pushed her over the cliff.'

'Why? Why would they do that?'

'I think they might have done more than that over the past couple of hours. Not being able to see any of the others, and Paul and Cecily and P.D. disappearing, makes me worry for our safety.'

'I don't understand. Why would they do that? How could they? Surely not,' Sandra said. 'They must be mad!'

'No, I think that's the reason they're on the trek. He was here to kill someone, and if I'm right he's getting rid of all of the witnesses.'

'He can't do that.'

'I'm afraid he did. Maggie's dead.'

'Maybe she's not. Maybe she's just hurt at the bottom of the cliff. We should go back and try and help her, Graysen.'

Graysen tensed and shook his head. 'No, Sandra. She's dead. Whoever or whatever Zed—and Miska—are, they are professionals. It was a head shot. Maggie had no chance at all. We need to be extremely careful, but we need to try and find the others. Maybe they need help.'

Chapter 18

Heading east

Graysen had found it hard to tell Sandy what he'd seen. Christ almighty, he was having enough trouble dealing with it himself, and knowing the trauma she'd suffered in her life, he worried how Sandy would cope. He'd encountered some dangerous situations in his travels over the years, but that had been more after Marion had gone. He hadn't cared much about his own safety; he'd witnessed accidents, and he'd seen death, but he'd never seen anyone murdered.

It was difficult to come to grips with what had happened. Zed and Miska had put on a front that everyone had fallen for. Newly married, saying they were medical doctors—he doubted that very much now—and Miska, so sweet and kind. Zed must have been carrying that rifle since they'd started out on the first day.

Sandy had gone a little way up the gorge for a toilet break, and Graysen sat with his back against the warm rock of the cliff, listening for any sounds. The wind had picked up and despite the sun it was chilly in the gorge. His senses were on full alert and his scalp prickled as the bush rustled to his left. He turned slowly, and encountered the steady gaze of a rock wallaby. His heartbeat slowed again as it watched him for a while and then turned and bounded up the gully.

A flash of white in the other direction pulled his attention that way, but it was Sandy's blonde hair catching the sun as she made her way back to him. She'd left her cap on her pack beside him. He reached for his pack on the ground and took out one of his two water bottles. One was full, and the other half-full. He took a small sip, not knowing how long it would be before they could find a running creek to refill them.

Sandy sat beside him; the colour had come back into her cheeks and she seemed calmer, but Graysen intended keeping a close eye on her.

'How much water do you have in your pack?' he asked.

'One empty and two full. I put an extra one in this morning because I knew we'd have a big climb.' She reached into her bag. 'Plus, I've got the two apples I took from Andrew's pack, and I've also got a packet of jubes.' She held up the bag of sweets. 'I haven't opened them. I was worried about how tired I'd get today.'

'And that ended up being the least of your worries. I've been sitting here trying to figure out what to do.'

'Should we try to get back to Standley Chasm so we can report what happened?'

'Yes. I've been considering that. The problem is we won't know what Zed and Miska are doing. Where they're going, or what their motivation is.'

'We also don't know for sure that Zed didn't see you up on the rocks. If he did, he'd know that you saw what . . . what happened.' Sandra's voice shook and she reached out for his hand. 'I'm okay. I'm not going to lose it on you. I just can't stop thinking about Maggie.'

'They could still be up on the track or they could be heading away.' Graysen moved closer and put his arm around her shoulders. The sun had warmed her T-shirt and skin, and he closed his eyes as she leaned into him.

'But if they did head off, where would they go? Jenny and Clive were ahead of them. Maybe they saw what happened too?'

'That worries me, because there was no sign of them either when I was up there looking. I wonder if they heard or saw something and headed bush too.'

'And you couldn't see Andrew either and he should have still been in full view on the trail. He'd only been gone about ten minutes and he wouldn't have gone out of sight in that time. It took us an hour to climb up there.'

'I know.' Graysen spoke slowly. 'What really worries me—as well as the other three disappearing—is that Zed headed off that way with Andrew's pack after he left. He said it was only a couple of hundred metres but he was gone a while. Also, he said he'd seen a cave. Did you see any caves on the way up today?'

'No. I did yesterday, but not today. We were on that ridge most of the way, and there were sheer drops on both sides.'

'Yes, there was. There were no caves. There was no reason why Zed couldn't leave the pack under that overhang where Andrew left it. It was tucked away okay where it was. I think he was after Andrew to stop him getting back to Standley Chasm to raise the alarm.'

'And I noticed that Miska sat beside his big pack while he was gone. I didn't think anything of it then, but I noticed it beside her because I was thinking how good those walking poles would have been today.'

'I didn't notice that, but yes, it's significant. He wouldn't leave a pack with a rifle in it unattended.'

'But I still don't understand. Maggie was still okay then. Why would he try to stop Andrew? Andrew didn't know anything.'

'The other three were already missing. When I spoke to Andrew, he told me he was suspicious about something. He told me he trusted me because he knew I was who I said.

Because he was familiar with my work and he'd seen my photos, he said he could trust me.'

'That implies that he was doubting that someone else wasn't who they said they were. Maybe they'd given him a reason to wonder? Maybe he'd overheard something or seen something?'

'Exactly, and Andrew's the only person who can tell us that. I'm concerned about him, and I'm pretty sure he's not on his way back to the Chasm. We can work out about how far he would have got before Zed reached him.'

'He took off at a jog. If Zed was after him, that would explain why he took a while to come back.'

'And if Zed did catch him, what happened?'

'Zed didn't take his rifle with him. What could he have done? Andrew was already suspicious.' Sandra sat up straight. 'Don't answer that. There's lots of ways, aren't there?'

'Maybe Andrew saw him coming after him and got off the track?' Graysen shrugged. 'We can hope. Maybe we'll hear a helicopter shortly.'

'A helicopter?'

Andrew said if he didn't find the others, he'd get the company helicopter to come out here.' Graysen rubbed his hand over his face. 'My gut tells me we won't be seeing it.'

'We could sit here all day and still not have a clue about what actually happened,' Sandra said.

'Unfortunately, yes, we could. But I don't think we should depend on help coming.'

'So, what do you think we should do?'

'I think we should try to get back to Standley Chasm, but we need to get there by a different route. We can't go back on the trail. If they *are* waiting for us, we'll walk straight into danger.'

'Is there another route?'

'That's what we have to find out. Because we don't know the terrain, we don't know how long it'll take, plus wherever we walk, I want to stay right out of sight. When we were up on that ridge, we were pretty much surrounded by some high country—the Chewings Range on the north side and that big mountain to the south. It's mountainous between here and Standley Chasm, whichever way we go. It might only be eight kilometres as the crow files, but it's high and hard country.'

'If they know that we're on to them, isn't that what they'd expect us to do though?' Sandra stood up and looked down at him. 'Should we think about going west and meeting Jodie at Birthday Waterhole?'

'It's a much longer route. Whatever way we choose, we're going to have a night out in the cold.'

'Couldn't we just keep walking? We'd be harder to see in the dark, and we'd keep warm.'

'It sounds good in theory, but walking in the dark, we won't have the sun to guide us and we could end up hopelessly lost, with little water and scant food. I'm not going to put you at any more risk, Sandy.'

'But if we don't turn up there, Jodie will raise the alarm if the whole group doesn't show, and they'll send someone out looking for us.'

'Unless Zed and Miska get there first.'

'And tell them we all went back to Standley Chasm for some reason?'

'Yes.' Graysen had already thought of a worse scenario if Zed and Miska went to Birthday Waterhole, but he didn't say anything. There would be a four-wheel drive truck there ready for the taking. Andrew had already said it was a private campsite, and there was a good chance there'd be no one else around. 'God, I feel so useless,' he ground out. He stood and looked around. 'We'll go through the gap that faces north in this gorge and head back closer to the main track, and be very careful. And as hard as it is, once we're under the main trail again, we'll keep an eye out for Andrew. He may have gone over and he may be hurt. Are you okay to start walking?'

'I am. The sooner we get back to civilisation and phone service the happier I'll be.'

Graysen blinked. 'Do you have your phone in your pack?'

'No. I put it in my kit bag last night after I texted my daughter and I forgot to charge it. You?'

'I haven't used mine since we left Alice Springs. It's in my kit bag too. I relied on Andrew saying he had the sat phone for any emergencies. I'm kicking myself now. We'd probably have service as we got closer to Standley Chasm. There was a new tower there. We'd probably have emergency access, and we'd be able to get a map of the terrain.'

'Don't kick yourself.' Sandra turned to him and slipped her arms around his waist. 'Never in a million years could we have expected this situation.'

'You're right.' Graysen rested his chin on the top of her head. 'Let's make a move. We'll go easy on our water, and share one of those apples now.'

She shook her head. 'I couldn't eat. My stomach is churning.'

'We both have to keep our strength up if we're going to get out of this.'

Sandra stared at him. 'And we *are* going to get out of this. I will not put my family through any more grief. My girls have suffered enough over the past ten years.' She dropped her arms from around his waist and picked up her backpack and took out an apple. 'Let's go.'

***

Sandra was surprised how calm she felt once they set off up the gully, following it in a north-easterly direction. With every stop, she knew they were getting closer to help.

'As soon as we can we'll head due east again,' Graysen said after they'd walked for half an hour. 'I can see a break in the gorge ahead, I think.'

'There seems to be a gap both sides.'

'Yes, we need to be careful in case there's a view from one of the ridges.'

'Do you think—'

'Get down!'

Graysen's command was low and urgent and Sandra dropped straight to the ground, Graysen beside her.

'I think there's someone near that gap in the gorge,' he whispered close to her ear. 'I'm sure I saw someone moving.'

'Do you think they saw us?' She kept her voice low.

'I don't know. I'm not even sure it was someone but I'm not taking any risks. Stay flat to the ground and keep your head down and we'll get over to those rocks. Can you follow me and drag yourself over as quietly and fast as you can? It's only about three metres away. There's a big enough rock to give us cover.'

She turned her head so her whisper was against his ear. 'I can do it.' Sandra's heart was thumping and a sharp rock beneath her was pressing into her right breast. Her elbow was stinging where she'd scraped it when she'd dropped to the ground. Luckily her pack was on her back so she didn't have to worry about it dragging on the ground or her water bottle making any noise.

'Go!' His voice was low and urgent.

Sandra put her head down and used her elbows in a commando crawl to follow Graysen. They crawled around to the back of the rock. There was a narrow space between the high rock and the jagged cliff face behind them.

He sat up and Sandra lifted her head and Graysen nodded, holding out one hand to help her. 'You're bleeding.' His breath was hot against her ear.

'I'm fine. I've just grazed my elbow.'

'I want you to wait here with my pack. I'm going to stay behind these rocks and make my way over there to see if there was someone. It's quiet, but they could be waiting for us to come out into the open.'

'No! It's not safe. He's got a rifle.'

'Ssh. I'll be careful. Stay here. I won't go far. I promise I'll come back. I won't take any risks.'

Before Sandra could reply. Graysen dropped a quick kiss on her cheek, slipped his pack off and dropped it quietly to the ground. She pushed her knuckles to her mouth, holding back the cry for him to come back, and not to leave her alone.

Trying to focus on the external, Sandra looked down at her T-shirt. Blood was splattered on the bottom right side where her elbow had bled. She pulled her handkerchief from her shorts pocket and quietly took out her water bottle and unscrewed the cap. Carefully she tipped a tiny amount of water onto her handkerchief, and then lifted the bottle to her mouth and took half a mouthful, moistening the inside of her mouth before she swallowed it.

She dabbed her elbow and then folded her handkerchief into a pad and pressed into against the graze. The process kept her focus on where she was and kept her fear at bay. Her leg muscles were tense, and she breathed slowly, trying to keep her senses at full alert.

The wind whistled through the gorge and she shivered. There was no sunlight in the small gap between the rock and the cliff.

Small stones rolled along the ground on the other side of the rock and she froze as slow footsteps crunched on the rough ground. She waited for Graysen's voice, but the only sound was shuffling footsteps on the small rocks. Sandra slipped her pack onto her back, and pushing her hands to the ground, rose to a crouch ready to run.

Chapter 19

Harbour View Apartments, Darwin

Dru stepped out of the lift, and pushed her hair back with her free hand as she juggled the takeaway container and her handbag. It was her turn to cook tonight and she'd cheated—as she did more often than not these days—because she was tired. She'd never slept as much as she had in these first months of her pregnancy. She knew that Connor wouldn't complain about the takeaway from their favourite Thai restaurant; he hated cooking as much as she did, and in the low season they ate out most nights. There were some excellent restaurants within walking distance of their apartment.

Their apartment.

Connor had hated the thought of not contributing when he'd moved into her apartment overlooking Darwin harbour.

'I feel like a kept man,' he'd said often.

'Good.' Her response was always a cheeky grin. 'I love having a kept man.' But she hadn't been able to say that after Connor had paid off her mortgage the week after they'd come back from their honeymoon two years ago.

Dru smiled as she tapped the security code into the pad beside the front door of their top floor apartment. The best time of the working day was coming home to Connor; he'd taken over the study and ran their security business from home. The security business that had led to their meeting when he had been investigating a diamond heist at the Matsu Diamond Mine where Dru had been employed as the chief rehabilitation engineer. She had been his chief suspect, but thankfully it hadn't taken him long to find the guilty parties, and fall in love with her.

Now Dru worked part-time as contract consultant to the Department of Primary Industry and Resources, and once this contract was over, she was going to take a couple of years off to be home with the baby, and become more involved in Connor's business.

As she walked to the kitchen to put the takeaway container on the benchtop, she could hear his voice coming from the study.

'I'm home,' she called out when she heard him disconnect the call. Taking out a packet of microwave rice, she waited as his footsteps padded down the hall tiles.

'Dru.' Connor's usual greeting of a kiss on her lips and then a gentle hand on her pregnant tummy, and a 'Hello, little bump,' was noticeably absent. He stood in the doorway, his chiselled face set in a frown.

'Hi, sweetie.' She set the microwave to cook, and crossed the kitchen to kiss him before she went to have a quick shower. 'Can you watch I don't explode the rice while I have a really quick shower?'

His arms went around her, but his kiss was brief.

'Have you had a bad day?'

'Dru, there's a bit of a problem that we might need to follow up.' Connor's arms stayed around her.

'A problem?'

'Greg's picked something up on his daily scan of the Feds. On the Larapinta Trail.'

'What?' She took a step back and looked at his serious expression. 'What is it?' A ripple of fear ran down her back. 'You're scaring me, Connor. What's happened? Is Mum okay?'

'I've been on the phone to Greg getting him to hack into the police network to get some more information.'

'Information about what?' Her voice rose in pitch.

'There's been an incident on the Larapinta Trial, and Greg's finding out as much as he can.'

'An incident?' she said slowly. 'What sort of incident?'

'Two people have died in a cliff fall, but the bodies apparently haven't been retrieved yet.'

Dru raised a shaking hand to her mouth. 'It's a long trail and I imagine there'd be a lot of trekkers on it. We can't think the worst. That's the sort of thing that Mum would do. Worry unnecessarily. I won't.' Her breath hitched on a sob, and Connor pulled her to him.

'That's my girl. That's the right attitude. Sadly, two people have died, and Greg's finding out what he can. He's watching it very closely. It hasn't hit the news wires yet.' Connor frowned again. 'There's something strange about the chatter on the Federal Police scan. It's marked as red alert "Highly confidential".'

She put her face against her husband's warm skin, his familiar smell comforting her as she fought back the chill that wouldn't leave her. 'I'm so glad he ended up getting a reliable satellite phone out there in his camp.'

Greg Francis was a partner in their security business. Once a colleague of Connor's in the Federal Police, Greg had succumbed to post traumatic stress disorder, and lived off grid near Wyndham in remote Western Australia. Since they'd left the force and Connor had started his business, he had initially used Greg's skills to retrieve sensitive information for him. Just before Dru and Connor had married, Greg had joined their business.

Through a couple of hackers he knew from their time in the Australian Federal Police, and with his excellent skills accessing the dark web, Greg had access to more databases than an everyday Google search would retrieve. Maybe not ethical—or legal—but Connor didn't care. Dru knew Connor's faith in ethical and legal practices had become jaded a few years back and whatever it took to get a job done, he and Greg would do it.

They stayed within the law . . . most of the time.

'What does that mean? The red alert stuff?'

'It means that no one is allowed to share any information or make any enquiries outside the room where the team will be working together. But listen, Greg said he'll call back within ten minutes. Go and have your shower and I'll supervise your exploding rice. And try not to worry.'

Dru forced a smile. 'Do you think we should ring the others yet?'

'I'll give the guys a call once I've heard back from Greg. Emma and Dee are still in hospital, aren't they?'

'Yes. Emma's going home tomorrow, I think. I hope.'

'No results yet?'

'Not that she's letting on.' Dru reached up and brushed her lips across his. Even at her height, Connor was half a head taller than she was. 'Thanks for contacting Greg. I'll be quick.'

Dru hurried to their ensuite and slipped off her work clothes. She stood side-on to the mirror as she did every night and smiled at her baby bump. Her throat closed as she thought of the deaths Greg had called about. There was no way it would be Mum; no one family could have so much tragedy, she told herself sternly.

She turned the taps on, and had a very quick shower, and it was only a few minutes before she walked back along the hall and into the study where Connor held the phone to his ear listening intently.

Walking across to the computer desk, she stood and put her hand on his shoulder; he was still listening—to Greg—Dru assumed, but he reached up and put his hand on hers.

'Okay, mate, thanks. Keep following through and let me know if there's anything we need to know.' Connor disconnected and put the phone on the desk.

Dru spoke slowly, it was hard to form the words around her fear that something had gone awfully wrong. 'What did Greg say?'

Connor stood and pushed the chair in. 'It's a young couple apparently. They still haven't retrieved the bodies but they can ID from who was on the trek. The company have advised there were two couples on the trek, but no names have been released. It's still being kept very quiet.'

Dru put her hand to her chest. 'Thank God.' Then she felt immediately guilty. 'You know what I mean. It's a relief, but it's sad. What happened?'

'Come on, we'll serve up and I'll get us a cold drink. Is it too windy to sit on the balcony?'

'I'd rather sit inside.'

'Okay.'

Connor was quiet as they served the rice and Massaman curry into bowls. They carried their dinner and glasses of water into the living room and placed them on the coffee table.

Dru leaned back on the sofa cushions and ignored the bowl sitting on the table. 'Tell me what else he said. I know you too well, Connor. There's something you're holding back.'

He reached over and took her hand. 'The local police aren't aware of what Greg's picked up. I don't know if we should even tell the family yet.'

'Tell them what?' Dru put her hand on her stomach and leaned forward.

'The two dead were trekkers on the Larapinta Luxury trek Sandra booked.'

'What? She'll be so upset.' Dru leaned forward to pick up her phone from the coffee table. 'She should be in phone service now that's happened. They wouldn't keep going.'

Connor pulled her back down gently. 'No, Dru. There's something else. They've closed the trail. The official reason is—and the local police know this much, Greg thinks—is because there has been an incident, but that's all they know. They've also been told to keep quiet about it.'

'What's the real reason?'

'The Federal Police are co-operating with Interpol who have a team on an international flight now.'

'A team on the way for what?'

'To try to catch a couple of operatives they've been watching for a while.'

'Operatives? I don't understand? Why would there be operatives on the Larapinta trail in Central Australia.'

Connor didn't look away. 'To carry out a paid kill.'

'What? That sounds like a movie! So, where's Mum?'

'That's what we don't know. It appears the whole group, including the guides are missing.'

'What?' Dru's mouth dropped open and she stared at her husband. Her voice shook when she finally spoke. 'Can Greg help us? What else can he find out?'

'He's on it. He's managed to infiltrate Interpol electronically and he's watching every communication, both internally and with the Australian Federal Police.'

'Without them knowing?'

'Sweetie, it's Greg, remember.'

'Right. As long as he tells us as soon as he finds out anything. We need to let everyone know and we need to get down there. Now.'

'No. *We* don't. Kane, Ryan, and I will go.'

'Jeremy?'

'No, Emma needs him.'

Dru nodded slowly. 'As much I hate to admit it, you're right. I'll tell Ellie she and James can stay here. Kane won't want her out at the farm by herself.'

'I'm proud of you, Dru. I thought I'd have a fight on my hands.'

Chapter 20

Larapinta Trail

Sandra's heart hammered as she waited. Her thigh muscles were screaming with pain as she tensed. The footsteps stopped and it was quiet. She stayed still and didn't make a sound, but she didn't know how long she could hold that position. A small stone crunched and she could swear a shadow flitted briefly on the rock in front of her.

Whoever, whatever it was, had walked behind her and was between her and the cliff. Slowly she relaxed her muscles and turned her head. A scream formed in her throat as she stared at the blood-covered face staring down at her.

'Help me . . .'

She fought back the scream and reached out to catch Andrew as he pitched forward and fell on her, pushing her backwards. The back of her head hit the ground so hard her ears rang. His chest pressed down on her face and covered her mouth and nose and she couldn't breathe.

Her pack was against her back and the metal of her water bottle was hard against her spine.

'Andrew,' she tried to speak but it was impossible; only a muffled sound came out. 'Have to get off me.'

Sandra gathered as much strength as she could muster and used her arms to take some of his weight as she rolled to her side. Andrew was a dead weight, but she managed to get her face clear. She could breathe, and she could also now see the mess his head was in. A tangled mat of hair caked in blood and dirt met her gaze as she tried to get out from under him. She could feel him breathing and an occasional groan came from him.

'Sandra!' Graysen's voice was low and urgent.

She tipped her head back and relief flooded through her as Graysen knelt behind her.

'Is there anyone out there?' she managed to gasp out as she dragged deep breaths in.

'No, it must have been Andrew I saw. I went the long way around. He must have seen us and come along the cliff.'

'He's badly hurt. Look at the back of his head.'

Graysen had managed to slide Andrew from on top of her, and she scrambled to her feet, and then looked around. 'You don't think there's anyone else here? Are you sure?'

'No. I had a good long look around, and we're well hidden from the main trail here.' He moved Andrew onto his side and that elicited another moan. Graysen crouched down and put his fingers against the guide's neck. 'His pulse is slow and steady, and if he managed to walk from that small gorge where I saw him, he can't be too bad.'

'He's exhausted himself. As soon as he saw me, he called out and fell forwards on to me.' Sandra's lips were trembling. 'Is he going to be okay?'

'He's alive.'

Sandra sat with her back against the rock as Graysen examined Andrew. He started at the head wound and moved down his body. 'He's got a really deep gash on his head, and a big bump, but his hair has matted over the wound and seemed to stop the bleeding. The blood on his neck and face is from that.'

As he touched Andrew's chest, he moaned again. 'Hurts.' His words were slurred.

Graysen paused. 'Good to hear you talking, mate.' He held up two fingers in front of Andrew's half-open eyes. 'Can you see my fingers?'

A nod.

'How many?'

Two bruised and bloody fingers lifted a fraction off his chest.

Sandra leaned forward as Andrew's head lolled forward again. 'He seems to be going in and out of it, doesn't he?'

'With the distance he walked along the gully, not to mention how far we are from the trail and his blood loss, he's exhausted and dehydrated for sure. I suspect he's got a concussion and a couple of broken ribs, which means pain, and pain will make him pass out. Even those grazes will be giving him a lot of discomfort.' Graysen examined Andrew's arms and hands and then his knees and lower legs exposed by his knee-length shorts. 'There's not one part of him that's not cut or scraped.'

'Do you think we should give him some water?'

Graysen nodded. 'If we were in a position to get him to emergency or wait for paramedics, I'd say no, but we're a long way from medical help. Andrew was our first chance; Jodie is our second.'

'What about a jube for him to suck for some sugar?'

Graysen ran his hand through his hair, a frustrated mannerism that was becoming familiar to her. 'I have very little medical knowledge. What about you?'

'Just what I learned bringing up my girls. I think if we use a tiny bit of the water to take some of the blood off his face—' Sandra stared and lowered her voice. 'Oh no! Graysen, look there's blood coming from his mouth. That's not good.'

As Graysen leaned forward Andrew tried to speak but no words came out. Only a muffled groaning noise as he lifted a shaking hand to his bloodied mouth.

'Broken,' he said.

'Yeah, mate,' Graysen said gently. 'You're pretty broken and smashed around, but don't worry. Your vital signs are good and we're going to get you out of here and you're going to be okay.'

Andrew's hand flailed around and the movement made him moan.

'What is it?' Graysen asked as Andrew grabbed his hand and held it tightly.

He pulled Graysen's hand to his face and tried to speak. 'Teeth,' Andrew managed to say, before he let go and his hand dropped to the ground.

Sandra let out a sigh of relief. 'His teeth! That's where the blood is coming from. His mouth is bleeding.'

'Can you open your mouth at all, mate?' Graysen asked.

Andrew put his head back and his lips came apart, slowly opening to a small gap. With a soft moan, he opened his lips further and fresh blood trickled down the side of his chin.

As they leaned over him Sandra held back a gasp. She closed her eyes, unable to look at the mess that they could see in Andrew's mouth. His top front teeth were broken to the gum, and three of his bottom teeth were sitting at an angle.

Graysen nodded, and his voice was even. 'Looks like you landed on your face when you fell?'

The grunt that came from Andrew confirmed that.

'Do you think you could sip some water and we'll clean up around your mouth. I think you really need to get some liquid into you, mate. You've done a fair walk. I know you can't tell us what happened, but don't worry, we'll get you to help.'

Graysen reached over and took Sandra's hand and gestured for her to follow him.

They kept their voices low as they moved closer to the cliff, away from where Andrew still lay on his back behind the rock.

'What do you think we should do?' Sandra said.

Graysen frowned. 'I think we're going to have to use quite a bit of our water to clean him up. Have you got any Panadol or Neurofen in your pack?'

'I've got one card of Panadol. I took two the other night when I had a slight headache. So, there should be ten left.'

'We can crush two or three up into water, even if it means he's got to try to suck the liquid from a hanky or something. I don't think he's capable of swallowing water from a bottle.'

'I could maybe trickle it into his mouth if he puts his head back. He definitely needs some painkillers, but you're right. We need to get him to help.'

'We do.' Graysen nodded. 'He can't eat, so we have to keep him hydrated and we have to get him medical help before that mess in his mouth gets infected. And keep the water up to him.'

'Can we afford to use all that water?' she asked with a shake of her head. 'Ignore that. We have to. Andrew has a much greater need than us.'

'We'll be fine if we stay here. There's a little waterhole down under the back of the gorge where I thought I saw movement. It was Andrew and he was being careful. He obviously didn't know who I was and he did a damn good job to get down here without me spotting him.'

'Is the water drinkable?' Sandra asked.

'I'd leave it as a last resort, but we're fine for water for the time being. I might empty your half a bottle into mine that's almost half empty and we'll use that to get water from the waterhole. We'll use that water to clean him up a bit to start, and hold off drinking it until it's necessary.'

Sandra dropped her shoulders as despair began to hit. 'And once we get him cleaned up what are we going to do, Graysen?'

'I don't know.' Graysen's jaw was set as he looked over Sandra's head. She fought the black feeling that began to creep through her. Finally, he reached out and pulled her to him. 'I've been thinking about it since Andrew turned up. We need to go for help.'

'But we can't leave him alone,' Sandra said.

'That's right and I'm very reluctant to leave you alone here with Andrew.'

'You'll have to. I'll be fine here with him.' She pushed away the thought of being stranded here in the gorge without Graysen, and without knowing whether he'd get back to the Chasm safely.

'With him having the injury to the back of his head and then landing face first to break his teeth, I'd say he's been hit from behind with a rock or something heavy.'

'And then fell over the cliff?'

'Or was pushed,' Graysen said. 'We'd better get back to him. We need to get him cleaned up and some Panadol into him. He's in pain with the mess in his mouth, and he's probably got a thumping headache from the wound and dehydration. He needs medical help before he gets an infection in his mouth, and to check out the head wound.'

'An infection that could make him very ill.'

'An infection that could kill him if we don't get help fast.'

Sandra reached out and gripped Graysen's forearm. 'We won't give it any more thought or discussion. There's only one thing for it, Graysen. You're going to have to leave me here with Andrew. No argument, please. We'll be safe hiding between that big rock and the cliff. You can get some extra water, and show me where the waterhole is. With water, and those jubes, I'll be right.'

He pulled away from her grip and stared at her.

'That's the logical thing to do, Sandy but I don't know that I could leave you here.'

'You have to. And if you won't, I'll go because if the three of us stay here, none of us will survive.' Sandra's words rushed out as she tried to convince Graysen. 'Andrew is going to get worse, and if we just sit here and watch him, what do we do then? Head for Standley Chasm when it's too late?' Her voice shook.

Graysen ran both hands over his hair, frustration obviously taking hold of him. 'I'll go early in the morning.'

Her shoulders slumped with relief that he finally agreed. 'You'll be faster without me, and I'll be fine,' she said softly.

'We'll settle in here for the night. We'll get Andrew cleaned up, and see if we can help manage his pain.'

Graysen's lips tilted in a small smile. 'How about we have some jubes and water for dinner after that?'

'Sounds scrumptious. Unless you want to go hunting?' Sandra smiled back as they each tried to lighten the worry.

'You want me to find us a kangaroo or a lizard? Problem is we can't have a fire.'

Sandra laughed with him.

'It's good to hear you laugh, Sandy. It's a shocking situation. I could kill that bastard for what he's done. I hope they haven't got away.'

'Or maybe we do hope that, because then they won't be up on the track waiting for us.'

'When Andrew's able to talk he'll be able to tell us exactly what happened, but I'd say he's been thrown off the cliff and left for dead. It would've taken Zed too long to go down to make sure he was dead, but he would have known at the bottom of that huge drop no one would find him, and he took the risk that even if Andrew was alive, he'd be too badly hurt to move. He did amazingly well to get to us.'

'It was just as well we were here.'

'We came down the gully not far from where he went over,' Graysen said.

'It's incredible what motivation can do. He has a wife and two children; I'm sure he would have been thinking of them. A parent will do everything for their children.' Sandra thought of her girls; she was thankful they had no idea of the situation she was in. Ellie wouldn't be able to help herself, she'd be in a helicopter on a rescue mission.

'And that bloody Zed was as calm and cool as a cucumber when he came back and said he'd stowed the pack.' Graysen's tone held disgust.

'What is it all about, Graysen? What do you think they are doing? They're obviously working together.' She took in a shaky breath. 'Are you really sure Maggie's dead?'

Graysen's eyes were bleak. 'I have no doubt of that. I worry about Paul and Cecily and PD. I worry about you, and I worry about Jenny and Clive out there too. I worry about Jodie. If Zed and Miska go to Birthday Waterhole—'

'She wouldn't be out there by herself under work safety regulations, would she? Surely not?'

'She has been before, but I suppose if you think about those times, it was where there was a camp with other people, and then the old Homestead. Standley Chasm was a proper campground too. I imagine Birthday Waterhole is more isolated so I'm hoping that she'll have another guide with her and that there'll be at least two of them.'

'But they're so bloody devious. They'll know it's an isolated camp. And that's probably why they chose this section of the trail to—' Sandra's voice shook as she tried to understand how someone could be so evil. 'They came across as normal, and Miska was so sweet. They're married and they're doctors and they love each other and yet they killed Maggie and then pushed Andrew off a cliff. Why?'

'And that's why I don't want to leave you here with Andrew,' Graysen said, but when she went to speak, he put his hand up. 'I know. I've accepted there's no alternative. I'll leave before first light tomorrow.'

'You won't be able to see where you're going. That's what you said before.'

'It will be light at dawn.'

'Graysen, please tell me you won't go up to the trail? That you'll stay down in the bush.'

'No, not unless I have to. I'll be able to follow the sun and head east and eventually I'll come to Standley Chasm. If I go too far to the south, I'll hit the main road so wherever I end up, there'll be a way to get the word out and get help for Andrew.'

'I'll be patient and I'll sit it out tomorrow and stay safe. You focus on getting us help. We'll be okay.' Sandra looked up and blinked as her eyes teared up. 'You be so careful. You're the one who's taking the risk. We're tucked away here safely; they can't cover all the trail looking for us. It's a huge area and anyway *they* don't know that *we* know what they've done.'

'Do you know what I think?'

'What?'

Graysen held out his hand. 'Come on, I'll tell you while we go back and check on Andrew.'

Sandra slipped her hand into his, enjoying the warmth and security of Graysen's hold.

'I suspect they don't want to be identified. As I flicked through my camera and noticed that those photos of Paul and Cecily were gone, there didn't seem to be as many photos as I thought on that card, but I was only looking for the ones of Paul and Cecily at the cliff. Now, I suspect it wasn't Paul. I'd say that Zed or Miska have deleted any photos of them from the card.'

Sandra frowned. They were almost back to the rock where Andrew was. 'But what about the others? Haven't they taken photos of everyone on their phones? I have. I snapped photos of everyone the other night around the campfire.'

'And where's your phone now?'

'In the truck,' she replied slowly.

'Exactly and where do we think they're going now?'

'To the truck.'

'They're obviously not stupid, Sandy. If they haven't already got to your phone, they will.'

'It just seems so complicated and contrived.'

'Murder usually is.'

Sandra thought back to the past and the events that had led to Peter's murder, and the things that Russell Fairweather had done to try to get his hands on the millions of dollars he would have gained had his scheme worked.

'And it's usually motivated by greed, isn't it?'

'It is.'

Andrew was asleep on his back, and his face didn't look as flushed.

'He looks okay,' Sandra said. 'No worse anyway. It's probably the first time he's stopped.'

'Let's start cleaning his abrasions and get some painkillers into him.' Graysen let go of her hand. 'We'll try to make him more comfortable. We can clear the small loose rocks on one side of him, so the ground is clear, and move him closer to that rock. It should hold some warmth for a while.'

'I'll give him my jacket and he can use it as a pillow.' She looked up at Graysen with a smile. 'The only thing is though, you'll have to keep me warm tonight.'

'I won't have any problems doing that, Sandy.' He pulled her close again and when she tipped her head back, Graysen's hand cupped her cheek. His lips were warm against hers and she let out a soft sigh against his mouth.

'The sooner our lives get back to normal and I can get to know you better, the happier I am going to be.' Sandra's lips were still close to his as she spoke.

'We just have to be positive and do the best we can. Come on, we'll get started. You sort the water bottles and I'll get the Panadol out, and then I'll clear those rocks away.'

Chapter 21

McLaren Mango Farm

'Ellie McLaren, if you don't sit down and stop pacing, I'm going to tie you to that chair.'

Ellie glared at her husband. 'I can't sit down, Kane. All I can think of is Mum somewhere out in the wild. She'll be so scared this will put her back. She won't cope if something has happened. We should've made her stay home. I should never have let her go on that stupid trek.'

Kane put his hands on her shoulders. 'And what? We wrap her in cotton wool for the rest of her life and lock her in a cupboard? You heard how happy she sounded on the phone and you saw the happiness in her face in that photo she sent. What Connor told us happened out there is a one in a million thing. And your mum was just unlucky that she was on that trek.'

'I don't care if she was unlucky or what it was, I just want her home. I just want to know she's alright.'

'Calm down, sweetheart,' Kane said. 'Think of the bub.'

Ellie put both her hands over her face and her husband's arms went around her as sobs racked her body. 'I know, Kane, I know. I know I have to be strong. After everything Mum's been through . . . to have this happen.' She lifted her face and held his eyes. 'I'm also going to worry about you flying the guys down there. Who knows what you'll find?'

'No darling, it's the best way. It's the quickest way we can look for her. And when we find her, we can bring her home quickly. And Connor, Ryan and I can be in touch with you girls the whole time. Now have you got your bag packed and James' gear packed? It's time we headed to Darwin.'

'Sort of. I've got no idea what I threw in there.'

'Now I want you to promise me when you're at Dru's, you'll rest. Put your feet up, even if you have to pay a babysitter to come and help you look after James. We don't want Dru doing too much either.'

'I'm not trusting anybody with our child, Kane. Life has taught me too much. We've both learned you can't trust easily. There's no integrity, and so much evil. Look at what we've been through in our lives. Poor David and Gina. David was the Territory's Chief Magistrate and now what's he doing? He's running a *gelataria* in a little village in Tuscany.'

'And might I say,' Kane said with a little glimmer of a smile, 'David is as happy as a pig in mud. What did Gina say in her last email?'

'*Maiale nel fango,* is his new nickname.' Ellie smiled this time. 'Pig in mud.'

'So see, everything can have a good outcome.'

'Maybe, but there is so much damage done to innocent people. Look what Russell Fairweather caused. And Heather, and Bill, and all those people who didn't do the right thing when we were trying to investigate Dad's death. And then Emma and that horrible man who tried to kill her with those snakes, and then Dru and that creepy guy in Dubai. Why does all this happen to us?' Ellie started to cry again, deep sobs shaking her shoulders.

Kane reached up and used his thumb to brush the tears off her cheeks. 'Okay, sweetie, I'll let you have a little cry for a couple of minutes and then I'm going to make you a cup of tea and you're going to sit for a while and calm down, because if you don't, I don't think I can leave you.'

'Oh yes, you have to, you have to go.' Ellie sniffed and wiped the back of her hand across her nose. 'I'll be fine, honestly. I promise. It's just getting used to what Connor told you. I'll be with Dru and we'll go to the hospital and visit Dee and the twins. James will keep us entertained at their apartment. Hopefully we'll hear some good news from Emma. I've just got to be positive and know everything is going to be okay. Connor hasn't told Jeremy what's happened, has he?'

'No, we decided not to put that on him because Emma is so intuitive, she'd know there was something wrong. We're better off not to tell them anything until we know what's happened. They've got enough to worry about.'

Harbourview Apartments Darwin

Two hours later Ellie had checked her bag was packed sensibly and James' favourite toys were in a crate. She'd sat and calmly drunk the cup of tea that Kane had made her while he rang Jock at Jabiru airport to check that he could hire a chopper. When Jock, their former boss, had heard it was to look for Sandra—Kane had been very vague with details after Connor's warning—Jock had said, 'Don't be stupid. Pay for the Avgas and that's all.'

Kane turned Ellie's sedan into the driveway of the Harbourview Apartments. Ellie picked up her phone and texted Dru as her sister had asked her to do when they arrived.

Immediately the security grill to the underground basement car park lifted and after negotiating the two floors of parking, Kane located the guest parking spot for Dru and Connor's apartment, and squeezed the car into the narrow space.

'Jeez, I'm pleased we didn't bring the Ranger,' he said. 'We never would have fitted in here.'

Ellie woke James up and he held her hand as Kane unpacked their bags.

'I suppose I can't say I'll carry James while you bring the bags,' Ellie said.

'No, you know you can't. I'll do a second trip. And don't you go picking him up while I'm away either.'

'I know.'

'I can walk, Mummy. I'm a big boy.'

Ellie smiled down at her little son. 'As long as you promise to hold Mummy's hand and not try to run ahead.'

'I promise.'

'Good boy.'

Kane managed to juggle the two bags and the crate of toys as he followed Ellie and James to the service lift. They were quiet as it rose quickly to the top floor of the multi-storey apartment block.

As the door dinged open to the corridor outside Dru and Connor's apartment, James realised where they were.

'Aunty Dru's house!' he called out excitedly. 'Ice cream!'

'Yes, darling, you and Mummy are going to stay with Auntie Dru for a little holiday.'

'And ice-creams at the park?'

Ellie pulled a face and looked at Kane. 'As long as Daddy says we can go to the park.'

'As long as Aunty Dru drives, I think that's an excellent idea. It'll keep you busy, Els.'

'We won't go to the shops. We'll just walk down to the Waterfront Precinct.'

'A good idea. Here, and down at the precinct, I know you'll be safe and I can get onto you quickly.'

'And hopefully you'll be home in a day or so and everything will be back to normal.'

'And that's what I want you to keep in your head. I don't want you to think of the "what ifs" and worst-case scenarios. Even though you don't think so, Sandra *is* a strong woman, and I know she'll be fine.'

The door opened as they reached the end of the corridor and Dru held her arms open. Ellie straightened her back determined not to cry again; she'd shed all her tears at their farm.

'Hi, Dru. I won't say it's good to be here, but we will have a nice visit.'

Dru cleared her throat, and Ellie noticed the sheen of tears in her eyes. It was very rare to see Dru cry. Since their father's death, she had worn a protective shell and very rarely showed emotion. Ellie was hoping that motherhood would soften her little sister.

'Connor's got some more information from Greg, and it should help the guys search, he thinks.'

Kane put the bags and the crate down in the foyer, and James ran straight to the toys.

'Jock's organised for the Yellow Waters R44 chopper to fly over to the airport here so we don't have to drive to Jabiru. Ryan's on his way up so we're going to leave in about an hour or so. It'll be too dark once we get down there to search tonight, and from what Connor said, we're going to have to keep a very low profile.'

Connor came down the hall. 'We are. I've booked us into the airport motel at Alice tonight and we'll get up at first light and head out over the trail.'

He swung James up into the air, hugged Ellie and then shook Kane's hand. He put his arm around Dru's shoulder. 'Okay, bub?'

'Yeah, I'm okay,' Dru said. 'Ellie, come with me to the kitchen. I'll get some afternoon tea for James.'

'Ice cream?' James said hopefully.

'We'll see, munchkin,' Dru said, holding her hand out to him. 'I'll make a pot of coffee, and one of tea, and some sandwiches for the guys. Or we could even get a takeaway Thai delivered before you leave.'

Kane paused before he followed Connor down the hall. 'I'm even starting to wonder whether we should go down tomorrow early in the morning. We won't be able to do anything tonight.'

Ellie shook her head. 'No, I want you three down there now. Please, you never know, she might turn up tonight. If she does, she'll need some family with her and we can't be there. God, whoever would have thought that Emma and Dru and I wouldn't be able to be there when Mum needed us?'

'Stay calm, Ellie. We'll be there for her.' Connor gestured to Kane. 'Come down to the study. Greg's sent some maps that go with the itinerary.'

'Tea for you, Ellie?' Dru called from the kitchen.

Ellie walked down the hall. James was sitting at the table with a bowl of ice-cream, but she turned a blind eye. Aunties were for spoiling.

'What would we do without a cup of tea?' she said as Dru warmed the teapot. 'I'm starting to turn into my mother.'

Dru smiled at her. 'That wouldn't be such a bad thing. In fact, you're starting to look more like Mum every year.'

'You're the one who looks like Mum with your blonde hair. But yes, we both look like her,' Ellie admitted. 'You got Dad's height.'

'And Emma's like Dad and Ryan. Here. Are you allowed to carry a tray of cups?'

Ellie nodded. 'That won't hurt.'

'Okay, go and sit down in the living room and I'll bring the sangers and tea and coffee in.'

'Is James okay here with you?'

'Of course he is.' She shot Ellie a grin. 'I've got lots of ice cream.'

Ellie put the tray on the low coffee table in the living room. She sat down on the leather lounge looking out through the wide window overlooking the water of Darwin Harbour. The sky was mirrored in the water today and the usual brown murkiness was masked by the reflection of the clear winter sky. Two cruise ships were moored at Fort Hill Wharf. Even though it was heading towards late afternoon, there were a lot of kids in the wave pool and a crowd of walkers in the park below.

'Life goes on,' Ellie said as Dru came into the room carrying the tea and coffee pots, and food on another tray. 'Look at the normality out there.'

'We're pretty lucky, Els. We've had a good couple of years lately. A new brother, a gorgeous sister-in law, and a tribe of babies on the way.' Dru put the pot on the end of the table away from where James had settled with one of his toys.

'A tribe?' Ellie raised one eyebrow.

'Well, the beginning of a tribe. Once this all gets settled, and now with our new generation coming along, we have to be positive. We've all got a lot to look forward to.' Ellie caught Dru's eye and she knew that they were both thinking about

Emma. 'Mum will be home soon and we can put all this behind us.'

Connor and Kane came in from the study.

'I've been talking to Greg again, and as far as he can check, the Larapinta Luxury trekking company has been quietly closed down.' Connor picked up the mug of coffee that Dru had poured for him.

'What do you mean closed down?' Ellie asked.

'No, wrong term, sorry. I should have said locked down. The office buildings have been closed, the staff have ostensibly taken leave, but Greg's discovered they've all been taken to a safe place.'

'Why, and what do you mean by a safe place?' Dru asked before Ellie could.

'Put it this way. Interpol and the Federal Police are doing everything they can to stop this hitting the media and that's why the local police aren't aware that there's been two murders. They've just been advised the track is closed. And to make sure no one goes on it.'

'A young couple,' Ellie said.

'A couple who were on the trek.'

'Can Greg find out anything about them? I mean are they sure it wasn't just an accident? Maybe they fell?'

'No, Ellie, there's something big brewing here. Greg said he's never seen this level of security in all the years he's been watching. Even when we were in the Federal Police force,' Connor said. 'We know how the relationship between Interpol and the feds work, and for this level of security and the huge effort to keep it quiet, something big is going down. From what Greg can get from the Interpol chatter and the communications with the Federal police, he's also hacked into—'

'Hang on,' Kane interrupted. 'Isn't this breaking the law?'

'Kane, be quiet. I don't care what Greg's doing as long as we find Mum. And you know as well as I do how good the law is,' Ellie added cynically.

Connor glanced at Ellie. 'Now that we've got the maps and know where the Feds have targeted, it gives us a good start. First up, we'll map a search grid and fly along the trail and a couple of kilometres to the north and south of each side. If anyone pulls us up, Kane works for Makowa Lodge at Yellow Water, and Ryan and I are businessmen who've hired him on a day trip to take a look at the West McDonnells.'

Connor picked up his coffee and Kane continued. 'The more you girls know about our plan, the better you'll feel. We'll be okay. And with any luck we'll spot some of the trekkers from the air.'

'Won't the Federal Police be searching from the air too?' Dru asked.

'No, not according to what Greg can make out, they'll only be doing a road and ground search. They have two targets and they're trying to keep a very low profile and not spook them. The police have road blocks south of the Birthday Hole turnoff and west of Glen Helen at the top of the trail where it goes south-west to the Mereenie Loop.'

'Why is it so hard to search the trail?' Dru asked. 'Is it really so isolated?

'Yes, where the bodies are is a walk-in area only. There's no road access and they can't have got away in vehicles because there's no access apart from some of the waterholes and trail stops. But there's none of them or road access on the leg of the trek where it all went down. The only thing that we're worried about is some information that's just been shared from the trekking company. None of the guides have turned up anywhere or been in touch with base since this morning. If there's problems, they all have sat phones that go on the trail every day, so as well as the two guides on the trek today there were another two guides who went to the waterhole where they were staying tonight. Four sat phones. None called in and none are answering. They've been trying to ping the phones to find their location, but haven't had any luck so far.'

'Destroyed?' Kane asked.

'Greg suggested that. They've sent another guide out to where the trekkers were supposed to camp tonight in one of the four-wheel-drive company trucks with a Fed police officer in a company guide uniform, but there's no sign of the guides who were setting up tonight's camp. The tents were half set up, but they've both disappeared. A female guide, Jodie, and Dave, a male guide. Plus, there's no sign of the first trekking truck that had the night's gear in it.'

'Well, where do they think they could be?'

'Ellie, nobody knows. They could have got spooked and taken off, but they didn't report in and there's no sign of them or the truck. It's anybody's guess. We know we have to go very carefully; our primary goal is to find your mum, and if there's anybody else out there that needs rescuing or medical treatment, we'll handle it as it comes. What Greg is certain of is that there are two professional operatives out there who were on some sort of mission. They suspect—or I reckon it's pretty much a certainty—that something's been witnessed and that the rest of the trekkers and the guides are—' he hesitated—'hopefully hiding in the scrub.'

Dru interrupted. 'Are what? That's not what you're thinking. Don't beat around the bush, Connor, we need to know.'

Connor put his arm around Dru. 'It's alright, sweetie. There's nothing to know. We don't know anything.'

Ellie looked at him. 'Can you just tell us *exactly* what Greg has discovered?'

'Okay, what we know is there's two operatives, but there's no positive identification of them. The names the trekking company have on their booking, and have shared with the Federal Police, and they have passed onto Interpol, are non-existent. No passports, no Social Security records. No records anywhere in the UK, in the US, or Australia. The names they booked under are unusual so it's an easy search. They were posing as man and wife according to the company, and said they were doctors from Scotland.'

'But they're not.'

'No, they're not. Greg's got searches running on other databases to see if he can intercept any other communication with those names.'

'So, they work for someone who does this sort of thing and they were after someone, you both think?' Ellie forced herself to stay calm. 'They wouldn't have been after Mum, would they? It wouldn't be Russell Fairweather?'

'Ellie,' Kane said. 'Russell Fairweather's in prison.'

'I don't care if he's in prison. That doesn't mean he can't communicate with someone. I wouldn't put anything past that bastard.'

'No, I think you're going out on a limb there, Ellie,' Connor assured her. 'Russell Fairweather wouldn't be in a position to hire operatives from overseas to come in just to get your mum. That's all over now. He has no money and he's locked away, but to reassure you, I'll get Greg onto that too.'

'Thanks. And yes, you're probably right about him. So, they were after somebody on that trek. Do they have any idea who the other young couple are? The ones who've been—' Ellie's voice broke. 'Oh, God, I hope Mum's okay.'

Kane put his arms around Ellie and she leaned in for comfort. 'I'm sorry. I'm okay.'

'They don't because anyone who's interacted with the trekkers are out on the trail. The Federal police get there this afternoon—they're flying into Alice Springs according to the chatter—and it doesn't take long to drive out to Standley Chasm. That's where they all set off from this morning,' Connor said. 'We've managed to get a hold of the trekking itinerary for this particular tour.'

Dru looked at him and shook her head. 'Duh, it's on the fridge, sweetheart.'

'Ah, so it is. I forgot. Anyway, Greg's got it too, so if there's been any changes, we've got the latest.'

Chapter 22

Larapinta Trail

After they'd made Andrew as comfortable as they could, Graysen walked down to the waterhole, keeping an eye on the cliffs above, and his ears tuned for any unnatural sound. He took his walking boots and thick socks off and walked into the water; it appeared to be a lot clearer in the middle than around the edge. The soft silt squelched between his toes, and as he filled the bottle, he wondered what else was in there.

Standing straight and screwing the cap on, he scanned the cliffs around him; he was exposed in the middle of the gorge. The wind was starting to come up, ruffling the water, and it was hard to hear anything apart from the rustling of the leaves and the scattering of small stones as they rolled down the cliffs into the gorge. The occasional thumping of a kangaroo or a wallaby jumping through the narrow end of the gorge broke the silence. If the wildlife were heading that way, perhaps it meant there were more waterholes, or perhaps it meant more feed in a wider valley. That was the way he'd be heading off in the morning, so he took note of how far up the gorge the break in the cliffs was.

Looking around once more, Graysen sat and let the wind dry his feet before he put his socks and boots back on. The temperature had dropped, and he hoped that the rocks and the cliff face would hold warmth for a while. It was going to get very cold tonight out in the open, with no cover and no groundsheet. The risk of lighting a fire was too high. If they were being looked for, it would be like providing a beacon saying, "here we are, come and get us".

Frustration filled him as he thought of leaving Sandra out here in the remote gorge with Andrew. Hopefully as soon as he got to Standley Chasm it wouldn't take too long to get a rescue team out here. He was just going to have to take good notice of where they were before he set off tomorrow, and note markers of his route as he headed east.

He could hear her chatting to Andrew as he walked closer. Her soft, sweet voice and the kindness in her words brought a smile to his lips.

'When Graysen comes back, we'll move you and you'll be more comfortable. When we get out of here, I'd like to meet your two little boys. It sounds as though they're a similar age to my grandson, James. When we go back, you'll probably be in the hospital for a day or two. Do you have any family there to look after the boys for you? If you don't, I'm sure Graysen will be happy to help me out and mind them while your wife visits you.'

Sandra was sitting beside Andrew and she looked up and smiled as Graysen approached. That strange feeling he knew from long ago hit him in the chest and he smiled back. She was a lovely person and he was starting to care about her way too much. Not just because he was looking after her; he'd known what a good person she was from pretty much the first minute he'd met her at the luggage carousel. It hadn't taken long for that to build into an attraction the more he got to know her.

He shook his head as he stood watching her. Despite Andrew's tangled and bloodied hair, she was gently smoothing her fingers over his forehead and his head, obviously avoiding the injured part of his skull. She'd turned his head to the side to keep the pressure off the wound.

Trying to get his focus off the attraction to her, Graysen wondered about the extent of Andrew's injuries and whether his head injury had caused a major concussion—or worse. If so, it would take more than a day or two in hospital for him to recover, but he guessed that Sandra was trying to reassure the young guide. Her puffer jacket was rolled into a pillow and it looked like she'd cleared a section of the flat ground around him.

'Hi, all done?' she asked with a smile. 'I found a branch and leaves on the ground over there and used it to sweep the ground clear.'

'Looks almost cosy,' he said. Graysen couldn't get over how well Sandra was coping with the situation. She'd told the group she was out here to find herself and her strength. Well, she'd certainly done that.

He held up the bottle. 'The water's not too bad. Worst-case scenario, I'd drink it.'

'Worst case?' She pulled a face.

'You should have enough in the other bottles for drinking until I get back.'

'Can you help me move him onto the cleared bit now? We'll need to move him sideways and then turn him around. He'll be a little bit more sheltered with his head near the big rock where I've made the pillow.' She stood and they both looked down at Andrew. 'I think he stayed asleep the whole time you were gone. I was talking to him in case he just had his eyes closed.'

She'd positioned her puffer jacket so that Andrew's head was facing away from the cliff.

As he looked down, he could see she'd laid out the contents of her pack. The packet of jubes, their one remaining apple and two bottles of water, two handkerchiefs, a tube of hand sanitiser and the card of Panadol.

'A home away from home,' Graysen said. 'You're very organised.'

'Years of practice with kids,' she replied. 'Although it didn't take long. We're travelling pretty light.'

They both looked down as Andrew moaned. His eyes were wide open, but dull.

'Okay, young man we're going to get you onto your bed and then we're going to clean down your wounds with some soothing cool water that Graysen got for you. Then if you can help, we'll get some Panadol into you, and you should start to feel a little bit better.'

Graysen was reassured when Andrew lifted his hand again in acknowledgment; it seemed he was having no trouble hearing and understanding, and responding.

He crouched down on one side of Andrew and Sandra took the other side. 'As soon as it's light enough in the morning I'm heading back to Standley Chasm and getting some help for you. Sandra's going to stay with you and you'll both be quite safe here.'

Andrew's eyes widened and he moved his head slightly from side to side; it was obvious fear held him in its grip.

'It's going to be okay, mate. I've had a good look around and we're going to be very careful. We know what we're up against. With whatever's happening, we'll be taking every precaution. So don't you worry, whatever Zed and Miska have done, there will be consequences. We'll all testify against them when it comes to that. *When*, not if.'

Andrew tried to say something but with the state of his mouth he couldn't get the words out. He closed his eyes and his hands clenched by his sides.

Graysen put a hand on his shoulder. 'Just stay calm, Andrew, that's the best thing you can do for us. Once we get you all moved and clean you up, you'll be feeling a little bit better and it might be easier to talk and tell us what happened.'

Graysen knew he was trying to reassure the young guide. There was no way his mouth was going to heal enough for him to talk clearly. He caught Sandra's gaze and nodded.

Andrew cried out in pain as they each took one side and moved him across to the cleared ground, but eventually they had him moved across and turned around, with his head on the soft jacket.

'Now, mate, I'm going to undo your shirt and pull your T-shirt up so we can check your wounds,' Graysen said.

Sandra undid the buttons on the khaki shirt and opened it wide. Graysen carefully rolled up Andrew's T-shirt, exposing his chest.

Sandra's eyes widened at the purple and red bruises wrapped around the front of Andrew's torso. A huge, jagged bruise and some broken skin sat on the left-hand side of his stomach.

'A broken rib,' Graysen mouthed to Sandra. 'Does it hurt you to breathe, Andrew?'

The guide managed to lift his left hand and make a negative gesture.

'Good.'

Graysen nodded to himself. It appeared the injuries to his body were grazes and bruises; it was the head injury and mouth that were of the most concern, and the state his mouth was in would hinder them administering the Panadol to him.

It didn't take long for Sandra to clean each graze and the dried blood with the handkerchief she'd soaked in the water Graysen had brought back.

Sandra put her fingers in his hair and felt around his head.

'You've got yourself a good bump there, Andrew, but I think my girls had worse when they were little.' She reached for one of the bottles of clean water.

'We're going to clean around your mouth a little now. Okay?' Sandra kept chatting as she wiped the dried blood from around his lips. 'My girls always pay out on me because I don't use tissues. I always have two or three hankies in my handbag and luckily, I had the same with my backpack. A travelling first aid kit.'

'When I meet your girls, I'll tell them what a trooper you were on our trek, and how those handkerchiefs came in very handy.' Graysen met Sandra's gaze as she lifted her eyes from Andrew's face to put clean water on a fresh handkerchief. She smiled at him and his heart squeezed a little. 'Now brace yourself. This might hurt a little bit.'

Andrew's eyes closed and his limbs tensed as Graysen used two fingers to prise his lips open. They'd both used the hand sanitiser in Sandra's pack to clean their hands.

Broken teeth protruded from Andrew's top gum and as Graysen gently probed around in his mouth, he could feel loose teeth on the bottom too. He couldn't believe that Andrew hadn't sustained a more significant head injury. He'd been able to walk and was lucid enough to respond to them. 'Sandra, can you please crush three of those Panadol while I finish up here, and mix them into a small amount of water.'

A moment later, she handed him the lid of one of the water bottles with the liquid in it. It was a difficult and painful process but after fifteen minutes of persistence, the lid was empty and Andrew had managed to take most of the liquid.

'I think what we'll do is save that water for Andrew and we'll share the other one. Tomorrow, I'll top my bottle up as I head out. That wind's turned cold and I don't think it's going to be hot tomorrow.'

'Problem is the cold night ahead,' she said. 'We have to keep him warm. We don't want him to get a chill.' She looked down at Andrew who seemed to have drifted off into a deep sleep. 'I think he's running a bit of a temp, but hopefully that Panadol will bring it down.'

***

Sandra took a deep breath as Graysen moved away from her and sat with his back against the warm rock of the cliff. It had been hard for both of them watching Andrew go through that painful process. As they'd worked, the sun had disappeared over the cliff, and now half an hour later, the shadows were lengthening. It wouldn't be long until it was dark. And it was going to be pitch dark. Cloud had come over as they'd worked, and even if the sky cleared, the moon was only a sliver.

'Come and sit with me. The rock's still warm.' Graysen's deep voice interrupted her musing. She repacked her backpack and placed it safely beside the rock. The rock that she was almost thinking of as home, as crazy as it seemed.

She walked over to Graysen and he held his arms open and moved his legs apart. She sat in front of him with her back to his chest.

'It's going to get cold pretty quickly, I think,' he said as she leaned her head back against his shoulder. It still surprised Sandra how natural she was with Graysen. There was no awkwardness or thinking about what she was doing.

'We'll have to lie either side of Andrew and keep him warm later,' she said. 'I hope he gets through this.' Sandra gave into a soft sigh and shivered as Graysen lowered his head and his lips brushed her cheek.

'We'll do what we have to, sweetheart. He's going to be fine.'

Another exquisite shiver ran down her spine as the endearment rolled off his tongue.

'Hopefully by this time tomorrow afternoon, he'll be in hospital,' he said.

'We can only hope.' Sandra snuggled closer to him and reached for his hand. 'I'll be fine here. I just worry about you out on that track.'

'I hate the thought of leaving you here, but I promise I'll be careful and I'll move fast.'

'Just don't get lost.'

'I won't. How about you try and get some sleep now or would you rather eat first?'

'I'll save a jube and the apple for later. For dessert, and to brush my teeth.'

'Sounds like a gourmet meal. I might choose the same from the menu,' he said with a low chuckle.

'I am a little sleepy now, so I'll try to doze for a while. You rest too. Tomorrow you take most of those sweets with you, because you'll need to keep your energy up.'

'We'll go halves.'

Graysen's chest vibrated beneath her back as he spoke and with the feel of his arms around her, she felt cocooned and safe.

'You know what?' she said. 'I should be a cot case after the state I was in a few years ago. I would have thought that something like this would have sent me spiralling down, but I don't know if it's because I'm stronger or if it's because I'm with you, but I'm managing to stay calm. I know that you'll look after me.'

'Your calm and your care for Andrew shows your strength.' Graysen's breath warmed the side of her face. 'You're a strong woman, Sandra Porter. Actually, you know what? No matter what Maggie said about you being called Sandy, I think she was wrong.'

Sandra bit her lip as she thought of Maggie. 'I can't believe she's gone. Maybe she's survived like Andrew did?'

Graysen nodded and she knew he avoided answering her. 'I prefer Sandra to Sandy. "Sandy" reminds me of that young woman out of that movie from years and years ago. The one who ended up dancing in the tight black cat suit. Marion loved it. I can't even think of the name of it now.'

'Love that you remember the black leotard!' Sandra laughed. 'It was *Grease*. My girls must have watched it a thousand times when they were in their teens. They'd be mortified if I went home and wanted to be called "Sandy".'

'Well, I'm going to call you Sandra from now on, because I think Sandra reflects the strong woman you are.'

'Thank you, Graysen. Your respect means a lot to me.'

'Come on, lie back and try and get some sleep against me. I can keep an eye on Andrew from here.'

As the winter evening drew in, the cold and the silence of the bush surrounded them. Sandra took a while to drift off, but gradually she relaxed against Graysen.

Chapter 23

The gorge

'His temperature is good,' Sandra said as Graysen followed her over to Andrew after they'd both dozed for a while. 'I'll crush some more Panadol ready for his next dose.'

The wind was picking up and Andrew was shivering. They sat each side of him as they ate their jubes and had a drink of water, before sharing the apple. There was something intimate about eating it together and Sandra smiled as she savoured the tart sweetness.

A strong gust of wind whistled through the gorge and there was a huge crack as a branch broke from a tree across from them. Sandra jumped and put her hand to her chest. 'God, I'm skittish.'

'At least it'll be light when I'm gone tomorrow,' Graysen said. She could just make out the silhouette of his head against the cliff behind them. Promise me that you'll stay here behind the rock with Andrew. Don't be tempted to go wandering. I'd hate to come back and find you not here. Or worse if they're still on the trail looking for us all.'

'I won't move.'

'When we're out of here I'm going to take you out for a beautiful dinner and we're going to get to know each other in normal circumstances. Just to check you still like me.' Graysen chuckled but there was an uncertainty in his voice. 'Without all the he-man stuff.'

Sandra looked up at him surprised but happy. 'So do you want to keep seeing *me*?'

'Of course, I do.'

'It's a long way to Darwin from the rest of the world.'

'I'm planning on spending some time up there. I was thinking about a photographic series of the northern Australian coast. Perhaps you'd like to come travelling with me.'

'After this experience I think I might be quite happy to stay at home for a while.'

Graysen nodded. 'I understand. Until Zed and Miska are caught anyway.'

'And you know what, Graysen? I don't need any fancy restaurant to get to know you better. If it wasn't for Andrew being hurt, and if we could have a fire, it would be quite a perfect venue.'

'I thought while we were there at our fancy restaurant you could tell me about your life. Tell me what you like to do when you're not out trekking. Tell me what makes you happy,' Graysen said.

'There's no reason why we can't have that conversation now. I want to hear about your life. I want to hear about the places you've been.' She lowered her voice and looked at him carefully. 'I'd like to hear about Marion. It sounds like you loved her very much.'

'I did. We were very happy and it almost destroyed me when she died.'

'Life can be cruel, can't it, Graysen?'

'Yes, it can, but the human spirit is strong and somehow we manage to get through our grief and life goes on. It sounds like a platitude but it's true. Time is the greatest healer. Time and new experiences. This trek, as hard as it's turned out, has been a wakeup call for me. I seem to have dug deep and found myself again.'

Sandra nodded. 'Me too. The main reason I chose to do this was to prove to myself that I could do it. That I could be strong and that I could manage away from my safe haven of home and family. Losing Peter and all the events associated with it made for a very difficult time in my life, and I dropped the bundle big time. I'll be honest with you, Graysen. I was in counselling for a long time and I was on medication. I pretty much stopped going out into the world for a couple of years. My girls were wonderful and they supported me as best they could with their lives happening around them at the same time. And trust me there was a lot happening. We seem to attract trouble.'

'You've told me a little bit about what happened and I can understand that. At least with Marion we knew she was dying. It wasn't a shock and we had that time together, not so much to make our peace with each other but to share and deepen our memories—his voice cracked a little— 'and that wonderful life we had together. I miss her every minute of every day, Sandra. and she'll always be a piece of my heart.'

'As Peter is in mine. We had a good life, and my only regret is that he didn't know about Ryan, his son, I'll tell you about that another time.' She shivered and Graysen's arm went around her.

'Try and get some sleep now. We'll lie either side of Andrew and try to keep him warm.'

Sandra nodded and put her backpack behind her to rest her head. The bare earth was cold beneath her legs and she knew it was going to be a very long night. She was grateful she had Graysen by her side to help her through it.

The knowledge that he wanted to spend more time with her filled her with joy. Not only had she found her inner strength on this trip, but she'd found a new friend. Maybe . . . who knew? Maybe a man who may one day be more than a friend.

Sandra shook herself mentally.

Don't be silly.

Of course, there was no romantic future or anything like that. Not at their age and not with his job, plus they were two very different people. Graysen Hughes, as well being a renowned photographer who lived out of a suitcase and had visited a hundred countries, and Sandra Porter, mother of three, grandmother of one, who lived in a small apartment in a suburban area of Darwin and had never had a passport.

The highlight of her days was maybe a shopping trip, or going for a swim in the pool at the apartment complex, but most of all visiting her wonderful family.

She wondered how Ellie was, and hoped she was staying well. It was awful not being able to pick up the phone and talk to the girls and she hoped they weren't too worried about not being able to talk to her while she was out of range.

Sandra sat up with a sudden gasp.

'What is it? What's wrong?' Sandra heard Graysen jump to his feet and he was instantly by her side. It was too dark now to see him. The light on his watch came on.

'Oh my God.' Her voice was panicked. 'I was just thinking what if the news has got back to Darwin? What if they know that we're all missing? They must. We didn't get to Jodie tonight and she'll have raised the alarm. What are we going to do? What if it gets to the girls?' Her voice rose in pitch and Andrew stirred.

Graysen faced her and put both hands on her shoulders. 'Take a deep breath, Sandra, the news won't be out there yet. It's only been a few hours, and I'm sure as soon as Jodie turns up and we're not there, there's going to be people out looking for us straight away. The company will have plans in place for such an event.'

'What, a murder?'

'No, missing trekkers. I wouldn't be one bit surprised to see a helicopter flying over at first light. If there is, I want you to get out there and wave and jump and yell as much as you can.'

Sandra took a deep breath. 'I'm sorry. Here I am bragging about how strong I've been and one thought about my girls worrying sends me into a panic.'

'Take some deep breaths. You know worrying's not going to achieve anything. Lie down and I'll lie beside you for a while. Andrew's okay, and I've had some sleep.'

Sandra lay back and closed her eyes. She focused on breathing evenly and tried to clear her thoughts. Graysen lay beside her and when his arms went around her, she began to relax and soon she drifted off into a peaceful sleep.

***

Graysen kept his arm around Sandra to keep her as warm as he could. The temperature was plummeting quickly. Once she was sound asleep, he'd go back to the other side of Andrew and try to give him some warmth. Sandra's cheeks were cool but the rest of her body was warm. He rested his cheek on her hair and breathed in her scent. She was a strong and beautiful woman and he was looking forward to spending more time with her.

Away from all this shit.

Sandra breathed peacefully in his arms and Andrew murmured occasionally in his sleep. Graysen kept his eyes open, fighting sleep. At the moment, all was quiet and safe, and he lay back and looked up. The clouds had cleared and a myriad of stars brightened the night sky. He lay there trying to plan the route he'd take tomorrow. Despite his promise to Sandra, he was tempted to climb up to the trail because that would be by far the quickest and the easiest way to get down to the chasm and help. He weighed up the chances of Zed and Miska being up there on the path. The trail would be the fastest route to Standley Chasm. It was probably worth the risk; he could keep an eye out and make sure that there was no sign of them.

Logic told him they'd be trying to do one of two things. Maybe they got away, and maybe they'd taken the truck from Jodie and headed off. Or maybe they were still roaming the trail trying to find the rest of them. Something had obviously happened to Paul and Cecily and PD because if they got back to the Chasm, there would have been help come by now. He had to worry about Clive and Jenny, and hope that Zed and Miska hadn't caught them up on the trail. Clive was a bigger man, but despite his size, they had seemed fit and moved quickly when they had to.

Being a detective, maybe Jenny had picked up something was not right. He could only hope that was why they'd taken off very quickly when Zed headed off with the pack and attacked Andrew.

The night settled in around them cocooning them in its darkness. The wind dropped and there was only the occasional crack of the occasional branch dropping, and rustling in the undergrowth as the wildlife headed out to feed and to drink. Sleep threatened, but Graysen fought it as best he could, but he must have drifted off because a short while later, Sandra's mouth was against his ear and her hand gripped his arm.

'Graysen!' The urgency in her whisper brought him back to full awareness. 'There's somebody here. I can hear somebody. Listen.'

'Stay completely quiet and don't move.' He turned his head to her ear and whispered. Cocking his head, he listened but all was quiet. 'Are you sure you heard something?'

'Yes. I heard voices. Look, look!' She stiffened against him and he sat up. 'There's a light at the end of the gorge. It looks like a torch.

Andrew started to murmur in his sleep and as he began to toss and turn, his murmurs got louder.

'Oh God, they're going to hear him.' Sandra sounded as though she was on the verge of tears.

'It's alright, sweetheart. We're enough away from where they are. The lights a fair way away.'

'I'm scared, what should we do? Move away from Andrew? Or is that the wrong thing to do?'

'Just stay calm. We're here behind the rock, they can't see us. I'll take a look in a minute and see what's out there.'

As he prepared to creep to the edge of the rock, Andrew let out a loud groan.

Graysen stiffened and Sandra was up beside him like a shot.

'I can't stay here by myself,' she said. 'I thought about putting my hand over Andrew's mouth but that would hurt him.'

Graysen slowly lifted his head and looked over the rock. About a hundred metres along the gorge to the north-west, a small light bobbed along, moving at a pace that indicated somebody was walking in the gorge.

'It can't be them. They wouldn't be looking down here in a gully unless they're looking for Andrew's body.'

It wasn't far from the place where Andrew would have gone over the edge of the track, Graysen thought to himself as the first ripple of fear ran through him.

He tensed as Andrew let out a loud yell. 'No!'

Graysen pulled Sandra back down behind the rock. 'Quickly, move along to the next big rock and get behind it Take your pack. If they come down here and find Andrew, they won't know we're there.'

Sandra dropped to a crawl and reached for her pack, but as she stood, her hands were shaking and she dropped it. The metal of her water bottle clanged against the rock.

Graysen and Sandra froze and waited. Andrew was quiet again. Maybe if he didn't yell out again whoever it was wouldn't come over here. From a distance the rock they were behind looked like part of the base of the cliff. Time crawled and all was quiet and still. Then footsteps crackled on the dry undergrowth and there were voices.

There was more than one person.

'Keep perfectly still,' he whispered quietly.

Andrew let out another loud groan and Sandra slid to the ground.

'I can't do this,' she said as he reached for her hands.

Chapter 24

Night flight

Ellie clung to Kane as he bent to pick up his overnight bag. 'You be careful, Kane. Check that bird before you fly and you bring our mum home.'

'Don't worry, sweetie. With any luck, we'll be home tomorrow. With the information Greg's messaged to Connor, we know what we're looking for, and exactly where to look.'

'Yes, we do.' Connor had been in and out of the study taking messages from Greg for the past hour.

'How will Greg stay in touch with you once you leave your computer?' Ellie asked as she let go of Kane.

'I've got a satellite phone. It's on the Iridium network, so, as long as we can get a couple of high points there and maybe even in the helicopter, we'll be able to stay in touch. He's not going to be able to send me detailed maps or information, but I've told him where we are and he'll keep an eye on the Interpol and Federal police chat, so I'll know what's happening at that end of things.'

Connor turned to Dru and hugged his wife as Ellie held her hand out to James. 'Come and give Daddy a hug. He's going on a little trip.'

'Bring me a present, Daddy?'

'Our son is getting way too materialistic, Kane,' Ellie said.

'I'm going to bring you and Mummy a very special present back,' Kane said as he lifted James high. 'Now promise me you'll be a good boy and do as Mummy and Aunty Dru tell you.'

'I promise.'

Dru's voice was low as Connor held her close, but she made Ellie smile. Connor and Dru were not a demonstrative couple in public; Dru had even baulked at a kiss at their wedding ceremony. Now her hands were on either side of Connor's face and Ellie turned away to give them a private moment.

'You be careful too. Don't go in all macho. Just because you've been in the field before, don't think you can go in boots and all. Just get Mum, get out of there, and bring her home.'

'That goes without saying, love,' Connor replied after Dru lifted her face away from his. 'Hopefully we'll have her back here tomorrow night. I'll stay in touch with you every couple of hours. If Greg needs to send me anything, I'll get him to send it to the computer and you can have a look and read it out and tell me if it's maps or anything like that or photos of who we're looking for.'

'Would it be easier if I took my laptop?' Kane asked. 'Ellie has it.'

'Thanks, but no, my PC has got encrypted software and a special internet connection to keep us hidden from whoever might go looking.'

'Fair enough,' Kane said.

'As Greg says, we're going to have to keep a very low profile, because we don't want anyone to know why we're out there. No one can know that we are looking for them; as far as anyone's concerned, we're in the Jabiru Yellow Water helicopter. I'm taking two guests on a private charter down to Alice Springs Airport first and then we'll map a flight path for first thing in the morning.'

Ellie hugged Kane tightly one last time. 'See you soon.'

'Okay, guys.' Connor's voice was brisk. 'Ryan has texted. He's at the airport. Let's get going.'

Ellie and Dru stood on the balcony and waited and watched until Connor's Landcruiser exited the garage and headed around the harbour and then turned east for the airport.

They made their way inside and sat on the sofa, each lost in their own thoughts.

They looked at each other as their phones both pinged at the same time. Ellie reached hers first as Dru headed for the kitchen bench to retrieve hers.

'Oh God,' Ellie said. 'It's Emma. She's asked where I am. She wants to come and see me tomorrow. What will I say?'

'Tell her to come here.'

'But what will we tell her about Mum?'

'We'll play it by ear.' Dru held up her phone. 'She's just texted me too. She needs us, Ellie. We'll just have to focus on our big sister for a while, listen to her and give her some time. The guys will be at least three hours before they message us. I'll keep an eye on Connor's computer and any messages from Greg while we wait for Emma to get here. Okay?'

Ellie nodded. 'Okay, I'll text her back too.'

'We don't have to tell her anything about Mum tonight, and she doesn't need to know you're staying in town.'

'Okay.' Ellie started replying. 'Will I say I'll meet her here or where?'

'Tell her you'll be in town, and I'll say I'm free tomorrow and I'll ask her where and when she wants to meet.'

'Good idea. Let her decide.' Ellie nodded slowly. 'It all depends what her news is, and whether it's good or bad.'

***

Kane walked around the helicopter following his usual pre-flight routine. The routine he'd never got out of since he'd been in the army in Afghanistan. He'd soon learned that checking and following all the routine checks at least twice, and he liked to do them three times—much to Ellie's amusement—made for a safe flight.

Ryan and Connor waited at the back of the chopper and when he gave them the nod, they slipped into the two seats in the back.

After they were secured and headphones in place, Kane checked with the tower and they lifted off. He turned immediately to the south, still in touch with the tower, and also keeping a visual on the sky around the chopper. There was too much air traffic around a city for his comfort, and he didn't relax until they'd cleared the outskirts of Darwin and were flying over the scrubby bush. A couple of times, smoke from the burn-off of the savannah woodlands had him changing direction further west.

As the sun set behind them, the smoke generated a spectacular show as it fired the sky to deep pinks and gold. Ryan and Connor were quiet, and he finally spoke through the mike. 'Probably a good idea to have a kip if you can, guys. It'll be about eight-thirty when we get to the Alice.'

As darkness gradually enveloped them, Kane relaxed into the flight. He much preferred night flying; he'd developed that preference when he'd been in the army in Afghanistan. Sometimes that seemed as though it was a lifetime ago. He was very content with his life as a mango farmer these days. His thoughts moved to Ellie and James and the new baby, and then to their worry about Emma. He blocked any worry about Sandra—as he'd told Ellie there was nothing to be gained by thinking of the what-ifs; he'd learned that in the army. You made your decisions guided by reality not by speculation. He would keep positive and prayed that this time tomorrow night they would have her back in Darwin with the family.

It only seemed a short time until the lights of Alice Springs appeared to the south, and Kane brought the chopper down to a lower altitude as he called in to air traffic control.

Once they'd landed, Ryan and Connor went to the terminal while Kane arranged to secure the helicopter for the night. He was concerned about leaving the chopper unattended at the airport but the security guy assured him that it was safe and that the airport was patrolled through the night.

'Where did you come from? Jabiru?' the guy asked.

'Yes, we're at the Makowa Lodge at Yellow Water.'

'What are you doing down here?'

'I've got a couple mates who want to have a look around the McDonell Ranges.'

'Which way are you going? East or west?'

Kane shrugged. 'Up to them tomorrow. They reckon the west is supposed to be the best. I'm just the pilot. I do as I'm told.'

'Six of one, half dozen of the other,' the security guy said. 'Me? I'd go to the east any day. Not as many bloody tourists that way, and some spectacular sights. Ruby Gap's a pretty spot, gorges, and a few lush waterholes.'

'Thanks, I'll let them know. I've never been down this way before,' Kane said.

'Then again . . .'

Kane was starting to regret getting into the conversation. He was keen to get back to Connor and hear the latest developments from Greg. 'Yes?' he asked with a quick look at his watch.

'Nice resort for lunch up at the top of the west if you go that way.'

'Isn't there a track there that people walk on to the west?'

'Yeah, the Larapinta Trail. We get lots of people come through the airport from all over the world. Can't understand it, myself. Why would I want to go walking in the scrub when I can drive out? Can't understand some people.'

Kane chuckled. 'Or fly. Thanks for your time, mate. We'll be back bright and early, and I'll pass on what you said to my mates. Nothing like local knowledge.'

'That resort I was talking about is called Glen Helen. It's not a bad place. I've taken the missus up there for Sunday lunch.'

'Thanks.' Kane made his escape and hurried across to the terminal.

Chapter 25

The gorge

Graysen held Sandra tightly as the footsteps came closer. The voices had stopped. As Sandra clung to him, she could feel the tension radiating out through his limbs, and his breathing was heavy, but almost silent.

'I heard something from over here, I swear it, love. It wasn't an animal.'

Graysen's relieved exhalation lifted the hair from Sandra's face. He let go of her and took a step to the left. She moved straight after him. Her heart was thudding, but sweet relief flooded through her.

'Clive? Jenny? Is that you?' Graysen's voice was still low.

The torch flicked up and shone on Graysen's face and then Sandra's.

'My God, Graysen! Sandra! Are you both okay?' Clive's voice was loud, and Graysen hushed him.

'We're fine.'

'We thought we heard moaning and we didn't know who it was.'

'Be careful where you walk,' Graysen said. 'Andrew's on the ground just in front of you.'

The torchlight dropped to the ground and Jenny's gasp filled the air.

'Oh my God.'

Clive let out a swear word as the light played on Andrew's battered and bruised face. Jenny grabbed for her husband and Sandra could see her shaking.

'Thank God, he's alive,' Clive said as he comforted Jenny. 'We heard Zed tell Miska he'd killed Andrew.'

'We don't know what happened because Andrew's mouth is badly injured, but we had pretty much figured it out. We think Zed pushed him over the cliff when he said he was going to stow the pack safely.'

Jenny left Clive and came over to them. Jenny put her arms around Sandra and her breath shuddered. 'That's three of you that are alive, thank God. We didn't know what had happened to the rest of you, but we were hoping for a good outcome.'

Clive moved closer and put his hand out, and shook Graysen's hand. 'It's good to see you fit and well, man.'

'And both of you as well.'

'Only thanks to my Jenny's instincts.'

Andrew moaned and Sandra let go of Jenny. 'It's time to give Andrew more Panadol.'

She crouched beside him and felt his forehead. 'He's a bit warm, but he's shivering and a bit delirious I think.'

While Sandra tipped the liquid she'd mixed earlier into the lid of the water bottle, Graysen dropped to his knees behind Andrew. 'Clive, if you can kneel beside me, we can gently lift Andrew's shoulders a little higher so he can swallow the liquid.'

Clive knelt beside him.

'Go slow and easy. I'm pretty sure he's got a broken rib.'

Andrew opened his eyes as Clive and Graysen propped him up at a forty-five-degree angle.

'Andrew,' Sandra said softly. 'Are you able to sip this a little easier sitting up?'

Andrew tried to nod.

Jenny sat beside Sandra and watched quietly as she slowly tipped a little of the Panadol and water mix into his mouth a sip at a time.

'We're done,' Sandra said to Graysen. 'Good man, Andrew, would you like some water too? To get the taste of the Panadol out?'

Another nod.

Clive and Graysen held Andrew for a few more minutes, until Sandra nodded. 'Okay, down slowly. Go back to sleep, Andrew. It's the best thing for you.'

Once he was settled, Clive took his jacket off and laid it over Andrew's chest and shoulders.

'His eyes are clear. I don't think he has a bad concussion.' Jenny said. 'And I just thought, I've got a beanie in my pack. That'll stop him losing warmth through the top of his head.'

It wasn't long before Andrew was wrapped up in Clive's jacket and wearing Jenny's beanie, and had fallen into a deep sleep again.

Clive and Jenny sat with Graysen and Sandra in a close semi-circle around Andrew to protect him from the chilly wind.

'Are you carrying much water?' Graysen asked when they were settled.

Clive nodded. 'That's why my damn pack is so heavy. We've got six bottles left plus our metal canisters are topped up too.'

'Clive has the water in his pack and I've got about ten trail mix bars and four apples in mine,' Jenny added. 'Have you pair had anything to eat this afternoon? What about your water?'

'We're low on water, and we shared an apple and a couple of jubes for dinner.'

Jenny picked up her pack and took out four trail mix bars. 'Here, you must be hungry.'

Sandra's stomach rumbled at the thought of food. 'Thank you.' She and Graysen opened the packet and Clive and Jenny sat quietly, holding hands as the trail mix bars were eaten.

'Thank you,' Graysen said.

Jenny smiled. 'I'll never doubt my dear husband again. I said there was no need to carry so much food and water because Andrew had the pack with lunch and morning tea, but he insisted.'

'I wasn't fussed on some of the food at the camps we've had along the way, and I need to keep my energy up,' Clive added.

'I'm pleased you did.' Graysen screwed up the wrapper, reached for Sandra's and put them in his shirt pocket.

'Okay, let's share what we know.' Jenny's voice was brisk. 'To try and make some sense out of what's happened. And to figure out what we need to do.'

'I guess you've been settled here because of Andrew?' Clive asked.

Graysen nodded. 'Yes, but we'd stopped here for the night before Andrew literally stumbled on us.'

'So, he hasn't been with you the whole time?'

'No.' Graysen quickly recounted what had happened and told them of his plan to head alone to Standley Chasm in the morning to get help. 'Andrew is a priority. He needs to be in a hospital.'

Sandra leaned forward. 'But we've been worried about coming across Zed and Miska.' She glanced across at Graysen. 'I've made Graysen promise that he would stay off the trail tomorrow.'

Graysen reached for her hand and Sandra curled her fingers around his. 'What happened to you pair?' he asked. 'Did you see what Zed did? Is that why you got off the trail? I did notice you took off pretty quickly after we'd stopped for morning tea.'

'Jenny's been wary of them since the first day,' Clive said.

'Zed and Miska, that is,' Jenny clarified. 'Paul and Cecily were just spoilt brats, a bit typical of the current "entitled" generation, but they were harmless.'

'Do you know they're missing too? And PD?' Sandra asked.

'Or we're assuming they are,' Graysen added. 'They'd supposedly headed back to the Chasm with Cecily with a turned ankle, but when I climbed higher, there was no sign of them on the trail. And if they had got back, I'm sure the company would have sent P.D. ahead to Birthday Waterhole to join up with Jodie, or sent another guide along the trail to catch us all up. If they were waiting at tonight's camp, the alarm would have been raised when we didn't turn up. It's just all too quiet out here. I don't think anyone is aware that the trek has come to this.'

'Seven of us haven't turned up. Maybe Zed and Miska continued on, and then told Jodie that we'd all turned back for some reason,' Jenny said.

Graysen frowned. 'It's all guesswork. All we know is that there's no one out looking for us. What made you think they weren't genuine, Jenny?'

'I know now I should have said something earlier. They just seemed off kilter to me from that first night. And then she seemed to take on a new personality when we headed out—all sweetness and light. Then when they said they were in

Aberdeen and Clive asked them where they were living, Zed said quickly they weren't there yet. They contradicted themselves a couple of other times when I was talking to them too. It's the sort of thing most people would maybe not even notice, but it registered with me, and my senses went on alert. I don't believe they were ever in Aberdeen and I doubt if they were doctors. No proof, just instinct.'

'Jenny was a top detective before she retired,' Clive said proudly. 'Worked on, and solved many high-powered cases, and received many commendations.'

'They just seem to be like cardboard cut-outs to me,' Jenny continued. 'They had no history. No personal comments apart from putting on the lovey-dovey "this is my wonderful wife and we're on our honeymoon" story. No substance.'

'You're very astute, Jenny.' Sandra moved closer to Graysen as the cold wind sent a shiver through her. 'My girls, and Peter too, always told me I was too trusting, but I do like to see the best in people.'

Graysen squeezed her hand. 'In normal social circles, that's not a bad thing.'

'I had forty years in the police force and thirty-five as a detective before I retired. I learned that many people hide behind a front for some reason or another.'

'Graysen and I were talking about greed being a motivator. I've had personal experience of that.'

'I looked up that case after you mentioned it the other night. Went back to the old files when we had service at Standley Chasm last night. Even though I was working in Sydney, I remember when it happened. It must have been very hard for you.'

'It was a difficult time.' Sandra cleared her throat as emotion threatened to take hold. 'What do you think Zed and

Miska are doing? Graysen saw something. Something so horrendous I still can't process it.'

'We overheard them on the trail, but we'd already hidden by then. What did you see, Graysen?' Clive asked.

'After you guys left, and Zed had been along the trail to stow the pack, I climbed higher. Like I said before, I couldn't see Paul and Cecily and P.D., but couldn't see Andrew either. I lifted my camera and panned around to the west.' Graysen's voice was flat and held no emotion, and Sandra wondered how he stayed so calm after what he'd seen.

'Zed had a rifle with a sight and he lifted it as I watched. I moved my camera to see where he was pointing just as the projectile hit Maggie in the head. Miska was standing beside her and as Maggie fell, she moved forward and pushed her over the edge. It was on one of the highest points just after the Bridle Path lookout.'

'I said maybe she's not dead,' Sandra said slowly.

'There's always a chance,' Jenny said. 'The human spirit is an amazing thing.'

'Andrew showed us that by getting this far with his head and facial injuries, and I suspect he has a broken rib or two.' Graysen turned to Jenny. 'Why were you hiding, and what did you see and hear?'

'You were about to head up to the knoll when Clive started to feel a bit unwell. I came back to see if you and Sandra would walk with us because I was worried he was going to pass out. Zed had his back to me and I saw the rifle with a big telescopic sight in his hand. And a silencer. No one has a setup like that unless they are going to kill somebody. He didn't hear or see me. I took off quickly and hurried back to Clive. By that stage he was really giddy and perspiring—I've thought about it and I wondered if Miska put something in his tea.'

'I told Jenny when I felt better that it had a bitter taste to it, but I thought nothing of it at the time.'

'She made tea for Andrew too, but Sandra and I didn't want one.'

'I grabbed Clive and made him leave the trail with me. We hid just under the trail behind some rocks until they went past. It was fairly tense for us, wondering if they would be looking off the track, and that's when we heard Zed say to get a move on because we were getting too far ahead.'

'Bloody tense isn't the word,' Clive said. 'My head was spinning, my stomach was churning and I was trying hard not to spew.'

'That's when we knew they were after us all. It was clear that they were looking for us and we knew we had to hide. There was a small stand of trees in a gully not far down, and I prayed we'd have time to get there by the time they came back. Because they'd know that we weren't ahead of them very quickly. I'd heard the muffled shot, and that seemed to give us the speed to get down.'

'I was as dizzy as all get out,' Clive said. 'I slid down most of the way and ended up falling and rolling the last fifty metres. I'm a bit bruised and sore, but nothing to compare to Andrew. I was on a grassy slope with a few rocks. That poor bugger looks like he came down a rocky cliff.'

Jenny took over. 'We got to the trees and I settled Clive behind a log with both of our packs and told him not to move or speak. I stood behind a tree that was wide enough to keep me out of view from above. If you remember from the past few days my hat and fly net are dark brown so when I looked around the edge of the trunk, I knew I was camouflaged. I watched them walk back and forth along the trail for almost an hour. Clive, God love him, was as quiet as a mouse.'

'I was so out of it, I slept for most of the hour until Jenny felt safe enough to come and lie beside me.'

'I was worried about you, love. You were crook, we had no phone, and Zed was up there scanning the countryside with a high-powered rifle with a telescopic sight.' She turned back to Graysen and Sandra. 'I was terrified the whole time he'd spot us and come down, but eventually they headed west. Every hundred metres or so, they'd stop and he'd look around through the telescopic sight. When he did that, I'd pull back a bit.'

Graysen interrupted. 'You said they were heading west? You're absolutely sure of that? They kept going west after they didn't find you?'

'Yes. And then they disappeared so the trail must have gone down off the ridge. I assumed they were heading to the camp site at Birthday Waterhole. I was terrified for Jodie, and I worried where Maggie was after I'd heard that shot. Plus, we worried where you pair had got to when you didn't appear on the trail either. When I went back to Clive and told him what I'd seen, we decided to stay put until he felt better and then head back this way and try to get back to Standley Chasm and report what we'd seen.'

'Plus, we also knew there was a risk they were hiding up there and sitting us out.'

Sandra couldn't imagine what that would have been like.

'It must have been dreadful for you.'

'In all my years in the police force I don't think I was ever as scared as I was in those three hours. Eventually we made a move and took off into another gorge that hid us from the track. We decided to walk in the dark to keep warm.'

'And to get closer to safety,' Clive added. 'It's lucky we found you. We got lost a while back and went down a couple of gullies that led nowhere.'

'That's why we decided to stay here for the night,' Graysen said. 'Without the sun I'd be lost.'

'Clive's got a compass on his watch, so we knew if we kept heading east, we'd get there eventually. It's so good to be here with you.'

'I was so scared when Graysen said he saw your light, but it was such a relief when we recognised your voices. I feel like there's safety in numbers,' Sandra said.

In the dim light, she saw Graysen and Jenny exchange a look, and she realised there was actually no safety when there was a rifle involved.

'We're still not sure of the way back and the fact that we stumbled on you is unbelievable. There are so many gullies and gorges. We haven't seen half of it from up on the trail. When we saw this narrow gorge, we decided it was a good place to rest and head out in the morning. We hoped it was out of the wind a bit.'

'I was starting to feel a bit crook again,' Clive said. 'I don't know what Miska gave me.'

'Something to knock you out,' Graysen said.

'Yes,' Jenny agreed. 'And that was another reason we stayed away from the trail. Whoever they are, and whatever they are doing, is well-planned. They're after someone and they're making sure that there's no-one left to witness what they've done.'

Graysen stiffened and Sandra stared up at him. His forehead was creased in a frown.

'I assumed that Maggie was their target,' he said.

'Never assume, Graysen,' Jenny said. 'It could simply have been an opportunity to remove her as a witness.'

Chills ran along Sandra's limbs, and her shiver was more from fear than the cold wind that still gusted along the gorge. 'But who could they have been after and why?'

'Any one of our group,' Jenny said. 'And the why is the payment they'll get. I don't think they were personally known to anyone on the trek, but for the right money, killers can be hired. If you knew how often it happens, you'd be shocked. Assassins are even brought in from overseas, and they fit that mould.'

Sandra shook her head. 'Even after my experience, I can't understand the inherent evil in people who will do that for money.'

Jenny's expression tightened. 'Some also do it for the power and the thrill of a kill.'

Sandra nodded as she recalled the year that Fairweather went after them. 'The guy who was hired to kill Peter and make it look like a suicide, the one who then went after my daughter, Ellie, and then kidnapped the Chief Magistrate's wife, was apparently a cold killer who would do anything for the thrill of killing. Fairweather had him in his pocket. He met a timely end in the jaws of a crocodile.'

'There can be natural justice,' Jenny said.

Andrew moaned and stirred, and Sandra reached for the water bottle. 'A drink, Andrew?'

His head dropped a small nod.

Graysen and Clive moved behind him and propped him up as he drank three capfuls of water, and then lay back, exhausted.

'How are you going, Andrew?' Sandra asked quietly. 'Is the pain manageable? It's another couple of hours until your next Panadol.'

Andrew's eyes were closed but his thumb and his forefinger made a circle above his chest.

'Jenny, I didn't think to ask. Do you have any paracetamol? I'm almost out.'

'Yes, Sandy, I have a whole box in my pack.' Jenny looked down at Andrew. 'Listen, I've been thinking. Instead of you staying here with Andrew when Graysen goes in the morning, why don't you go with him? You're both younger and fitter than us, and we can give Andrew the Panadol, and water, and look after him until you get back with help. You've found a secure possie here.'

'What do you think of that, Graysen?' Sandra was excited by the prospect of heading out with Graysen.

'If Clive and Jenny are happy to stay here, it makes sense for us both to go.'

'We can give you half of our water and some trail mix bars.'

Graysen held Sandra's eyes with his. 'What would you rather do, Sandra?'

'I'd rather leave with you. We can organise help and I can ring my girls.' She turned to Jenny. 'That sounds selfish. If you would like to go, I'm happy to stay.'

'No, Clive's not up to it, and I'd rather stay with him.'

'Okay.' Graysen nodded. 'We have a plan. Now we'd better get some sleep.'

Chapter 26

The last gorge

It was a long night, but strangely, having Clive and Jenny there and the five of them cocooned safely in the narrow gorge had taken away the tension. Even though the temperature had dropped, and the wind continued to gust, somehow it didn't seem as cold with the extra bodies huddled together.

There'd been no need for Graysen to set his watch alarm because he dozed lightly all night, and seemed to wake every fifteen minutes. He was constantly aware that they could be found. The small light flickering should be okay, but he still worried. Every rustle, every stone moving, and the creak of the tree branches had him on edge. Before they called it a night, they chatted quietly, and Clive and Jenny told them more about themselves before they eventually all lay down to rest.

As the sky lightened almost imperceptibly Graysen looked down at his watch and then gently shook Sandra. She seemed to have slept well; he'd only been aware of her waking twice through the night. The first time they had given Andrew another dose of Panadol and water, but the second time she had sat bolt upright and stiffened. He'd sat up like a shot and listened and looked around, but she'd shaken her head.

'Only a bad dream,' she'd murmured. 'Sorry.'

He'd held her close as they lay down again, and it was only a minute or so before her breathing was deep and even as she slept again. Now Sandra opened her eyes and smiled at him in the faint light. Her smile was sweet and he reached down and his lips hovered over hers.

'Good morning, Sandra. Are you ready to go on our trek?'

'After you cook me a hearty breakfast,' she said, reaching up and kissing him.

Graysen smiled. 'It's good to see you chirpy this morning. I promise as soon as we get to Standley Chasm, I'll get you whatever you want for a hearty breakfast.'

'After we've called for help, I'll take you up on that. I think I might be ready to eat by then.'

'Back in a while.' Graysen headed bush.

***

Sandra stood and stretched and looked down at Andrew as Graysen walked away.

The young man opened his eyes and she was sure she could see a smile in them.

'..andra.' He managed to say but Sandra put up her hand.

'Sssh. You're looking much better, Andrew. That makes me happy. Graysen and I are going back to Standley Chasm this morning and we should have a helicopter here for you hopefully within four or five hours.'

Andrew tried to make a sound and lifted both hands and make a sideways motion.

'It's okay. We know to be very, very careful. If we take a bit longer than I said, it means that we are taking extra care, so please don't worry.'

'We won't be able to help ourselves worrying,' Jenny said as she sat up and rubbed her eyes.

Sandra nodded. 'I know. We've got three people's lives depending on us and we'll get there. I give you my word. Did you get some sleep?'

Jenny reached out and squeezed her hand. 'I did, but crazy dreams. The sooner we get home to Sydney and in our own soft bed, the better. Next holiday will be on a crowded beach, I think!'

'Safety in numbers?'

'For sure. Sandy?' Jenny's expression held curiosity.

'Yes?'

'If you and Graysen ever get to Sydney together, we'd love to have you stay.'

Sandra's cheeks heated. 'Early days yet, Jenny. Who knows what will happen?'

'I can see that you care for each other. Don't let it go.' She stood and brushed her hands down her cargo shorts. 'Anyway, the offer's there. I'll give you our mobile number before we all head off home.'

'Thank you. I'll do the same. And if you and Clive are ever in Darwin . . . the same invitation stands.'

Jenny grinned. 'I like our positivity. 'It's going to be a good day, Sandy.'

'It is. I'm just going to head up there for a toilet stop before we go.' Graysen had headed away from camp in the other direction.

'Here, take my torch. 'Jenny pulled a small flashlight from her pocket.

'Thanks,' Sandra said as she headed bush.

It was still dark half an hour later when she followed Graysen to the end of the gorge, but there was a promise of pink dawn light in the sky. They had said a brief goodbye to Jenny and Clive, and Sandra knew Andrew was in good hands. Jenny had given them two apples and some trail mix bars, and Clive had loaded Graysen's pack with four bottles of water. 'You'll need it more than we will here, and with any luck, you'll be back before noon.'

Jenny and Sandra hugged each other, and Sandra crouched beside Andrew and ran her fingers over his hair before she dropped a kiss on his forehead.

'We'll see you soon, Andrew. Stay well.'

Graysen pointed to his camera bag. 'There's no point me taking my cameras with us,' he said. 'I've got the memory cards in my pack, but if you could keep an eye on my cameras, Clive, I'd appreciate it.'

'Not a problem, mate. Be careful and we'll see you soon.'

As they reached the end of the gorge, Graysen pointed out the waterhole where he'd collected the water to wash Andrew's wounds yesterday. They walked steadily in the faint dawn light, not speaking as they made their way east. Soon they came to a narrow gorge that led north towards the direction of the main trail.

'I've spent a lot of time through the night thinking about which way we should go,' Graysen said as they stopped. He reached out and took her hand. 'We can go back to the trail but it's going to be a very big climb. There's also the danger that they might be up there looking for us. On the other hand, it's a long track and the chances of meeting them are probably very low odds but there is always that chance. What do you think?'

'I don't know,' she said. 'I'll leave it up to you. I do worry that we'll get lost, and come to a dead end if we go bush. Maybe it's worth the risk?'

'If it was just me, I'd have no hesitation,' Graysen said looking up at the ridge way above them. 'But I don't want to put you in any danger.'

'And I don't want you to be in any danger,' she said squeezing his hand.

'Six months ago, I would have forged ahead up there, and not given any thought to, or cared about putting myself in danger. Even three months ago, I wouldn't have cared if I'd lived or died. Coming out here—and meeting you—has changed me.'

'What are you trying to say, Graysen?'

'I know we've only known each other a short time, but you've put some meaning in my life again. I don't want to rush things, but I needed to say that before we head up to the ridge. If we get out of here safely, I'd like to explore that, because if we didn't it would be hard to let you go. Now we need to get going. Up the hill to the trail?'

Sandra leaned into him and put her arms around his waist. 'Yes, together. We will survive this. We will get help for Andrew and we will make sure that those people will get what they deserve. Going through what we went through when Peter was murdered has given me a deeper strength and a belief in good. I know I struggled for a long time, but I know I've dug deep and tapped into the strength these past few days. Being with you has enhanced that for me too and I'm going to dig deep and keep this strength in place. I don't mean my physical strength. I mean my ability to cope mentally, and my emotional strength. I hope that you stay around and help me find it. It would be really good to have you in my life. Now, before we start climbing . . .'

Sandra lifted her hands to Graysen's face and cupped his cheeks gently as she stood on her toes and pressed her lips to his. They stood there in a close embrace for a long moment until Graysen pulled away and Sandra reluctantly stepped back.

'Let's make a start,' he said quietly. His expression held something that sent an exquisite feeling all the way to her toes.

'Keep looking around and listen. There should be other hikers up there, but at the first sign of any danger we take off together.'

Sandra looked at the big climb ahead.

I can do it.

As they walked north back through the gorges and gullies and began the first gentle climb up to the Larapinta Trail, the sun cleared the eastern horizon and provided them with the most spectacular sunrise they'd seen so far. The sky started off pink and then segued to a golden yellow until above them a mass of bright pink and yellow clouds reached as far as they could see.

'The promise of a new and good day,' Sandra whispered to herself.

Above, the colour of the cliffs slowly changed from dark brown to red as the sun touched them with its first gentle rays. The sliver of the crescent moon began to fade as the sun strengthened.

Graysen paused and shaded his eyes as he scanned the cliffs above them from west to east and back again.

'Not a single trekker in sight yet, although it's probably too early for anyone to have come this far. If I'd known we wanted to be camouflaged on this trip, I would have bought darker walking clothes,' he said as they reached the end of the sandy gully they'd crossed. 'We stand out against the rocks and the trees in these light shirts if anyone's looking down.'

Sandra stopped beside him. 'That gorgeous sunrise is an omen for us. I think we need to stop worrying and just go. We'll be cautious but positive. Now come on, let's pace this out.'

Graysen's eyes widened and a broad smile spread across his face. 'I agree. Let's go. We'll keep a steady pace and not stride out too far.'

The floor of the narrow gorge had a steady incline and the cliffs closed in and hid them from above. Sandra was happy to maintain a steady pace but gradually as the incline increased, her legs began to ache.

Graysen paused and looked up with a frown. 'We'll take a quick water break when we reach the end of this gorge.'

'What's wrong?' Sandra was able to pick his concern without him saying anything.

'I wonder if we are walking the wrong way? I think we might have chosen the wrong gully to follow. The cliffs are getting closer together, and I'm worried we're either going to come to a dead end or a big drop between us and the trail.'

'Do you think we should turn back? We don't want to have to do this climb, go down and have to climb the same distance again. It'll slow us down.'

'It's starting to look like that. My gut feeling is to turn back. We're climbing too sharply, too quickly.'

It's okay. We haven't come very far.' As she spoke her stomach let out a huge gurgle.

'Definitely time for a break.'

'Just time for a drink and an apple.'

After a quick break, they stood discussing whether to keep going or turn back.

'It'd be easier walking back downhill for a while. If we do, we'll take a left where there was that gap with the grassy gully about half a kilometre back in the cliffs.'

Graysen's fingers tapped the side of his thigh. 'Or do we keep going and hope that this doesn't end at a drop. Even if we do have to turn back if we keep going, we'll have a good view of the landscape around us.'

Sandra shook her head. 'No, let's keep low. If we keep going and then have to turn back, that's an hour or more wasted.'

'Right. We'll follow my gut. I just hope I'm not leading you astray.'

Sandra couldn't help her smile. 'Maybe not today, but being led astray does sounds enticing.'

Graysen's face was a picture and then he chuckled. 'Okay, I can do that when we're out of here. Just call me Danny.'

Sandra frowned for a moment and then she elbowed him as she understood. 'You did watch *Grease*!'

He looked sheepish. 'I didn't want to admit to it, but yes, I did, several times. Marion loved it.' He held her hand as they walked.

Soon they reached the gap at the side of the gorge and Graysen nodded as they took the turn.

'Yes, we should've come this way to start with. Even though it's going a little bit further away from the south, we're sort of doubling back a little bit but it's a lot clearer and lower further ahead.'

Soon it was full daylight, and the sun was warm on their faces as they headed back to the east. There was little conversation as they walked steadily for an hour. Sandra had hit her stride. The gentle incline was easy on her leg muscles, and the occasional stop for a sip of water kept her feeling surprisingly good. Knowing that they were getting closer to safety and help for Andrew spurred her on.

Eventually they came to a wide grassy area and Graysen stopped and gestured to the left. 'I think we'll head over that way. There's a bit of a gully running along the base of the hill. If we stick to the middle of that grassy hill, we'll be too visible from up on the trail and it's one thing I don't want to do.'

'Pretty much sitting ducks, if they happen to be up there.'

'Yes.' Sandra turned and followed Graysen towards the gully where there were some scattered trees.

Suddenly he grabbed for her hand. 'Run. Quick.' The urgency in his voice had her taking off at a run beside him.

The shade of the gully was welcoming as they reached the gorge, out of sight of the trail above.

'What's wrong?' Sandra put her hand to her chest as she pulled in a ragged breath. 'What was it?'

'I saw something glinting up on the trail.'

'And a person?'

'I didn't wait to see. Hopefully it was the sun on a trail marker.

'So, are we going to keep climbing or head off in another direction?'

Graysen took his hat off and ran his hand through his hair. 'If we head back down and look for another route past that mountain, we could be out here another night. Logic tells me they won't be up here this far east looking for us. Jenny said they headed west. We'll just have to hope and pray that she was right.'

They climbed for an hour, keeping in the shade, their senses on full alert. Sandra's legs were aching, the muscles taut in her thighs and her calves pulling with each step. She began to stop more regularly for a sip of water.

Graysen opened his bottle and took a deep drink as she leaned against the cliff.

'Not much further and we'll reach the trail, and then the good news is it's all downhill to Standley Chasm.'

'I'm okay, just a bit hot and tired. You wouldn't believe that after the cold of last night I'd be complaining about being hot this morning.'

'I think you're entitled. We're doing good.'

The incline followed a northerly direction and when they were almost to the top the track widened considerably. To their surprise a small waterhole surrounded by thick grass glinted in the morning sunlight on the southern edge.

'Maybe that's what you saw.'

'Hope so.' As they pushed through the long grass, Sandra kept her eyes on the ground. It was hard to see where she was putting her feet and the last thing she wanted to do was step on a snake.

'Just another thing that could go wrong, isn't it?'

'What's that?'

'Snake bite.'

Graysen took Sandra's hand again as the incline grew steeper. They were only about fifty metres from the top and she was sure that he was pulling her up a little bit.

'At least the grass is deadening our footsteps,' he said quietly close to her ear. 'Try and be as quiet as we can now.'

'You don't have to drag me up. I'm fine. Save your energy,' she whispered.

'I'm good. Knowing we're so close is getting the adrenalin pumping. What I want you to do is wait in that narrow alcove about twenty metres ahead.' He pointed with his other hand. 'Can you see it? Just up there a bit past that straggly tree.'

She nodded.

'I should get a bit of a view from up there.'

'Be careful,' Sandra said as they reached the small gap.

'I will be. Just wait here quietly. I'll only be a few minutes, and it'll give us a bit of a view as to where we're going and reassure me that there's no one up here looking for us.' He leaned down, kissed her and was gone.

There was a flat rock on one side of the alcove. Sandra sat down and stretched her legs in front of her. She took out her water bottle and took a big drink, and then looked out over the view. Her eyes narrowed as she let her gaze follow the ridges ahead, and she jumped up. About a kilometre to the north she could see four pointed peaks a few metres apart. Excitement thrilled through her. The morning they had set off up the steps from the Standley Chasm campground, she had noticed those four short, jagged peaks on the eastern side of the chasm. Once they were on the trail, they were so close to their destination.

Close to help, and safe.

Even though Sandra was in the shade, the temperature was climbing steadily and perspiration trickled down the back of the neck. She put her hand up and wiped the moisture away as she waited for Graysen to reappear. The excitement of being so close to their destination was replaced by a niggle of worry when he didn't return.

Five slow minutes passed and she tried to rein in her impatience, focusing on her breathing. It was a good opportunity to have a rest, and build her energy for the fast walk down hill to the campground.

Surely when he was up there, he'd be able to see if all was clear. Maybe he'd spotted someone and he was laying low.

Sandra tensed and held her breath as an unfamiliar noise came from above.

Chapter 27

From the air

Connor suggested they hire a car before the airport closed. 'We don't know what we'll find tomorrow, and if we need a vehicle, it's not far to come back to the airport and collect it.'

'And we can go and get some food now,' said the ever-hungry Ryan.

'Good plan,' Kane agreed. 'Won't hurt to have some food and water onboard tomorrow.'

'And we can get some pies or something now,' Ryan said hopefully.

Connor looked up at him with a grin. 'I thought we'd had dinner?'

Ryan shook his head and grinned. 'That was a snack, mate. All right for you sedentary blokes who sit at a desk all day. Kane and I need our food.'

After takeaway pies and coffee, they spent the night in a family room at the airport hotel and were up at dawn. The hired four-wheel drive was in the car park, ready if they needed it, and they booked the hotel room for another night just in case.

'Hopefully, we'll be home by tonight,' Kane said.

There'd been nothing new from Greg, apart from the news that the chatter between Interpol and the Federal Police had quietened.

Kane's concerns about the safety of the chopper were unfounded. All was well as they made their way across to the tarmac the next morning. The security guard gave them a wave.

'Have a good day, guys,' he called from his booth between the car park and the hangar beside the helicopter.

Ryan and Connor carried a backpack each, one full of water, and one with snack food. Kane had suggested getting a first aid kit; he carried that across to the chopper and stowed it under the front seat.

'You've got the map folder, Connor?' he asked.

'I have.'

'You pair can navigate. I've never flown here.'

Ryan and Connor made themselves comfortable as Kane did the pre-flight check. He focused on the R44 sitting on the tarmac in front of him. He walked around it slowly, checking the skids and the rotor blades before opening the cowl on the fuel tank to fill it with Avgas.

He hadn't flown much since that horrific day he'd had David beside him and they'd gone out looking for Ellie and Gina. The rage that he'd experienced when he'd discovered that the chopper had been tampered with had frightened him, and after that he'd focused on the life that he and Ellie had made at the farm.

Although the delay frustrated him, Kane took his time preparing for the flight. His time in the desert in Afghanistan, and his experience at Makowa Lodge had taught him to be thorough. He filled the fuel tank and did another pre-flight check before he was satisfied that the bird was safe to take up. He lifted his head and surveyed the landscape to the west as he walked around the machine. His stomach churned as he thought of Sandra somewhere out there, and he prayed that they would find her quickly, and that she wasn't hurt.

He took time to do a third check of the chopper.

He did a final instrument check and handed the earphones to Connor beside him, and Ryan who was strapped into one of the back seats.

'I logged a flight plan along the whole route of the trail; they didn't say anything about the air space being closed or the trail being closed.'

'It's been kept pretty quiet,' Connor said. 'I'm assuming that they haven't caught the pair they're looking for yet, or things would be back to normal.'

'So, we're looking at the track, and anyone walking on it?' Ryan asked.

'And do a sweep, a kilometre or so on your side. I'll take the south, Ryan,' Connor said. 'Kane, you focus on the trail if you can see it clearly ahead.'

'It's fifty kilometres to where they set off from yesterday morning, and that'll take us about half an hour from here, but keep an eye on the first bit of the track. We can't discount any possibility. The starting point for the Larapinta Trail is eighteen kilometres north of the airport. I'll tell you when we fly over the Old Telegraph Station at the eastern end of the track. About five minutes from now.'

Ryan and Connor took out the binoculars Connor had packed, and few minutes later, the chopper swept to the left and Kane spoke into the mike.

'The track starts near those buildings; past the telegraph poles you can see and then ahead a bit, it goes under a road bridge. Then you'll see the Ghan railway and then the track heads twenty-six kilometres southwest to where they spent the first night at Simpsons Gap.'

Kane focused on the trail below, and there was no sound from Ryan and Connor as they swept over the landscape below.

Ten minutes later Kane broke the silence. 'Coming up to Simpsons Gap in a couple of minutes. No sign of life on the track.'

'Ditto,' Connor said.

'Nothing here,' Ryan added.

'From here to the old homestead where they stayed the second night, the track gets rougher and more remote, a similar distance to what we've just searched but more mountainous. I'm going to take the bird up a little higher, so you'll really need the binoculars.'

Connor nodded beside him, and then his voice crackled through Kane's headphones. 'What do you think about landing at the old Homestead and having a look around? It's shelter and there might be someone holed up there.'

Kane agreed. 'Worth a try. But we'll be careful. If there's anyone there and they ask what we're doing, you're a couple of businessmen looking for a resort site. The track turns a bit north from here.'

They all focused on the landscape below, but like the previous section of the trail, all was quiet. Half an hour later, Kane pointed ahead. 'There's the old homestead, there's no vehicles there. What do you think?'

'Why don't you do a low flyover, and see if anyone comes out?' Connor said. 'If not, we'll keep going along the trail until we get to Birthday Waterhole and if we don't have any luck, we'll come back after that. It's a fair way before where they went missing.'

Kane brought the bird down low, and did two sweeps over the homestead and a kilometre in each direction. Ryan and Connor kept their eyes on the ground below.

'Nothing,' Connor said.

'Right, we'll go back to where we left the trail at Jay Creek. Next leg after that is where they trekked yesterday after Standley Chasm.'

'Where it all went pear-shaped,' Ryan said.

Kane kept his eye on the trail as the bush below got thicker and the landscape became more mountainous. A couple of times he lost the trail and had to ask Connor for the map co-ordinates to circle around and pick it up again.

'Not a soul to be seen,' Ryan commented.

'South-west for ten and then we fly over Standley Chasm,' Kane said.

'Campground and café there. That's where the Feds will be set up,' Connor said. 'I reckon they'll take a bit of interest in us.'

'Worth landing and seeing what we can suss out?' Kane asked.

'No, because there's a chance they'll ground us, and we won't even have looked in the critical area,' Connor said.

'Roger that.'

'Maybe stay a bit higher, but not too high that we can't see.'

Kane looked down as he flew them over the car park at Standley Chasm. 'You're right, mate. You can see something's happening down there.'

Half a dozen four-wheel drives and three police cars were parked close together at the end of the road beside the entrance to the campground.

Kane lifted the bird and pretended not to see as two of the men below gestured for him to land.

'Good move, mate,' Connor said. 'Something's definitely afoot down there.'

Within a minute, the radio crackled. 'Makowa Lodge bird, Makowa Lodge bird, this is NT police, repeat, NT police. Please return to Alice Springs and await instructions.'

Kane turned to Connor and raised his eyebrows. 'Instructions, boss?'

'Don't reply. We can deal with the fallout after we've searched the next bit of the trail.'

'Okay, northwest and we'll double back at the summit of Brinkley Bluff.'

'Where were the bodies? Did Greg have any information on that?'

'They were spotted about four kilometres along the track on the northern side,' Connor replied.

'Ryan, keep a lookout that way,' Kane said.

'Roger.'

The track climbed from Standley Chasm and followed a ridge, and it was easy to see it from the air.

'There,' Ryan called. 'Down there.'

Kane lowered the nose of the chopper and looked to the right. A small group dressed in white overalls were walking through the bush, carrying what looked like two stretchers.

'I'd say that's the couple we first heard about. They've retrieved the bodies,' Connor said. 'Once we do this leg, we'll land somewhere, and I'll call Greg and see what he's heard.' His chuckle held no mirth. 'He'll know by now we've been spotted and challenged.'

'I can't believe Sandra's climbed that,' Kane said as the track below rose steeply to the mountain they were approaching. He peered down and pulled back the speed a little as a movement on the track below caught his attention.

'Connor,' he said urgently. 'About a hundred metres ahead. Can you see? There's someone on the track. I'm going up higher. There's something metallic in his hand.'

Chapter 28

Darwin Waterfront precinct

Dr Emma Langford walked into the coffee shop near the wave pool at the Darwin Waterfront Precinct just before eight a.m. She walked in and ordered her usual caramel latte, and then took the number to an outside table before easing herself carefully down onto the plastic chair. She looked around and smiled; she should have let Jeremy come with her, but when he'd suggested he come with her she'd said, 'No, I can tell my sisters alone.'

The poor sweetheart had been working hard at the hospital as well as dealing with her health issues, and he would have enjoyed sitting here in the sun with her. Anyway, he was on duty at ten, and she didn't want to rush away. It had been ages since she'd had girl time with her sisters. It was a shame Mum was away; she would have enjoyed meeting up with them.

'Thank you.' Emma smiled as the young girl put the coffee on the table in front of her.

'Did you want to order breakfast too?' she asked.

'I will. I'm meeting my sisters and I'm sure we'll eat.'

Emma sipped her coffee and lifted her face to the morning sun. Since yesterday afternoon when she'd made the decision to take some time off work, the world somehow seemed a brighter and sweeter place.

'Aunty Em!' She turned with a smile as James ran across the lawn towards her, followed closely by Ellie and Dru. A surge of love for her sisters brought tears to her eyes, and she blinked them away before Dru could see them.

Standing carefully, she bent down and kissed James' cheek.

'Hey, you pair. What are doing in town so early, Ellie? Are you okay?' Emma stared at her two younger sisters. Both of them were pale and didn't look happy. 'Are you both okay? What's going on?'

'James, you can go and play on the grass and I'll order you some pancakes,' Ellie said quietly.

'With ice-cream too?'

'With ice-cream.' Ellie smiled, but Emma knew her sister well enough to know something was wrong.

'I'll get our drinks, Els,' Dru said after she'd hugged Emma. 'Tea?'

'Yes please. And can you order James' pancakes too, please?'

'Another latte for you, Em?' Dru asked.

'I'm all good but I'm going to order some brekky in a while.' She could sense the girls were skirting around her, and then all of a sudden, she realised why.

'Hang on, you pair. Sit down, Dru, for a minute before you go and order.'

Ellie and Dru looked at each other, but they both sat down.

'You're worrying about what I have to tell you, aren't you?' Emma put her cup down. 'I didn't want to tell you on the phone. It's too important for that. I wanted to share my happy news in person.'

Ellie sat up straight. 'Happy news?'

'Yes, it's good news. The cyst was benign. The down side is, he had to take my ovary, but I've still got one left and I've been given the all clear.'

Shock ran through Emma as Dru grabbed her hand and started to cry.

Dru? Dru never cried.

Tears ran down her youngest sister's face and her bottom lip shook as she stared at Emma.

Ellie got up and came around and put her arms around Emma and kissed her cheek again. 'Thank God.' She moved across to Dru and put a hand on her shoulder. 'Come on, Dru. It's good news. Don't cry.'

Emma caught the look that passed between Dru and Ellie as Dru took a deep shuddering breath.

'You two are scaring me. Is Dee okay? Is there something else wrong?'

'Can you get me a cup of tea while I talk to Em?' Dru asked Ellie.

'Sure, keep an eye on James for me. Won't be long.' Ellie patted Dru's shoulder as she headed for the counter. She turned at the door. 'And Em, that is the best news *ever*.'

'Okay, Dru. Spill. I can't remember the last time I saw you cry.'

'I was just overwhelmed. Knowing that you're okay is such a relief, and I can tell you something I've been holding back.'

'You're pregnant. I know.' Emma sat back and folded her arms and she knew her smile was smug.

'Ellie told you?'

'No. I just knew by looking at you. The day we went to see Dee. I know that glow, plus you had boobs.'

'Ha ha. Dr Smarty Pants.' Dru folded her arms and rolled her eyes.

'That's more our Dru.' Emma chuckled. 'I'm happy for you, Dru. When are you due?'

'September. I wanted to tell you, but didn't want you to know when you had that bloody diagnosis hanging over you.'

Ellie came back and sat down. She held three menus. 'I'm starving. So, what did you tell Emma?'

'What she already knew,' Dru said.

Ellie put the menus on the table and looked at Dru. 'She already knew? About what?'

Emma narrowed her eyes. 'Is there something else I don't know? Are you okay, Ellie? I wondered why you were in town so early.'

Dru and Ellie looked at each other.

'Okay, now you're worrying me. What's going on?'

Emma held herself still waiting for what was coming.

'I'm in town because Kane and Connor and Ryan have gone down to—' Ellie paused. 'They've gone down to the Larapinta trail to try and find Mum.'

'What! Find her?'

Heads turned in the outdoor coffee area as Emma yelled.

She lowered her voice. 'What do you mean find Mum?'

'There's been problems on the trek, and no one can get in touch with any of the trekkers.'

'It's not been on the news. Did they call you?'

'No, Em. It's hush hush.' Dru spoke quietly. 'Connor learned about it through his security business. We don't know what's happened, so they've gone down there to try to help.'

'Oh, God. I feel so guilty. I was so wrapped up in my own worry, I actually let one of her calls go to voicemail while I was waiting for my results. What the hell's happened?'

Dru and Ellie took Emma through the whole story, and as much as they knew. Emma felt sick by the time they'd finished. She reached over and pushed away the menu Ellie had put in front of her. 'I can't eat now.'

'Me either,' Dru said.

'How about I get James' pancakes to take away, and we'll go back to your apartment, Dru?' Ellie stood and went over to the grassed area where James was playing with his cars.

'Yes, I'd like to be near the computer in case Greg sends anything through. Do you have to work today, Em?'

Emma shook her head, still trying to process that their mother could be in danger. 'No, I'm on sick leave for another week, and then I've decided to work part-time to give my body a chance to heal and get my hormone imbalance sorted. I'll call Jeremy and then stay at your place until we hear something. If that's okay?'

'Of course, it's okay, I wouldn't want it any other way,' Dru said.

Chapter 29

Hope

Sandra focused on breathing in and out evenly as the noise grew louder. She put her hands over her ears and fought the rising panic. Was she really hearing that overpowering noise or was it the pulse in her head? She'd experienced that when she was recovering after Peter's death. The panic built and her chest tightened as she struggled to block the sound. An ache rose from her stomach and settled behind her breastbone, and she dragged in breath after breath until she saw stars. She reached for her water bottle and unscrewed the lid and drained the bottle, but still, she couldn't calm herself.

She looked up to the track again but there was still no sign of Graysen. An eagle wheeled high on the thermals above the mountain to the north and she focused on the large bird, trying to calm herself as the noise in her head began to recede. Eventually her breathing slowed, and as the noise faded away to almost nothing she looked up to the trail, but there was still no sign of Graysen.

What if Zed had been up there all the time sitting, waiting, for them? What if he'd pushed Graysen over the edge?

A whimper escaped Sandra's throat and she was ashamed of herself for being such a coward. Her heart thudded in time with the faint noise in her head.

She took a deep breath, screwed the cap back on her water bottle and put it into her backpack. She took out one of the jubes and put it on her tongue hoping the sugar hit would make her feel better. She closed her eyes as the sweetness filled her mouth.

A pebble rolled nearby and Sandra jumped, turning her head from side to side and then looking up. Graysen's head appeared above and her relief was sweet as he hurried down to her. She was so ashamed of her sudden weakness; she wasn't going to tell him how close she'd come to losing it.

'Quick, come up with me,' he said. 'There's a helicopter coming. We need to be up on the trail. I think they're turning around and coming back.'

She stood suddenly and put one hand to her head as her head spun.

Graysen grabbed for her. 'Don't faint on me now, love.'

Her head stopped spinning as he held her close and the steady thud of his heart calmed her more. He reached down and slipped her pack over his shoulders with his.

'Are you right to climb up that last fifty metres? I want them to see us both.'

Her strength was retuning, but so was her fear. 'Are you sure it's safe? It's not Zed and Miska?'

'I'm sure it's a search helicopter. I could see three men in it. It's not them.'

As Graysen helped Sandra up the last of the incline to the track, the loud thudding noise filled the air around them as the helicopter approached.

It hadn't been in her head; she felt foolish, but relieved.

'Quick, we're almost there. Even if they don't see us, I can see Standley Chasm ahead. We can walk there in about half an hour.'

'Yes, I could see those low serrated peaks from where I was sitting.' Calm kicked in as Sandra started to feel normal again.

The thudding got louder, and the air seemed to vibrate around them as they reached the bank at the top of the incline. Graysen held out both hands to help Sandra up the last step to the trail.

As she lifted her head, a yellow helicopter approached, hovering low and moving closer to them every second.

Sandra squinted as she looked up and she put her hands up to shade the sun from her face. 'What on earth? It's Ellie's helicopter. Not hers, I mean. It's the one she flew at Yellow Water. At the lodge where she worked.'

'There's probably a few up there now,' Graysen said. 'It looks like they've started searching for us.'

'That's the only one we've seen, and we haven't heard any the rest of the time we've been out.'

The helicopter came lower, hovering over them, and a man leaned out of the passenger side, gesturing ahead along the trail.

Sandra's mouth dropped open and she yelled and jumped up and down, waving her arms. 'Connor!' She grabbed Graysen's arm. 'I don't understand it, and I can't believe it but that's my son-in-law. In fact, I think it's my sons-in law and stepson. Kane's a pilot, like Ellie.'

'Your sons-in-law? Don't they live in Darwin?'

'Yes. I have no idea what's happening.' The sound was deafening now and they had to yell over it to hear each other speak.

'The company must have contacted our families when we didn't turn up last night.'

'It's too quick,' Graysen said. 'They wouldn't have had time to get here. Look, they're landing a bit ahead where the track widens out. That's what he was pointing at. I still think we need to keep out of sight. If anything is going to draw attention to where we are, and Zed and Miska are still around, that helicopter will have got their attention.'

***

'She looks okay.' Kane brought the bird in to land on the wide flat section of the trail he'd spotted about five hundred metres away from Sandra and the man. 'Connor, get on your sat phone and let the girls know she's okay.'

'Right, I'll be brief.'

'Hang on a minute, we need to find out what's happened first and who he is. And maybe we need to make sure she's safe with him,' Ryan said.

'Let's give it five minutes, and we'll see what's going on.'

'We don't know who he is, so keep your wits about you when we get out of the chopper,' Connor warned.

Kane killed the engine and they waited until the rotor slowed. Connor jumped out and ran in a half-crouch, followed quickly by Ryan. Kane wasn't far behind them, and he kept his eyes on the man that Sandra was clinging to.

They hurried along the track towards them, and Connor was the first to reach her. Sandra let go of the guy and fell into Connor's arms; Kane could see the smile on Sandra's face from where he was.

'What an earth are you all doing here? How did you know that we needed help?' She reached for Ryan and he held her until Kane reached them.

Sandra hugged Kane, but the guy behind her spoke. 'It's not safe here. We need to get out of sight. Maybe one of you can stay here with me while I explain what's going on, and you can take Sandra back to safety at Standley Chasm.'

Kane looked at Connor as Sandra turned.

'Graysen, this is Kane, Connor, and Ryan. Boys, this is Graysen Hughes, who's kept me safe since—'

'Good to meet you all,' Graysen interrupted Sandra. 'Look we really have to get off the track. We've got a badly injured guide down there, and there's a guy with a high-powered rifle.'

'It's okay,' Kane reassured him. 'We've been up the trail another three kilometres, and back as far as the Old Telegraph Station, and up to the old Homestead. There's no sign of anyone on the trail at all. It's busy with police down at Standley Chasm, and we saw them carrying someone out about a kilometre back.'

'Look, to cut to the chase, we need to get back to safety,' Connor said. 'We know what's going on and you're right, it's dangerous. The main thing we need to do is to get you pair into the chopper and away from here.'

Graysen shook his head. 'No, I'll stay here. I have to show you where to go. We've got another couple, and one of our guides with fairly serious injuries about four kilometres into the bush.' He paused and looked at Kane. 'I think the best thing would be if you take Sandra back to Standley Chasm, and one of you stays with her to make sure she's safe, and then you come back, and I'll guide you to the others.'

'Fair enough,' Kane said. 'Is there anywhere we can land close to them? Ryan, I'll get you to come with me and Sandra, and Connor can stay here and fill Graysen in.'

Ryan nodded. 'I'll take care of her.'

Graysen gestured down the southern side of the escarpment. 'I sussed it out on our way out this morning, but it was pretty dark when we left. There's a flat sandy bit at the end of the one of the gorges fairly close to them. I think it would be firm enough to land on.'

Kane raised his eyebrows as Graysen turned back to Sandra and put his arms around her.

'I'll be back with you soon. You stay safe. Don't trust anyone. Maybe don't talk to anyone until I get back? If they insist, pretend to be too upset or crook. Okay?'

Kane and Connor exchanged a look as Sandra put her arms around his neck and lifted her face to his. She brushed her lips over Graysen's. 'You be careful. Come back to me as quick as you can. It's going to be strange without you.'

Fast worker, Kane thought.

'You'll be fine. You've got someone to look after you. We'll be quick. We'll have to do it in two trips, but we'll be back soon.' Graysen turned to Ryan. 'Do you have a phone? There's service at Standley Chasm.'

'I do.'

'Ring for an ambulance and let them know that Andrew, the guide, has facial, mouth, and head injuries as well as a suspected broken rib. They should be able to be there from Alice Springs before we get back.'

'Should we take him straight to the hospital?' Kane asked, impressed with the cool organisation of this Graysen guy.

'I think we're best not to have him in the air for too long. I don't think he's got a bad concussion, but I'm not a medico. Jenny, the other woman with us, was a detective and she's got all her emergency care quals. She thinks he's okay, but let's get the paramedics waiting for him as quick as we can.'

'Right, sounds like we need to get moving.' Kane held his hand out to Sandra. 'You right to go, Sandra?'

She looked hesitantly from him to Graysen, and when Graysen nodded, she took Kane's hand. 'Yes, the sooner we go, the quicker Andrew will get help.'

***

Graysen stood with Connor as the helicopter lifted off and turned in a wide arc and headed back to Standley Chasm with Ryan and Sandra on board.

Connor's expression was cool and assessing, and as soon as the noise of the helicopter receded, his first question came as a surprise.

'So, Graysen, what's the go between you and Sandra?'

Graysen pushed back the anger that threatened to rise. There was more important information to share than his relationship with Sandra.

'The go?' His voice was equally cool.

'Yes, there's obviously something going on.'

'I'm sure Sandra will share what she wants to with you when she's ready. But be assured, I think very highly of your mother-in-law, and I've done all I could to protect her over the past horrendous days.'

Connor nodded. 'Fair enough.'

'We joined the tour together and we were buddied up. We've got to know each other well in a short time,' he said by way of explanation. 'Now I don't know how much you know, but yesterday one of our trekkers was killed by one of the others on the tour. Three others are missing, and Sandra and I took off into the bush. Andrew, the guide, stumbled into the gorge where we were holed up yesterday, and then last night, Clive and Jenny, the other older couple turned up.' He drew a breath. 'I'm assuming that it's got out on the news when none of us turned up at Birthday Waterhole last night. Jodie must have reported us missing.'

'Jodie's one of the guides?' Connor asked.

'Yes, and the chef on the trek.' Graysen ran his hand through his hair. 'God, it seems like days since we were walking and camping at night. It's only been thirty-six hours since I saw him kill Maggie.'

'You witnessed it?'

'Yes, through the zoom lens of my camera.'

'You said, "him"?'

'Yes, his name was Zed, but I doubt if that's his real name. We think it was a contract killing, but the thing is we don't know who the target was supposed to be. Maggie is the only one that we're sure is dead. I think Sandra was even worried that she might have been in his sights at one stage.'

'Okay.' Connor unbuttoned his shirt pocket and took out a small satellite phone. 'Before I tell you what we know, what was that woman's name?'

'Maggie. Margaret Ferguson. From Sydney.'

'Excuse me a moment.' Connor turned away, but Graysen could hear his conversation.

'Greg, we've found Sandra and one of the other trekkers. We're about to take the chopper and retrieve three more. One's injured.'

A pause.

'Yes, she's fine, and yes, I know, we saw them bringing them out. Two of them. Anything else?'

Graysen was surprised when Connor chuckled. 'Yeah, that was us. They told us to land immediately, but Kane ignored the radio. Listen, the target could be a Margaret Ferguson. Yes, from Sydney, that's the one. Rightio mate, over and out. I'll talk to you when we either get back to Standley Chasm—depends what plays out there—or when we get back to the airport at Alice Springs.'

Graysen stared at Connor. 'You're Sandra's son-in law?'

'Yes. Dru, her daughter, is my wife.' Connor's look was challenging.

'Who else are you? Who were you talking to, and how do you know all that? And who else did you see brought out? Two what?'

'You're pretty astute, mate. Look I'll fill you in, but it's not to be shared, okay?'

Graysen hesitated and then nodded.

'I'm ex-Federal Police and I now have my own security business. Yesterday, my colleague came across some communications between Interpol and the Feds. Greg knew Sandra was on a trek, and he confirmed it was the one she was on. The first information we got was that there had been two fatalities, and I assume that's the two bodies we saw being carried out about a kilometre back towards the Chasm when we flew over the track. No one knows about the woman you said was shot.'

'She was. I witnessed it. It was a clean head shot and then Zed's partner pushed her over the escarpment.'

'If you saw that, you're in danger, and by association, so's Sandra.'

'We've already figured that out. We guessed that they were going after the rest of us. Whether that was their plan all along, or something went wrong, we don't know.'

'That remains to be seen. Now, just so you know, when we get back to Standley Chasm, we're gonna play this very low-key. Nobody knows what's happened, it's not on the news, and the Feds have closed the place down. They are obviously doing everything they can to get this pair before they get away, but Greg—my colleague—and I think, they've slipped through the net already.'

'And you know all this for sure?'

'Yes, and I'm sorry to tell you, that at the camp you were supposed to meet at, they've found two bodies out there.'

'Oh, fuck,' Graysen said. 'Jodie and the other guide.'

'We assume so. There was no truck there, and the Feds found it burnt out at the beginning of the Mereenie Loop. That's the back road to Kings Canyon. They've obviously stolen another vehicle, and I'd say they're long gone. I wouldn't be surprised if they were out of the country by now. Interpol are looking at all the flights. If they identify them and find them on a flight, they might be able to apprehend them at their destination.'

'And you all know all this how?'

'Better off not to know, Graysen.'

'Who are these people?'

'Cold ruthless killers who'll stop at nothing, so you and Sandra and the others need to be very careful.'

They both turned as the sound of the returning helicopter came from the distance and Connor spoke quickly.

'One more thing you need to know. As far as anyone we talk to at Standley Chasm knows, the three of us were just on a flight across the trail and we saw you and Sandra waving for help. I won't be disclosing that we knew anything. Absolute coincidence that it was our mother-in-law.'

'Unbelievable.' Graysen nodded slowly. 'I can keep my mouth shut.'

They waited for the helicopter to land, but before they boarded, Graysen put his hand on Connor's arm. 'You said two bodies were brought out?'

'Yep.'

'But there were three together who went missing. Maybe one of them was involved too?'

'I'll get the names off you and let Greg know when we land. He can follow that up when they get the bodies to the Chasm, and we know who it is. Who were the three?

'A young married couple on the trek and an indigenous guide.'

'Right, let's go.' Connor put his head down and they ran for the waiting chopper.

Chapter 30

Return to Standley Chasm

Ryan had been super-protective of Sandra since they'd arrived at the Chasm. As luck had it, three helicopters had circled the campground, and Kane had landed on a flat area behind the hill about five hundred metres along the road from the highway and dropped them off.

'Are you right to walk in, Sandra? I can get out and help Ryan get you there.'

'No, I'm fine. That flat road is a walk in the park compared to the past few days. You go. Andrew is the priority. If you have to explain everything, it'll slow you down getting to him. I'll handle it.'

'Okay. Stay safe. Just remember we weren't down here looking for you. The three of us were on a scenic flight over the trail.'

'Got it. Now, go!'

'Yes, ma'am! It's good to see you. Ryan, I think you can make that call now.'

As they walked slowly along the road to the campground, Ryan pulled out his phone.

'I'll quickly text the girls to tell them you're fine and then after I've called the paramedics, we'll call them back.' He put his arm around her shoulder as soon as the text was sent.

As they walked, Ryan dialled triple zero and reported that an injured trekker was being conveyed to the Standley Chasm campground.

'All done. Now let's get you to some food.'

'And a loo,' Sandra said.

'You're amazing, you know that? We know a bit of what you've been through, but you look as fresh as a daisy.'

'I'd kill for a shower, a meal, and a nice hot cup of tea.'

'We'll get that sorted as soon as we face the welcome committee ahead.'

Sandra looked up. Two men in work shirts and cargo shorts were running towards them.

The men stopped as Ryan and Sandra approached them.

'The campground is closed due to an incident,' the taller of the two said. 'Do you have any identification?'

'I do.' Ryan pulled out his wallet. 'But I'd prefer to leave it until we get my stepmother to help.'

'What's the problem?' the second guy asked.

Sandra pulled herself straight. 'The problem is that I've been lost out there in the bush for the past day and a half. My sons happened to be down here for work, and saw my partner and I on the trail. They've gone back to get the rest of us, and one of the guides is badly injured. Ryan's called for help, and hopefully an ambulance is on the way.'

'I think you'd better come with us.'

'I'm happy to, but first I need a shower and a cup of tea, and some painkillers.'

'You're hurt?'

Sandra made her voice shake. 'No, I'm dehydrated, and I'm starving and I have a thumping headache.' She pretended to stumble and Ryan grabbed for her.

'Help me, please,' he said. 'We'll make a carry chair and get her to help.'

Sandra lowered her head and closed her eyes.

'Step back please, sir. Your name, ma'am?'

'Sandra Porter.'

'Right, thank you. Four-hand seat carry. We'll have you to the facilities shortly, Mrs Porter.' The two men positioned themselves behind Sandra, and she looked over her shoulder to see what they were doing. They faced each other as one grasped his left wrist with his right hand, and then reached for the other man's right wrist with his left hand forming a seat. Before she knew it, she was being conveyed to the campground, with Ryan by her side.

She hadn't realised how exhausted she was as she finally gave in to her tiredness. There was no need for pretence.

##

Half an hour later, Ryan and Sandra were sitting in the café with a member of the Federal Police force. She'd been to the amenities; Ryan had been waiting outside for her and walked her over to the café where they were now preparing a meal for her. Their rescuers—or whoever they were—had given her a towel and a hair brush, and a clean khaki shirt. Sandra had been to the toilet, washed her face and hands and brushed her hair, but her hands wouldn't stop shaking.

As she lifted the tea cup, it sloshed over into the saucer.

'We'll leave you to rest, Mrs Porter.' The tall man who'd identified himself as Jake Sandhurst stood and pushed his chair in. 'When the others come back, if you're up to it, we'll interview you and take a formal statement.'

Sandra nodded. 'Thank you, I appreciate your consideration.'

The trail was closed, but there were still campers at the campground. A middle-aged couple were having lunch at a table across from them, and the woman looked at Sandra curiously before she leaned across and whispered to her husband.

Sandra looked away.

'We've allocated one of the empty cabins to you, if you'd like to have some rest and some privacy before the others come back,' the policeman said, looking across at the couple.

'Thank you.'

He handed a key to Ryan. 'Number twelve, the second one along.' His eyes narrowed. 'Look after her. It was an incredible coincidence, wasn't it? That you found her?'

Ryan's expression was as innocent as a child's. 'It was. We knew Sandra was here on a trek, but we had no idea what had happened. We couldn't believe it when we saw them on the trail and realised it was her.'

Jake nodded and walked down the stone stairs and across to the tent that had been set up near the police vehicles.

Sandra tried to lift the cup again, but her hand was still shaking and she gave up. Ryan smiled at her and lifted the cup and held it to her mouth.

'You're a good boy,' she said. She drank as he held the cup and indicated that she'd had enough. The woman across from them was staring now. Sandra stared back, and then turned to Ryan. 'How's Dee? Is she sick of herself yet?'

Ryan's rugged cheeks flushed a dull red. 'Shit. Sorry, I mean damn. We'd better ring the girls back. They'll be on edge. But I'll ring Dee first, and you can have a very quick talk to her.'

Before Sandra could speak, he'd called on his mobile. 'Dee, Sandra's with me and she's fine. Can you talk to her quickly, before we ring the others? She asked how you were. I thought you could tell her.'

Sandra took the phone as Ryan handed it over. 'Hello Dee, how are you, darling?'

'I'm very well, Sandra. I'm feeling good. When will you be home?'

'Soon.'

'Good, you can meet your two new grandsons.'

When Sandra looked up, there were tears in Ryan's eyes. She smiled at him as her eyes filled. 'I knew I shouldn't have come away, but oh, darling, I'm so happy for you. You're all well?'

'We are. Still in the hospital, but the boys are making wonderful progress. I've got to go, but I'll see you soon. Love you, Sandra. I'm so pleased you're okay. We were all worried.'

'See you soon. I'd better call the girls now.'

Sandra passed the phone back to Ryan and gripped his hand. 'I'm so happy for you both, Ryan. Dee sounds good.'

'It's been a pretty special time,' he said.

'And you need to get back to your family. Now, can you dial Ellie first for me? I know she'll be home.'

Ryan smiled. 'They're all at Dru's apartment. The Porter girls have been amazing, Sandra, but they *were* worried.'

Ryan began to press the buttons on his phone, but Sandra's attention was taken by the sneer on the woman's face at the table across from them.

'Typical, isn't it? Look at him. Drunk at lunchtime! And after all we do for them. Last time we're coming to the Red Centre, Albert.'

Sandra turned to see who she was looking at. She jumped to her feet, and called out loudly, 'Help! Help him. Ryan quick.'

She took off as P.D. lurched down the three bottom steps that led up to the trail. One arm dangled uselessly by his side and one side of his face was a mess of grazes and bruising. He fell head-first on to the ground and lay there.

Chapter 31

Back to Alice

The rest of that day was a blur for Sandra. The highlight of the afternoon was Graysen stepping out of the helicopter. He came straight to her and took her into his arms. They were interviewed together—Graysen had insisted—and it appeared that the coincidence of the arrival of her family was accepted, albeit reluctantly.

Fragments of information surfaced through the afternoon. She cried when she heard that Paul and Cecily's bodies had been retrieved. Andrew had been taken to Alice Springs hospital as had P.D. They were both in the intensive care ward. The opinion of the Federal Police was that Zed and Miska were long gone.

'We're working in the dark,' Jake had told them. 'We have no photographs of them. Any that were taken by your group were all on phones that were destroyed in the torching of the truck. For the next few weeks at least, I'd like you to be vigilant. Both of you, Clive and Jenny, and the two guides are the only ones who can identify them.' Jenny and Clive had been interviewed too.

Eventually, they were all allowed to leave, but Jake Sandhurst told them that they would be in touch again.

'Where will you be, Mr Hughes? I noticed that you have no permanent address.'

Sandra's insides had curled when Graysen looked at her and answered him. 'I'll be in Darwin.'

'One last thing,' Jake said. 'We know that the target was Margaret Ferguson.'

Sandra caught her breath. 'Oh, Maggie. Poor Maggie.'

'Her husband is "assisting" us with our enquiries.' He exchanged a look with Graysen.

They waited at Standley Chasm while Kane flew Jenny and Clive to Alice Springs. Ryan went with them and was collecting the car they'd hired and driving them to the hotel where'd they'd all met only a few days ago.

'It seems like a lifetime, doesn't it' Sandra commented as she and Graysen and Connor sat together in the café waiting for Kane to come back. She had just had a long conversation with her three girls, and James too.

Graysen hadn't let go of her hand since they'd sat down. She'd finally stopped shaking, and after talking to the girls, was feeling much better.

'A lifetime of events has happened. I can't believe it.' Once her girls had calmed down and stopped crying, they hadn't been able to hold back. 'And none of you boys said a word, Connor.'

'What's happened?' Graysen asked moving his leg against hers. She knew how he felt; she didn't want him to go out of her sight and took every opportunity to touch him, squeeze his hand, or hold his gaze.

'Well, in a nutshell. I have two new grandsons, two babies on the way—only one of which I knew about—and a daughter who's been ill and didn't tell any of us until she got the all-clear!'

Connor leaned forward. 'Ryan, Kane, and I were sworn to secrecy. Anyway, Sandra, you'll be home with them all tonight.'

'No. I'm not going back today.'

'Ryan's going to book a commercial flight so there's room for you.'

'No. I'm driving back with Graysen. We'll stay at the hotel tonight. Get our gear sorted. What's left of it anyway, and then we'll drive to Darwin tomorrow, or maybe even the next day. Depends how we're both feeling. Isn't that right. Graysen?'

Sandra bit back a smile at Graysen's expression. A mix of surprise, happiness and innocence—for Connor's benefit, she suspected—flitted across his face.

'Yes,' he said seriously. 'That was our plan.'

Connor hesitated, obviously thought better of arguing, and then replied. 'Okay, I'll let Ryan know he doesn't have to book a flight.'

'He has a family he needs to get home to,' Sandra said. 'You all have your families, and I'm honoured to be a part of it, but you have your own lives to live. I'll see you all in a day or so.'

Graysen squeezed her hand, and she ran her thumb lightly across the back of his warm skin. She thought back to the conversation she'd had with Frank, her investment adviser, and the reason she'd first decided to trek the Larapinta Trail.

It had been time to make some changes and make a life for herself. The future beckoned now. Who knew what this relationship with Graysen would develop into? All Sandra knew was that she had achieved her goal. She had found herself, and the bonus of a new friendship along the way.

'Despite the horrid events of the past few days, I have no regrets.' Graysen held her eyes.

'No regrets at all,' she said quietly.

Crowne Plaza

Graysen was as nervous as a teenage boy on his first date. Sandra had shocked him when they checked in at the Crowne Plaza. As they'd walked across to the reception desk together, after parking the hire car that Ryan had left with them, she had looked up at him.

'Just book one room, Graysen. I don't want to be myself yet.'

He'd swallowed and wondered what to do as they approached the desk. To his relief, he was able to get a two-bedroom suite. He didn't want to presume, and he didn't want Sandra to feel insulted, but that way he'd covered all bases.

She was quiet as they travelled up in the elevator with the suitcase Sandra had left in storage at the hotel before the trek, and Graysen's pack and camera bags. Sandra carried the small pack she'd used on the trek.

Graysen used the security card to open the door and she crossed the room to the window and let out a sigh. 'Luxury!'

'Air conditioning,' he said with a smile.

'And a bathroom with a bath. Which is where I am going to spend the next two hours.'

'And then I'd like to take you downstairs for that special dinner I promised you. What do you think of that?'

'Dinner sounds lovely, but could we maybe do room service on the balcony? I think I'd like to be more private.'

'That sounds like a better idea. And I promise we'll have a better meal than jubes and apples and water.'

'Don't think that was bad, Graysen. It was the company that made the night for me.'

He held himself still as she walked over and put her arms around his neck.

'One thing this trek taught me'—her lips quivered—'especially Maggie, and Paul and Cecily, is that life is precious, but so uncertain and there's no point wasting time. Do you remember what you said to me this morning as we set off?'

'I do, and your response made me blush.'

She moved in closer to him, and her breasts pressed against his shirt. 'Tell me what you were worried about, *Danny*.' Her voice lowered to a whisper.

'I was worried about leading you astray, *Sandy*.'

'And I said?'

'Maybe not today, but being led astray does sound tempting.'

'Whoever would have thought it would be today?' she said.

Graysen bent and leaned in to her lips, but Sandra stepped back.

'No, we are going to do this properly. I'm going to run a neck-deep bubble bath, and you're going to open a bottle of champagne, and bring me a glass.'

She turned and twirled with a sexy smile, and he thought he had never seen anything so beautiful as this woman in a khaki shirt, dusty shorts and trekking boots.

Sandra opened the bathroom door, and her smile was seductive. 'Oh, look what's in here. You'd better get two glasses. It's a bath for two!'

##

By the time their dinner was delivered, it was almost ten p.m. The hours had passed quickly with an hour-long shared bath, a bottle of champagne, and a very enjoyable interlude of being led astray in a soft and luxury king-sized bed.

Sandra yawned and pulled the plush bathrobe close around her as Graysen held out the platter of cheese that had followed their meal. They each wore one of the soft bathrobes that came with what Sandra had discovered was the luxury suite.

'I'm glad we're facing this way,' Sandra said as she looked up at the brilliant star-studded sky. Her eyes were heavy and she forced them wide to take in the beautiful vista above them. The balcony overlooked the McDonnell Range, but they faced the east, and not the west where they had spent the days of the trek.

'To see the sunrise? We never got to Mt Sonder,' Graysen said. 'Will we come back and see that one day?'

'No. I don't think I could trek here again, too many sad memories. That's why I'm pleased we're looking away from the trail.' She shook her head as he passed the cheese plate again. 'But I have read about a couple of tracks in New Zealand that might be good.'

'As long as you let me come with you,' he said.

'That's a given.' Sandra yawned again. 'Sorry.'

Graysen stood and held out his hand and she took it. His fingers wrapped around hers and she smiled.

'Now I know we've got two rooms—'

'Yes?'

'Which bed are we going to share?'

Sandra smiled. 'You choose, but I do have one thing to say.'

'What's that?' Graysen's arm looped over her shoulder as they walked inside.

'I have a wonderful king-sized bed in my apartment and if you're coming to Darwin, I'd like you to stay with me.

However, unfortunately, my guest room is set up as a sewing room, so there's only one bed.'

'Hmm,' he said. 'I guess we'll have to share then. What about your girls?'

'No,' she said cheekily. 'There's not enough room for them.'

Chapter 32

Two months later-Darwin

'Sandra, have you seen my lens cloth?'

'I put it on your camera bag last night.'

'Ah, I can see it. I was having a boys' look.'

Sandra smiled. One of the things she'd discovered about Graysen over the past two months he'd been staying at her apartment was that he was disorganised. She'd never picked that on the trek when they'd first met. He'd been good for her, because she knew she spent too much time having everything in the right place and not being able to go out unless the apartment was perfectly clean and tidy. She'd also discovered he was impetuous, and a spur of the moment person, like the morning he'd woken up beside her and said, 'Let's go to Bali today!'

Just as well she'd got her passport. They'd been over there in time for dinner. Sandra had learned to be flexible, and with her newfound independence and Graysen living with her, their life together was very happy.

Her phone rang, and she walked into the bedroom and took it off the charger beside the bed.

'Hey, Els.' Sandra sat on the bed ready to settle in for a chat. 'How are you, sweetie?'

'Fat and bored stiff.'

Sandra chuckled. 'It's going to get worse before it gets better.'

'Mum? You know how you said with that couple who did all the stuff on the trek no one could identify them because there were no photos?'

'Yes, that's right.' The usual dread settled in Sandra's chest. 'They've got clean away, and Jake and Greg both say they'll be back in Europe by now. It makes my blood boil that they killed five people and got away with it.'

'Mum, listen, I think you better ring that Federal Police guy. I was bored and I was cleaning out my old texts and you sent me a photo of everyone sitting around a campfire. There's two young couples in it and all their faces are really clear.'

'Really. Oh, wow. I'd better call Jake. Can you text it to me now?'

'Done.'

'Thanks, love. Now you take care of yourself and we'll see you at Dee and Ryan's on Saturday night.'

'I will. Say hello to Graysen for me.'

Sandra's phone pinged with the incoming text as she disconnected the call.

Her fingers were shaking and she went to open it, and then she decided not to.

'Graysen? Are you still there?'

'Yeah. I'm in the kitchen. Do you want a ham and cheese toastie?'

'No, thanks.' She stood by the door and waited until he turned.

'Sandra? What's wrong? Who was on the phone? Is everyone all right?'

'Yes, everything's okay. It was Ellie. She was cleaning up her phone and she had a photo that I'd forgotten I took.'

Graysen rinsed his hands and came over and held her. 'What's it a photo of? You're as pale as anything.'

'Remember the night we camped out? At Simpsons Gap and there was that beautiful sky?'

He nodded. 'I do.'

'I took a photo of the sky that night and I sent it to Ellie. It also had the campfire and everyone in it. Apparently, the faces are really clear. I'd totally forgotten about it. I can't bring myself to look at them. Not now. Knowing what they did.'

Her hands shook as she handed over the phone to him.

Sandra felt sick as Graysen stared at the phone. 'I think we'd better ring Jake Sandhurst. This is gold, Sandra. They'll be able to run those photos worldwide.'

'I might ring Connor too. What do you think?'

'Try Jake first. I'm still a bit uneasy with how Greg and Connor work on the fringes.'

Sandra's hands were shaking as she pulled up Jake on speed dial. He'd been in touch a few times since they'd been back, but there'd been no developments.

Jake's phone rang out and she left a message. 'Jake, it's Sandra Porter. I need to talk to you asap I've got a photo I took.'

Graysen looked worried. 'No luck?'

'No.'

'Okay, give Connor a call, and see what he thinks. Greg can probably start running the photo in his dark databases. The sooner they're locked up, the happier I'll be.'

'Can you call him? I don't feel so good.'

Graysen put his arm around her and Sandra rested her head on his shoulder. 'Connor. It's Graysen. We need some advice, mate. Sandra's got a photo of the killers. She'd forgotten she took it, and Ellie had it on her phone. She's called Jake, but he's not picking up.'

Graysen nodded as he listened. 'Yes, that's what we thought. Okay text his number to Sandra and we'll send it now.'

Her phone pinged immediately. 'That's Greg's mobile number. Are you okay if I send it now?'

She nodded.

Graysen's fingers flew over the keys as he texted the photo that Ellie had sent. 'Okay, all done. How about a cuppa? You look awful.'

'Thanks, darling. I feel awful.'

'A cuppa coming up.'

Before the jug had boiled Sandra's phone rang. There was no caller ID number and she frowned.

She picked it up as Graysen picked up the jug and poured the hot water over her teabag.

'Hello?'

'Sandra. I want you to listen very, very carefully. It's Greg. Is Graysen there with you?'

Sandra swallowed. 'He is, why?'

'I got the text and I'm running the photo. I've already got two hits under two different names, but you don't need to worry about that. Can you please put your phone on speaker so Graysen can hear?'

'Just a minute.' Sandra's fingers were shaking so much, she missed the speaker icon the first time she stabbed at it. 'Okay, it's on.'

'Listen to me. Your new phone has a bug on it. Not a physical one, but it's tagged so that all of your calls and texts are being listened to. I'd say yours is too, Graysen, and Jenny and Clive's. I've found them, and IDed them and I've put an electronic marker on the phone that's tracing yours. That means that they are listening to this conversation too. And by the look of things, they're almost to your address already. Hello, Zed and Miska, I hope you rot in hell. Graysen, I want you guys to leave your phones behind and get the hell out of your apartment. Now. Go somewhere where's there's a landline and call Connor and he'll patch me through. I've called the Feds and the local police, and they're on their way. Now get the hell out of there, and walk, don't take your car. It's probably tagged too.'

Sandra put her hand over her mouth as shock and fear hit her stomach and her bladder. 'I have to go to the loo.'

'No, we don't have time.'

'I *have* to. I'll run.'

Graysen's hand did the frustrated hair thing, but she ran to the bathroom. As she went to flush the toilet, there was a knock at the apartment door, and she froze.

Graysen's voice outside the door was low. 'Come on Sandra, we'll go over the balcony. They're at the door already.'

Her hands were shaking, her lips felt frozen and her legs didn't want to work. All she could think of was, is this what Peter felt like when he knew he was going to die?

'Come on, sweetheart. You can do it.' The balcony was off the main bedroom and about two metres off ground level.

Graysen opened the door and stopped dead. Sandra looked past him. A tall woman with a white blonde crewcut was sitting on the balcony on one of the chairs. For a moment, relief flooded through Sandra, and then she backed away as Miska's voice came from this unfamiliar face.

'Sweet, sexy Graysen, why don't you go and let Zed in, and I'll talk to your lovely Sandra. How sweet is it that you've found each other? Is she a good fuck?'

Sandra ran into the bedroom as Graysen tried to engage Miska. 'You might as well leave now. The police are on the way.'

'We have three minutes,' Miska said in a cold voice, 'and we don't leave unfinished business. After we deal with you two, we'll go and visit the lovely Ellie and then deal with Connor and Greggie boy. They've impressed us. They're very clever.'

When Sandra heard the bitch say she was going to Ellie, she stood straight and walked into her wardrobe. Reaching into the high Italian leather boots that had sat there unworn for the past five years, she retrieved what she was looking for.

Someone was still pounding on the front door, and Miska was talking to Graysen as if they were at a friendly social function. Sandra did what she had to, and then walked back to the balcony door.

'Ah, here she is.' Miska lifted the handgun that was sitting in her lap.

Graysen's back was to Sandra as she lifted the pistol from behind her back and fired directly into Miska's face. The boom deafened her, so she wasn't sure if the pounding on the door had stopped, or if she simply couldn't hear it. She walked over and stood looking down at the sightless eyes. 'No one threatens the ones I love,' she said.

Graysen turned and gently took the gun from Sandra as the sound of sirens reverberated through the air.

Epilogue

Sandra stood on the wide veranda and looked out over the beautiful lawn. Graysen was down near the front gate hosing his beloved plants. The lawn and gardens were a joy to look at, and she was proud of Graysen for what he'd achieved since they'd sold her apartment and bought this house together.

She'd spent all day yesterday cooking, and not left the kitchen until ten o'clock last night, preparing for the day and excitement bubbled as she called to Graysen. 'Come and have a shower. They'll all be here soon.'

'Almost done, love.'

'The celebrant will be here in fifteen minutes.'

The man she loved turned and blew her a kiss. 'I hear you.'

Sandra almost hugged herself as she walked back along the veranda of their beautiful home; it was the perfect venue for the ceremony today and she couldn't help the smile across her face.

As much as the events of two years ago had been difficult, and a breakdown had threatened after she had killed Miska, Sandra did not for one minute regret her actions. No charges had been laid, and the police had taken Zed into custody, and he was serving three life sentences in a maximum-security prison. For a long time, Sandra could not forget the dismissive look he'd given Miska's body. She'd gone back into counselling but had managed to avoid medication this time, and had recovered within six months.

Having Graysen by her side and loving her had been the best medicine she could have asked for.

In a way, she wondered if she'd always known that one day, she would have to prove her strength. Despite the awful fallout on the trek and two months later when Zed and Miska had come back to kill them once the missing photo had surfaced, she did not regret going on the Larapinta Trail for one moment. She knew now she could rely on her strength. Having a wonderful man in her life was a bonus that had come from those difficult days in the bush together.

That man ran lightly up the front steps and walked along the veranda and put his arms around her. 'Those plants are doing beautifully,' he said. 'I thought it would be too hot in that corner.'

She knew her smile held secrets.

'What are you looking at me like that for?'

'Because I love you. Graysen Hughes, world-renowned photographer, content to potter around his wife's garden. Did you ever think you'd see the day?'

'No, I didn't. Look what you've done to me, woman.' She tried to run as she saw the look in his eye. He grabbed her and kissed her.

'Look what you've done to *me*,' she said stepping back and putting her hands on her hips.

'I've loved you, and I've made love to you, but not enough,' he said with a mock frown. He looked at his watch and said, 'Come on, you said we've got fifteen minutes.'

Sandra ran down the veranda, but Graysen caught her and kissed her again.

She giggled. 'Stop it, I want to tell you what you've done to me.'

'Okay, what have I done?' His eyes danced with amusement and he waggled his eyebrows. 'I know what I'd like to do.'

'I had a little apartment that I could keep clean in ten minutes and now I've got this huge home on two acres and I spend all my time keeping it clean for you.'

'You love it.' His hands cupped her cheeks. 'Admit it, you love seeing the kids run on the lawn, and you love having your family on the veranda. Now what's happening today?' he teased.

'As you well know and the reason why you mowed the lawn and did the gardens so it was perfect, the family are all coming. Emma's little Amy is getting christened.'

'I'll let you into a secret,' he whispered. 'I'm as excited as you are. Now come and have a shower with me.'

Sandra was dressed with a minute to spare when the celebrant turned into the driveway,

##

Two hours later Sandra sat in her chair on the veranda, filled with contentment and joy that was hard to describe. James, at six years of age had put himself in charge of Dee and Ryan's two-year-old twins, Angus and Wyatt, who followed him wherever he went. Ellie's little Verity was sitting on the step with Dru's Ruby, playing with a baby doll. The cousins were close in age and chattered away in their own language; words that no one else could understand.

Emma was in pride of place with Jeremy hovering at her shoulder. Little Amy was dressed in the christening gown that each of Sandra's girls, and then each of her grandchildren had worn. Sandra smiled as she remembered helping Dee change the twins halfway through the christening so they could both have a turn.

'Are you happy, Mrs Hughes?' Graysen's lips brushed her cheek and he pulled her up from the chair. 'I'll sit down and you can sit on my knee.'

Sandra sat and love filled her heart as she looked around at her family. She held Graysen's hand as she sent a silent prayer upwards.

'Peter Porter, we made a lovely family. You'd be so proud of them now.'

Sandra blinked away a tear, and turned to her husband. 'Thank you, my love,' she whispered.

'What for?'

'For loving me, and for loving our family.'

Graysen reached around and she turned her head to meet his lips. They both smiled at the chorus of her girls, their loving partners and her stepson, but ignored them as they always did.

'Get a room, you pair!'

THE END

If you've read and loved the Porter Sisters series, I'd love to hear from you **annie@annieseaton.net**
Or on Facebook
https://www.facebook.com/AnnieSeatonAuthor

Acknowledgements

The Red Centre and the MacDonnell Ranges, or *Tjoritja* in *Arrernte,* is one of the most remote and beautiful locations in Australia.

I have been supported by so many people in the writing of this final book in the bestselling Porter Sisters series. I would like to acknowledge them here.

To the many friends I have made in the writing world who constantly support me on my journey; I often say I have found my "tribe" and I value the daily contact with like-minded people all over the world. Again, a special mention and thank you goes to my critique partner, Susanne Bellamy, and to my proof readers, Roby Aiken, Kristen Woolgar, and Anna Welch.

It would be impossible to write without support in your personal life:

To Ian, the love of my life and my partner in research as we travel this magnificent country seeking stories each winter. I could not do this without you.

To our children and their partners, and our grandchildren: thank you for your love and support.

Again, my love and appreciation go to my wonderful aunt, Maureen Smith, who not only supports me, but supports so many Australian writers by reading, loving and sharing their stories.

I read many books and visited many websites about the Larapinta Trek, but specifically useful for my research were:

http://johnmcdouallstuart.org.au/

D. Larraine Andrews [Google books]

Great Walks of the World.

G.J. Coop. *Wandering the Larapinta* [eBook]

THE PORTER SISTERS 1-4

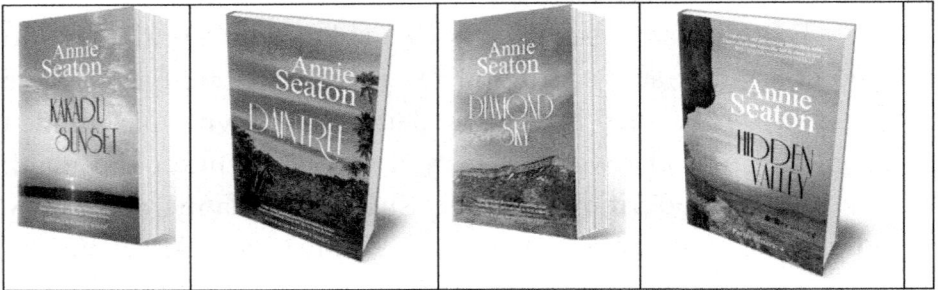

Printed in Great Britain
by Amazon